The Other Side
of the Fence

A Historical Novel of
Chinese Immigrants in the Northwest
During the Mid-1880s

To Jack
AD 750
long time friend
and best customer
of K720x!
Joyce Nowacki

by
Joyce Nowacki

D1733197

Copyright

Copyright © 2010 by Joyce Marsh Nowacki,
dba Write Offsite Publishing
Printed in the United States of America
ISBN 1451594941
ISBN 9781451594942

All rights reserved. Except, as permitted under the US Copyright Act of 1976, no part of this publication may be reproduced, distributed, or transmitted in any form or by any means, or stored in a database or retrieval system, without the prior written permission of the publisher or author.

This is a work of historical fiction. Any similarities to real persons, living or dead, are coincidental and not intended by the author with the exception of actual names used from history. No disrespect is intended. All incidents, characterization and events are products of the author's imagination, however, some may be based on actual historical events and places.

Dedication

For my husband, Wayne, who believed in me, helped with research with visiting actual sites where events took place in the 1880s, and he prodded me to keep writing.

Honorary Dedication

To Denny Barton, an avid reader who looked forward to reading this book but passed away before publication. With permission by his daughter, Linda Barton, a fictional character is named in his honor.

Help with Pronouncing the Chinese Names:

Jie =	Jay
Wong Pai	Wong Pie
Hong Haoli	Hong Hal-ly
Ming Yun	Ming Young
Ang Li	Ang Lee
Yue	You
Zhifer	Zef-fir
Lein-Hua	Lynn-waah
Mie	Mee
Sua	Sue
Zharg	Sargee
Chyo	Kioo
Jaoi	Jay-oe
Kai =	Kie

A Note About Names in the Timeline of this Story:

Chinese last names are traditionally before their first name. This shows the clan to which one belongs. Eldest sons sometimes are the only child given a name. Other siblings might be referred to as "son number two", numbered according to birth order. Junior is not used and children are often named after family members. It is common that girls were only given numbers, and given a name when to be married.

Prolog

Wong Jie's husband, Pai Number Two, parked their new 1946 Dodge pickup at the edge of the road on the east end of Pinegrove Cemetery. She glanced up at him and took a deep breath as he opened her door, then grabbed the rake from the back of the truck. Tall, stiff weeds snapped under her steps. Pai went ahead with the rake, breaking a trail.

"It is so dry. Like when I was a girl, before that bad fire."

"Yes." Pai surveyed the area. "It's sad our parents must lie under such parched earth, and again without the rocks I placed to mark their graves. Vandals probably," he shook his head.

Behind them in the cemetery, Ponderosa pines lifted branches to the sun and sent lean shadows across ornate tombstones. Between some of them, sunflowers drooped, and near others, leaves floated from lilac bushes landing among dried iris plants now bent to the ground.

"I think the graves are near." Jie's voice drifted in the breeze.

"Only a few more feet." Pai waited for her to catch up with him. "There." He pointed to a thick clump of grass. "This looks like the right spot." He swung the rake to remove more weeds.

Together they sat on the ground he had cleared. Jie laid down the bouquet of daises she had clutched in her hand. They chanted a prayer, and then sat in silence. "I'm exhausted. My mind and body both hurt. I'm only of forty-three years but hunting for the graves always makes me weary." She bowed her head almost as though prophesying, whispered, "I will be buried here too, but first I must make sure all who will hear know of our family heritage."

1

PART

ONE

1882

Chapter 1

The wail of the Burlington Northern Santa Fe hurtling through town awoke Jie. Opening her eyes, she scooted up to lean on the pillow braced against the headboard and yawned. Now at ninety-six, it seemed an effort to stay alert. From the bedroom window, she watched people greet each other outside the Methodist Church. "This must be Sunday. It's hard to keep the days apart." She yawned again and eased into a stretch, careful not to cause another leg cramp. Jie's active mind mulled over the past and present sometimes mixing the two, often confusing herself, so she spoke the words aloud even though no one would hear. "Yes, Sunday. Good. I must tell Molly when she comes," she smiled thinking of her favorite granddaughter. "I must tell her today...about my dreams...of my father, Haoli...his friends...the railroad."...

Hong Haoli dared not wipe the sweat pouring past his dark almond eyes and bony cheeks. He stole a furtive look at fellow workers along the hundred-foot cut. The trench they were digging would be leveled as a bed for the coming railroad through Westwood, Idaho Territory, a fast growing settlement. "Everyday I see more wagons loaded with families and their belongings come into town," Haoli chanted to the others in Mandarin as another passed along the roadway.

Beside him Ming Yun did not answer. Although not a wisp of air stirred, Haoli noticed Yun not perspiring in this August heat, and idly wondered why, as he emptied his shovel.

The hundreds of other Chinese working beside him looked no different than Haoli. All were small bodied, clad in

5

black baggy trousers and tunics reaching below the knees. They shuffled along in woven sandals with leather shields over their feet, while conical straw hats kept the sun off their heads. Each wore long, ebony hair pulled back in a *queue,* braided pigtail, tied with a strip of black cloth or leather. The Irish, French, Germans, and other whites had plaid shirts and woolen pants, and caps to shade their eyes. They worked at the top of the cut, and drove the mules. Heavy boots kept their feet safe from rocks.

"Dig, you gopher." Swartz's bullwhip sliced the summer air and nipped a piece of skin off Ming Yun's cheek. "Dig, ya slant-eyed devil." The foreman lowered his whip and watched as Ming Yun stumbled, a hand covering his wounded face. "Yer no better than tailless monkeys," he shouted, wiping his own face on a dirty rag, before wadding it back into his pocket. His piggy mouth pinched in disdain.

Haoli's eyes met his friend's, Wong Pai, and saw murder in them and something more, something deeper. The merest shake of Haoli's head told Pai to swallow his hatred. Haoli quoted a proverb from the ancestors to his friend. "'If you are patient in one moment of anger, you will escape a hundred days of sorrow'." He knew from experience the white boss would not hesitate to hurt, maim, or kill the Chinese.

His back ached, hands blistered, feet swollen, and dirty sweat covered him. He ignored his pain and never complained. Instead, he chanted as he shoveled earth away from the railbed. All he had to do was keep in rhythm, dig, and breathe deeply until the dinner triangle rang. He gulped air, filling his lungs as taught to his people by Chuang-Tzu centuries before, and sang out, "The drawing of a deep breath promotes long life and good health." He found truth in this cleansing of blood and body as he recited it. He glanced at Ming Yun again and saw his face was dry and sickly pale yellow, where it should have been reddened from the sun's heat.

The wide cut now had banks piled into fifteen-foot hills on each side. Above him, a few lordly pines left by the loggers stared down at the blasting teams. Coolies filled slips, gigantic scoops on sled-runners pulled by mules, to carry the dirt and rocks to the banks growing higher.

Each man forced his shovel into the rocky soil and heaved the loads onto the slips to be dumped at the top of the growing incline. A Brawny Irishmen held the slips' handles, "Faster, you fools, think we have all day?" With a hearty laugh, he whipped the mules into motion making Ming Yun's shovelful miss the slip. He was still laughing as he ascended up the ramp to empty his load.

Haoli lifted another shovel of dirt to the slip. "The cook's wagon will ring the noon signal soon. We can rub our weary leg muscles then." The waiting mule ignored him. The driver sat on the huge boulder Haoli and Pai had worked hours to remove from the bed-way. After six hours of unceasing labor, it would be good to rest. There would be twenty minutes to swallow bits of venison, vegetable rice rolls, and tea before the next six hour pace.

Beside him, Ming Yun paused and leaned his weight against his shovel. His head drooped to his chest. Haoli started to speak but stopped as Yun lifted his head, eyes rolled back as he collapsed, landing on his shovel.

"Awk!" Haoli hollered and rushed to Yun, lying on the ground, eyes stared unseeing at the sky.

Wong Pai and Ang Li tossed their tools aside and ran to their friend. Others stopped working and stared.

Wong Pai sat and lifted Ming Yun's head in his lap. He felt Ming's face then snatched his hand away. "He is hot."

Kneeling, Haoli grabbed Yun's wrist. "His beat is slow and breathing shallow," he half-shouted to Pai. "Ming, Ming, do you hear me?" Haoli looked up, consternation on his face as his friend gasped for breath. "His heart jumps."

Every worker within a hundred feet now stood, and looked intently at the gathering group. Haoli dropped his friend's wrist and looked into Wong Pai's face. "He is gone. My cousin has gone to the ancestors." He choked as he spoke the words. Haoli stood and shouted, "He is dead," loud enough so all could hear.

Wong Pai bent his face next to Yun's, still in his lap. "I am not surprised. I saw four crows circling our work camp this morning."

"He must be buried by our traditions." Ang Li bowed his head with grief and respect to his comrade. All the Celestials did the same, their hands cupped to their chests in prayer.

"The dead must be honored at all costs," Ang Li announced. "We will not dishonor the ancestors *again* by not conforming to tradition."

"Slackers!" Swartz yelled running back down the cut to where he'd just left. "Get back to work. What goes on here?"

Haoli's voice rose. "We must bury our dead."

"You there, coolie, get back to work." Swartz backhanded Ang Li, who was closest to him.

Ang Li fell to the ground but rebounded like an acrobat in almost one motion. Defiance lit his dark eyes as he squatted beside Wong Pai, who continued to hold Ming Yun.

One by one the workers dropped their tools and bent to the ground, like dominoes. All but Haoli sat in silence for their dead mate. He turned to face the boss man.

"Get back to work," Swartz bellowed, cracking his whip wildly in the air. "Work now, you slacker dogs."

To control his anger Haoli cupped one hand in the other against his chest, hoping Swartz thought it to be showing respect. He stepped up to the foreman then spoke bravely. "We must bury our friend. We must have ceremony of forty-nine days, pray, and burn food, clothes, and money for his journey or the ancestors will haunt us."

"Heathen ritual. O'Toole won't allow it. Get these men back to work. Bury him under the next slip load."

Hong Haoli faced his countrymen and spoke in Mandarin, telling them that they would not be allowed to celebrate Ming Yun's death with a traditional Chinese burial. "What shall we do?" he asked, still in Mandarin, aware of Swartz's glowering scowling and tossing his whip from one hand to another behind him.

Wong Pai did not clasp his hands nor bow his head. He traced the whip cut across Yun's still face with his finger. "We will sit until the world stops turning. We will give Yun proper ceremony. We will not work even if boss man flays our skin with his whip until we die. We do not work." Heads under pointed hats nodded in agreement and mournful chanting began. Haoli turned to face Swartz and translated Pai's words.

Swartz's mouth pouted, his face turning purple. He cracked his whip and again ordered them back to work.

Haoli moved closer to the body. "We do not move one grain of dirt until Ming Yun is entombed." Ang Li and Wong Pai rose and carried Ming Yun's body into the shade of the embankment. Hong Haoli then reported to Swartz in a firm voice, "We will not mourn the required forty-nine days, instead we will take three."

"No you won't." Swartz waved frantically up to the superintendent, Jack O'Toole, at the top of the hill. O'Toole started down the grade, slipping and sliding in the loose rocks.

Fifty-some of the whites, using any excuse for a rest, laid down their tools and moved in closer for a better view.

Swartz shouted louder. His face swelled, again, nostrils flaring. The Chinese exchanged sly glances at this white man having a fit. Most did not understand his words, but comprehended his actions.

Superintendent O'Toole burst through the line of mule drivers to where Swartz stood. "What goes on here?" His face stony, eyes narrowed under a blue cap with NP embroidered in gold on the front.

"A chink died of heatstroke. This is just another work stoppage, this time under the pretense of mourning. Stupid fools," Swartz snorted disgust.

O'Toole hiked over to Haoli, still the only coolie standing. "This won't help, boy." He cocked an eyebrow. His voice harsh, but nonthreatening. "We're already behind schedule. Folks are depending on you to get this railbed in. You must work."

Haoli pointed at the body, "We must not anger the ancestors."

Then O'Toole turned his fury on the whites who watched with grins on their pudgy faces. "You trashy bogeymen. Who gave you permission to stop work?"

Like reluctant children at school, they started back to moving the skids of dirt but with less energetic, muted 'gees' and 'haws' to the mules.

"You there, coolie," O'Toole turned back to Haoli. "Order these men back to the railbed."

"Not do," Haoli shook his head.

"What?" roared O'Toole. "You back-talking me, boy?"

Haoli faced his crewmates. The chanting paused. He chattered something in Mandarin. No one replied. All stared at the ground, and again began their chant—louder.

O'Toole rubbed his chin, thought a moment, turned to Swartz and spoke so quietly, only Haoli overheard. "If we don't give them time to bury their dead, they'll run off and then where will we be?" He lowered his voice even more. "But if they stop work again, by glory, you'll...you'll be digging dirt along with 'em...that you'll be."

Swartz's eyes now mere slits, nodded to O'Toole then bellowed at Haoli. "You three," he jabbed a finger at Haoli, Wong Pai and Ang Li, "I'll give you one hour, go bury him in the woods. Take any longer and you'll work extra hours for the next two weeks!"

With Pai and Li's help, Haoli lifted Ming Yun to his shoulders and started up the cut toward camp. His cousin's head hung over his shoulder, eyes staring. Haoli turned to see the Chinese crewmembers rising to their feet, picking up their tools, and going back to their chores on the bed. "Good," he told Wong Pai and Ang Li, "working will save us from more troubles."

Both nodded in agreement as they climbed up the incline.

At the top of the cut, Wong Pai took Haoli's burden and started across the field of stumps to the camp past the creek.

Wong Pai laid Ming Yun's body on a blanket that Haoli had placed beside a tent. The friends moaned in a sing-song chant for a time, until Haoli raised his hand to speak.

10

"We cannot please the ancestors in only one night. There is no time to mourn, no time to gather paper money, burial clothes, or prepare food. His spirit will not be free until we can do this. We will bury our friend where we can remember the site and come later to collect his bones."

"Yes," Ang Li spoke, glancing over his shoulder as though expecting someone to stop him. "We will bury him before darkness. All see where." He pointed to a tall pine on the same side of the creek, near the entrance to the camp. "We shall place him there. When his flesh is free from his bones, one of us must come back and gather them to please the ancestors. Until then, his ghost will roam this wild country, looking for rest. Haoli, you must do this."

Haoli bowed his head and shoulders, "Yes, we must lay him to rest in the white-man's cemetery with a proper ceremony...as an American." Taking upon himself this great responsibility, he looked to his friends and saw their agreement.

Chapter 2

"Do you know where they had to bury Ming Yun? It was disgraceful, Molly." Jie sighed and took a sip of tea then began...

Before dusk, Ang Li and Wong Pai placed a small coin between Ming Yun's cold, blue lips, that he might pay his way into the next world, and wrapped the body in the blanket. They transferred it onto a stretcher fashioned from poles and willow branches. Pai began a chant to the gods. All joined in. Haoli led the mourning march through camp to the creek, and laid their burden under the chosen pine.

The blistering heat had abated somewhat but it was still uncomfortable. Haoli was thankful that soon the sun would hide behind the mountain, offering relief.

Others had dug a shallow grave, to better allow the flesh to decay and make the bones easier to collect. With only the sighing of the pines for music, the members placed Ming Yun in the burial place.

When earth covered him and stones marked the site, Haoli addressed the hundreds who had joined them. "We have no paper money to burn so he will be able to pay his debts. Will a few of you who have a dollar bill tear off a tiny corner to replace the traditional offering? We will burn it to calm the demons."

Three men pulled money from trouser pockets, hidden by tunics, ripped off a piece and handed them to Haoli. Two others tore pieces of fabric from their tunic hems adding to the offering so Ming Yun would be clothed in his new world. All chanted a prayer as Hong Haoli lit a fire of wood chips. Smoke rose as flame consumed the money and cloth sprinkled with a bit of rice that Ang Li saved from his lunch.

Ang Li shook his head. "We need three days to honor our friend, but bossman will not allow it. We will work again tomorrow, but work slow for two days. Tonight, we will stay in our tents after supper and pray to the ancestors not to haunt us. Tell them we have done all we can. We will not fail them." His voice rose. "Pray he gets used to his new life in the underworld." A chant began. "This we will do. This we will do." All joined the incantation as a few filled in the gravesite.

The next day, the friends picked up the Mandarin chant of the others, their shovels and picks moving slower. Haoli was sure Swartz thought they only chanted in Chinese to keep the pace of their shoveling. If he understood the words they spoke, he would know sometimes it was of home and family, sometimes of hatred and rebellion, or messages to each other...today they mourned for Ming Yun.

Haoli understood English better than most of his comrades and had overheard the bosses say they were nearly a year ahead of the rail layers. The loggers had advanced to rougher terrain. The Chinese rail encampments spaced about every fifteen miles, rotated crews as they moved along the railbed. Haoli chanted out to Ang Li and Wong Pai, "we are like leaping frogs at play as each team completes their job and moves on to the next one. But I like this place best."

The Westwood camp was about a quarter-mile away, across the creek at the base of Storm King Mountain. White workers had shacks closer to the edge of Westwood, some stayed in the hotel or boarding houses, and many had their own home and families in town. "I think it is the mountain and creek that make this place like home. It is the prettiest we have seen so far in this America."

"Yes, it would be a good place to raise a family," Pai sang, keeping time with his shovel. "Too bad our women are not allowed to come. A shame we shall never marry."

"Aye," Haoli agreed as he heaved the rocky dirt from his shovel, letting his thoughts drift back to the different crews. His mind was busy figuring who had camped here before them. First, the loggers, then mule drivers pulling stumps. All had already left here, probably creating other camps wherever they were working now. Stacks of hewed ties showed evidence the tie cutters had also gone ahead. Tie cutters were more fortunate, with lighter labor than Haoli's leveling group. They had cut crossties from the logs left by the loggers and piled them along the roadbed to be used when the rail layers arrived.

Now, Haoli's team must level the bed, whether it was digging through hills like this one or filling crevices. Like his friends, he would never disgrace his clan by breaking the work traditions of the ancestors. He bent his back and his mind to the task, with an attitude of subservience to powers higher than he, the way of Confucius.

"We should have stayed in China," Wong Pai chanted, "in Chiang-Men, they promised us great wealth if we'd come to America's land. Gold they said. I do not see any here. And, I miss my family."

Haoli answered in mantra fashion, "We do work hard, and long, but our bellies hold more food than when in China."

"We will never see riches. Our pay is not enough to buy even a chicken," Pai sang out.

Haoli was quick to drone back. "At least we are not with the explosives any more. Just move your shovel and soon we will be done." He tossed another shovelful onto the waiting slip as if it was no effort. He was glad he had left the blasting team. It had frightened him. When the strength of mules didn't do the job, the whites sent them to use black powder or liquid nitroglycerin. He'd seen too many clansmen mangled or killed, and was quick to join the diggers when more manpower was needed to level this hill. Now, the backbreaking labor to make the bed as flat as possible proved to be exhausting, but it would not *kill* him. Thoughts of Ming Yun flashed in his mind. Or would it?

Haoli stopped his daydreaming to listen to the Irish bosses. "The tracks are nearing the Columbia and Snake Rivers to the south, in Washington Territory," the shorter foreman said. Haoli recalled the area. It was in the frostiness of early springtime when his crew had cleared trail there, only months before.

"Building the bridge across the Snake is delaying them. That river is dangerous with its cold and depth," the short one spit on the ground.

"She's a swift one alright," the piggy-faced one answered. "The rails could be connected with the East before that bridge is completed."

Haoli shook his head at the joke, thinking 'they should let us Chinese build it.' He took a breath filled with dusty, stagnant air hanging in the dig and wondered how he could endure this dry heat, greater than China's. He paused, glancing over his shoulder, saw that the supply wagons were arriving.

"Maybe they bring mail." Wong Pai chanted, also seeing them.

Jie yawned and stretched, then looked at Molly. "Do you know what happened then? Mr. Barton whose son, Denny, became my friend years later, told me all about that day when first the supplies came to town."...

Smothered in a dust cloud of its own making, the supply wagons stretched near a quarter-mile with the mid-August noon sun bent on mummifying all. Behind it, herders kept cattle moving, allowing them to nibble the rich native grass growing among the rocks.

George Mudgget, a stocky man with arms like oak limbs, rode in the chuck wagon at its lead. His long face sliced by tight lips, except when cursing the horses, studied the road ahead for deep ruts. He elevated his lame leg, balancing it against the seat, trying to ignore the pain. He grumbled, "I should never have tried to break that devil of a horse last year."

"Yep," Bill Brocket agreed for the umpteenth time, riding shotgun beside him. Brocket stood occasionally, stretching and surveying the line of the dozen wagons behind them. Before leaving Fort Spokane last week, Mudgget calculated the number of animals needed to feed the 7,000 laborers in all the railroad camps to the Northwest. "The 2,000 white-bogies are not as easy to please as the 5,000 coolies." He hoped he had figured correctly to furnish the camps at Moab, Mud Lake, the diggers at Westwood, the tie men at Granite, and the loggers at Cocolalla Lake. He also planned a portion of the supplies for the village of Westwood as a courtesy from the railroad.

Keeping animals alive as they herded them across the prairie proved a tricky business during the trek from the Columbia River. Four wagons carried caged poultry and wiener hogs that he had traded farmers for dry goods along the way. Feeding the animals and keeping them alive involved an all-day chore. More wagons were packed with barrels of flour, salt, sugar, rice and tea—that everlasting chinaman tea.

Their scheduled delivery stop at the Mud Lake camp, where the railbed had been cleared, came into view. Crews were leveling the final area to lay track. Next would be the railroad camp at Westwood. By three o'clock, they had traveled to within a mile of the settlement.

At the edge of Westwood, the trail took a sharp left turn, crossed a creek over hewn logs, and then bent back to the right. At the first intersecting road, Mudgget turned his team to the right. One dry-good wagon and one with caged animals followed, leaving the others on the main roadway to rest. As they made their way up the small incline, Brocket whistled through gapped teeth. "Well I'll be jiggered. I don't see how it grew this big since last fall. She's not a settlement anymore, she's a town."

The growing village stood proudly on the rise. Signs hung from porches and above doorways announcing Brownson's Mercantile, the newspaper office of the Silver Blade, next to Orenstein's Saloon, all on the side south of Main Street, the new railbed stretching along behind them. Across on the north, stood the Wright Hotel and the offices of C.L. Heitman & S.C. Herren, Attorneys at Law. Betty's Café, a barbershop, The Silver Bar and another saloon. Nogle's Blacksmithing stood at the east end, a lean-to shed with a forge and tools in front of a corral. Scattered on both sides of the streets up and down the slope squatted dozens of one and two-room houses.

Mudgget stopped in front of Brownson's Mercantile on Main Street. Brocket was first to jump from the wagon and stretch. Mudgget lumbered down and limped his way along the mules, patting each as he passed, more to keep his balance than heed for the animals. He brushed the muzzles of each lead, and then he turned and walked in the direction of a man wearing a dirty white apron hurrying toward him.

"Mighty glad to see you," Brownson reached out to shake hands with Mudgget. "Supplies are getting pretty short. Danged if I know where all these folks are coming from," Brownson huffed. "Thinks they are all going to get rich soon as the railroad comes through. Thinks they'll buy up the land. But they'll get a surprise." He displayed a toothy grin under his handlebar mustache with prefect curls over each cheek.

"Why is that?" Mudgget asked he had been watching the mustache wiggle as the man spoke.

Brownson pointed at two men standing off to the side of the Silver Blade, "Fred Post and Charley Wood, there, they own most everything. And now, Alfred Potter coming over there, bought up almost every acre they didn't own. He nodded at a third man who was approaching from the café.

"In front of the saloon, over there," he glanced in the direction, "that's Orenstein and Barton, a couple of our first legal homesteaders. Filed titles, too. Most everyone else is new here." He rushed on without waiting for a reply, still shaking Mudgget's hand. "When's the tracks expected?"

Mudgget finally pulled his hand from the excited storekeeper. "Fall time, maybe. Tell Brocket, here, where you want things put."

By this time, over a hundred people had gathered on the street, chattering in low voices. The shipment wagons made an unusual sight. Three boys poked sticks through the cages at the hogs. A woman shooed them away with a promise to warm their britches. Several men stepped forward and offered to help unload the supplies. Brocket directed which barrels and crates to unpack.

"How many folks are here now?" Mudgget asked. "I don't think you had even a five-hundred last I came through."

An intelligent-looking man with clear blue eyes and a balding head paused beside Brownson. Hands in the pockets of his clean pressed trousers, he watched the goings on.

"Ben McGuire, here, just got himself elected mayor," Brownson bragged. "He took a head count."

The new mayor drew himself up straight, befitting a politician at being introduced, pulled his hand from his pocket and stretched for a gentleman's handshake, which no one accepted. "What total you get, Ben?" Brownson asked.

McGuire's deep voice, like a bear growling, answered, "Near 5,000, best as I could figure, oh, and the couple thousand coolies. They don't stand still long enough to add 'em up but their paymaster gave me the number. He shook his head up and down as he finally pumped the wagon master's hand. "Good to see more supplies. Rails get to Spokane yet?"

"About a hundred miles out. Supplies are coming by rail now up from the coast through Othello and Yakima, so you won't starve. I see you have a saloon. Join me?"

Brownson, McGuire and all the folks now standing in earshot laughed, but Mudgget noticed he hadn't gotten an answer. Oh, well, he had six cases of Jack Daniels in his own supplies. That'd see he didn't go dry tonight after business. He quickly forgot about going to the saloon. "What's the best route to the rail camp now?" he asked.

"Go back to the main road and turn right. It is not far. You'll see the rail diggings to the southeast over yonder. When you see it ahead of you, look for the trail up a short hillside, on your left, towards the mountain. It'll you take right to the chink camp." The mayor nodded, grinning as if the coolies were of interest to him.

Mudgget climbed back onto the wagon seat, clicked his tongue at the mules, and slapped the reins. The animals picked up the pace as if sensing the end of the journey. "Guess we'll have to wet our whistles with chink tea 'til we can get to our private stock."

Brocket gave him a big grin and wiped his sleeve across his forehead.

As directed, Mudgget headed the team toward the railroad dig. They went about quarter of a mile before coming to where the coolies delved, creating the cut. Seeing the banks of the railbed diggings through what had been a hill, it looked to be an impossible task. "I thought the Good Book said that only God could move a mountain, looks like the coolies do it just fine." Brocket laughed at his own joke.

"Yeah," Mudgget retrieved his red paisley bandanna from his pocket and wiped his face with the filthy rag. "Those coolies look like moles digging their way out of the earth." Both made deep-throated chuckles at their own wittiness. On their left, a stumped-lined creek twisted its way along the side of the road with only a few pines too scrawny for lumber remained.

The China camp sprawled out on a flat area that pushed away from the town to the north across a roaring creek lined thick with fir and pine trees. Storm King Mountain rose abruptly covered in two-foot-thick pines, too high to see the top from standing so close to them.

His handkerchief soaked, Mudgget wiped his face with a sleeve. He scanned the area as the wagon train moved through the camp.

"Where'd all these coolies come from?" Brocket whistled through his missing tooth again. "Guess that storekeeper wasn't kidding when he said a couple thousand camped here."

"I guess. Oh well, it doesn't take much to feed them. Rice, a bit of meat, and plenty of that greenish weed they call tea." Mudgget guffawed, "but it keeps them healthy."

Brocket always chortled at his boss's jokes. He let out a loud howl and shook his head in agreement.

"The Irish and others can eat rice instead of potatoes. Do them good, the big mouths," Mudgget added with a grunt. He'd see they didn't get into his private stash. "Drunkards. Every one of them." The words slid off his tongue. He tapped the reins again and the mules picked up their pace.

Brocket sniggered but didn't look at his boss.

Mudgget led his procession toward the chow shack at the far end of the camp. He passed crudely built log shacks that sheltered the white crew bosses.

Hundreds of tents staked in perfect straight rows filled the field facing the creek to the base of Storm King Mountain leaving room only for a pathway to the cook shack and the huge dining canvas in the center.

Behind the cook's area, two Indians skinned a deer. Already, two quarter-sections of venison roasted on iron spits above glowing beds of coals. Another half-section hung from a cross-pole between two tamaracks near the place where the Indians worked.

Chinese, dressed in their usual black trousers and tunics with coned hats, went about with purpose. Some washed laundry in the creek, some gathered wood and others performed different chores of caring for the animals. The camp seemed empty but for these workers. "Not many coolies here. Must be the day off for these not out on the dig." Brocket verbalized Mudgget's thoughts.

At least a dozen men set about the coolie kitchen preparing vegetables. Kettles of rice, cabbage and carrots steamed on iron grates above open fires next to the venison pits.

"Look at 'em," Mudgget muttered to Brocket as he watched the Chinese men working. "Maybe they took lessons from ants."

"Yep, like little black ants. Isn't that something?"

Mudgget and Brocket dismounted from their perch on the wagon and Brocket set off to supervise the unloading. Mudgget's men began separating the cattle, hogs, and chickens designated for this camp at corrals past the cook's shack.

Several coolies joined them to help with the work and feeding the animals.

O'Toole came from his log shack to greet Mudgget and Brocket.

"Sure glad you're here. I was just preparing to go back to the dig. Can't leave those bogeymen in charge without me too long or trouble erupts."

Mudgget noted O'Toole wasn't smiling and didn't sound too friendly. "What do you have this trip?"

Mudgget began counting on his fingers as he listed the total of his supplies for all the camps. "We've about 200 feeder-chickens. Some could make good laying hens. Near eighty wiener-pigs growing fast, maybe you can raise a sow or two from them." He looked O'Toole in the eye trying to see if the man would be smart enough not to butcher the whole lot. He couldn't decide so continued. "And, half as many barrels of rice, and as many filled with various dried sea fish, flour, sugar, and tea. Figure to drop off about half our load here, this being the largest camp." He frowned, "Also, brought a big packet of something sent up by Ah Quin in San Diego. Some kind of herb, I venture. Or opium?"

"Ah, the chink that runs the medical tent will be glad to get it. That chinaboy is pretty good with his herbs and witchcraft. I don't care if the devil himself prescribes it, it keeps the men well. One good thing about those yellow midgets, they don't get sick often. Guess it's all that tea they swill. He cured a broken leg with some kind of herbs and a bunch of needles a few weeks ago. Weirdest thing I ever saw. The man was back on his feet in just over two weeks. Too bad he couldn't help the one who died yesterday from heat. The fools won't complain, just drop dead."

Mudgget followed O'Toole into the sweltering shack and took the only chair. He balanced his gimpy leg up on the cot. "Might have to see him myself," he muttered. "Going to have to send a younger man next trip if this leg doesn't get better."

"Maybe you ought to let that chink take a look see."

"Not yet," Mudgget shrugged and rubbed his thigh. Then he brought O'Toole up to date on developments out in the civilized world. "Congress adopted the Edmunds Act to keep those Mormons from having more 'n one wife. And, the Exclusion Act bars Chinese immigration for ten years. Lucky for the railroad, these chinks are already here, but they'll have to pay the tax now required. One-hundred-thousand coolies made it through. I think that worried Congress into passing the law."

"I almost forgot. You bring any mail?" O'Toole asked anxiously.

Chapter 3

"Molly, did I ever tell you how my father met my mother, a great love story." Molly curled up next to her grandmother with her notebook and waited patiently while the elder woman thought quietly then began her tale, describing it as if they were watching the scene...

The crews returned from the dig late the day Mudgget's supply wagons had arrived. Most went to their tents after eating supper. Some reclined on in the shade to light opium pipes, others talked quietly, while some fell asleep exhausted. The creek burbled from the northeast on its way towards Westwood. The setting sun turned clouds brilliant pink and orange, fading to gray and violet as the early autumn air turned crisp.

Haoli and Wong Pai leaned against stumps and chatted about home and families. Ang Li joined them.

"Mail!" a foreman yelled, then began calling names and tossing envelopes toward answering shouts.

Haoli paid no attention, knowing he would receive nothing. A year ago he had written to his father, telling him he was working for the Northern Pacific Railroad in the western part of America. He did not expect to hear back. His letter probably never reached China, and if it did, father would not reply and Mama would not be allowed to write. And, she'd have no money for a stamp.

Haoli had a strong notion his papa received payment to have him hired away to work on American railroads. But that was all right. He figured Mama and his siblings had benefited from the money as well as from his pay he always sent them. Then he thought of his beautiful little sister, Yue. Ten years younger than himself, she had followed him everywhere. He missed her most.

"Hong Haoli."

Hearing his name, Haoli straightened and jumped to his feet. He watched as the foreman tossed a yellowed envelope. He kept his eyes glued to the letter as it was pitched from hand to hand until it reached him. He held it as though it were an ancient treasure. Gripping it in tight fingers, he ran through the camp, leaped the creek, and hid among the scrub trees. This was too private to share. What if his father died? Or worse, Mama?

He read "HONG HAOLI, NPRR, ID TER, USA" written in Mandarin and rewritten in English by someone. His hand trembled as he untied the string, opened the flap, and took out the letter. Chinese characters in thick black ink seemed to leap from the rice paper.

Greetings son Hong Haoli. Foods supplies are few. Father sold Yue to a tong. She must work in den in Dai Fou. Can you find her? She not born for misuse. Miss you much. Love, Mama.

He recognized Mama's strokes on the page. She was always so delicate with her brush. Not many women had reading and writing skills and his mother honored hers with perfection. Haoli stared at the familiar characters, letting the words sink in. Papa sold Yue! I must find and rescue her, but how will I get to *Dai Fou,* San Francisco, as Americans call it?

Then with a positive thought he brightened and sat straighter. Spirits of the ancestors will help. They will not let a young girl be the toy of men. least not white men. Little sister Yue, only twelve years next Lunar Year's day of birth. Tears raced down his cheeks.

Footsteps alerted him. Wong Pai approached. "What's wrong Haoli, someone steal your only pig? The letter?" Wong Pai frowned and sat down beside his friend.

Haoli did not answer or look at his friend. They sat in silence, watching the evening light disapper. The *Shi-yue*, October air, chilled them.

Finally Haoli spoke in a low whisper. "My first letter from China is evil news." He tapped the paper's folded edge against his knee.

Wong Pai reached over and laid his hand on Haoli's arm. He gave the arm a quick squeeze and released it. "What did it say?"

For several minutes Haoli did not answer. Pai slapped at a mosquito. "Buzzing bugs," he swatted his arm, again missing the pest. They watched the changing sunset. Blackness slowly slipped across the land, veiling the mountainside camp.

The darkness filled Haoli's heart with more despair. "It is my sister," he finally whispered so low Wong Pai had to lean close to hear. "Father sold Yue to a tong in *Dai Fou*."

"No! Not so!"

"It is true."

"Better she be dead. Your father is a devil. You must find her."

"That is what Mama writes, but how?" After a long pause Hong Haoli spoke with resolution in his voice. "I will find Yue and bring her here. After the day of payment, I will go. Two weeks more. I can plan."

Both got to their feet and moved through the timber, crossed the stream, and strolled toward their tents.

Wong Pai stretched his arms above his head and yawned, "I'm worn. Sleep will be good," he mumbled, yawning again.

"Tomorrow's work will come too soon."

Each crawled into one-man tents, bedding down on mats with woolen blankets.

Like the mosquitoes buzzing around his head, weary thoughts interrupted Haoli's sleep. Did Mama really mean "tong?" And, "den?" No! Surely they would not use little girls. But Mama had written it so. The letter was sixteen moons old.

Then his mind's eye raced to Mama and the family. In China, hard times had hit. Food was scarce when he left over two-years ago. His absence helped the family with one less to feed. Now Yue. Could he fault his father for this ill deed?

Yue. How many of those houses were there in *Dai Fou?* He would seek out every one until he found her. Poor Yue. Her long black hair had framed her face. She was tall for her age, and a beauty since she was born. Mama must be wrong. Yue would not be in the dens, such evil places.

Haoli burned inside, imagining torments Yue may be suffering. Perhaps things had changed. Maybe she was no longer there. I will learn the truth, he vowed.

Sleep eluded him until dawn appeared. He reflected more on their years together as children. She always shied away when visitors came to their hut, hiding in the loft they shared with their five siblings. The children helped their father in the rice paddies. Yue, frail in spirit and body, worked beyond her strength. As an adult, Haoli appreciated his childhood. It had taught him to work hard and be in subjection to those over him. But Yue, she did not deserve mistreatment.

"Haoli." Wong Pai awoke him, calling his name. "You did you not sleep well?"

"No, not much." Haoli slipped from his tent.

A quick splash of cold water at the creek in a dugout pool for washing, followed by a meager breakfast of tea, roasted venison strips and rice would not fill the hunger in Haoli's spirit.

The continued dinging of the cook's triangle alerted the crewmen it was time to leave for the dig. Haoli spread his blanket and mat on top of his tent to air and joined Ang Li and Wong Pai in the quick jog toward the worksite. Haoli and close friends paused to honor Ming Yun in his grave for a moment, then ran to catch the crew. At the dig they joined the hundreds of others from camp, picked up shovels and pickaxes and set to work. Haoli's body labored, but his mind was filled with images of Yue.

Chapter 4

In Jie's room at the front of the old house, Molly lay sprawled on her stomach across the foot of her grandmother's bed. A red chenille bedspread left marks on Molly's arms, but blue jeans protected her long legs. Sashes held back the lace curtains so Jie could watch movements in the street and across the creek. "What happened next, gramma?" ...

At the end of the 1882 October's high moon, the day of pay finally arrived. Haoli had devised his scheme. He'd collect his railroad compensation, suffer the required Exclusion Act fee, and be sure to get a receipt. "A Chinese without his papers could result in imprisonment or death," Haoli told Pai as he folded his slip and put it in his pocket.

Visions of building a new life with Yue in this beautiful land filled his thoughts. "I don't want to ever again work on the railroad," he vowed. "Maybe open a laundry or find a government job." His life would be different, someday even send for his mother and siblings to come to America. The plan played out perfectly, simple to accomplish, as he dreamed it.

Collecting their money took up most of the morning. Wong Pai, wanting adventure, decided to accompany Haoli as far as Fort Spokane, maybe further. It was already past the noon sun, shadows cast were shortened as Haoli and Wong Pai left Westwood on foot.

"Goodbye," Ang Li waved at the edge of town and turned away before they disappeared round the bend in the roadway. Haoli had insisted Ang Li stay with the rail crew. "I know your mother depends on the money you send from your earnings," he had argued.

Late afternoon they arrived at the Mud Lake rail camp. The cook welcomed the two travelers with a meal of Irish stew. Haoli took a bite, licked his lips and smiled. He had tasted it many times in camps, but it always weighed strange on his tongue. "I am surprised the rails are not here," he said to a countryman near him.

"Not yet. That's why we have only twenty-five on this crew. The engineers moved the rest onto Westwood for digging." The cook set the steaming pot next to the men and plopped himself onto a bench. "I hear the rails are coming into Fort Spokane by next spring. Our bunch is leveling the final bed for them. Rumors say they lay ten miles of track on a good day."

"Maybe we will see the finished tracks on our journey." Haoli took another bite, appreciating the foreign food and nodded his approval to Pai and the cook.

Pai repeated the gesture as he ate.

The Mud Lake crew welcomed Haoli and Pai to spend the night. Appreciating the hospitality, they helped with camp chores. At daybreak they were on the road with a breakfast of cold biscuits with sliced rabbit meat in hand to eat on the way. The cook packed a tote for them with dried and rice wrapped tight in grape leaves.

A few miles west of Mud Lake, at the Moab camp, busy crews transported rocks and gravel for a higher ridge in the railbed. "See that." Pai pointed at the mound they had made. "In Westwood we are digging, down and here they are creating a hill."

Haoli shook his head in agreement. "Looks like they are building a trestle? Maybe over the stagecoach roadway?"

At the Moab camp, the cook packed some venison jerky for their journey. "Dried meat will not spoil you can keep it for thin times," he told them.

A few miles down the trail, a farm wagon loaded with milk cans, and crates of vegetables and eggs, heading their direction along the stagecoach road. Haoli and Pai stood aside to let it pass.

The farmer tipped his soiled felt hat in greetings. "Going my way?" He smiled and added, "Fort Spokane?"

Pai nodded, but not sure if the man could be trusted he held back.

"Climb aboard." He indicated with a nod at the straw packed about his load to keep it fresh.

"Thank you," both the Chinese men used their best English and clambered on the back, each settling for a seat near the driver.

"Oh. You speak our language well. Tell me boys, where are you from and what are you doing here?"

"We work on railbed in Westwood," Haoli was first to answer. Then he told how he came from China on the ship, crammed tight with too many people, and about the diggings for the railroad.

"What's China like? Is it hot like here? Does it snow?" The man slapped the reins over the two oxen's backs to pace them.

The two smiled meekly. Wong Pai relaxed, put away his fear, and answered all his questions. He described the countryside filled with rice paddies, the family he left, and how clever the people were to make use of everything they grew. Pai shared his memories for the thirty miles to Fort Spokane.

When Pai and Haoli tried to pay for the ride, the farmer refused the money stating that learning about China and her people was payment enough.

At Fort Spokane, both hired on with a freight company to drive wagons to the Columbia River. Hauling cargo to be shipped by the massive river barges to Portland, Oregon, would give them transportation. "Better than walking, eh Pai," Haoli tired to comfort his companion.

They arrived at Ainsworth, a few miles from Pasco, where the rail crew was building a bridge across the Snake River. "Yesterday there was an accident," Pai told Haoli what he had learned at the coolie camp. "Over a hundred of our clan-railmen were killed when a pillar they were setting slid. It took the south side of the bridge into the swift, high waters."

"That is not good. It will delay the rails even more, I suppose." Haoli studied his friend's face. "Are you staying? They will need more men, I think."

"I decided not to join this crew and return to Westwood." Pai leaned against the back of the cargo wagon and looked thoughtful. "I have come far enough, my adventure is over. Digging rocks and dirt is better than what the cold waters offered here. I will ask if the cargo wagon master will hire me for the return trip."

"Good idea. Go now, the boss does not look busy."

It was not long before Pai returned with news that he would leave in the early morning, driving a team back to Spokane. Haoli managed to barter labor for a ride on the river barge down the Columbia to the Portland. He would worry later about getting to San Francisco.

At the Portland Harbor where the *Kitty Ann* loaded passengers for San Francisco, Haoli counted his money. It was not enough. He dug frantically in the pocket of his tunic for more coins. Empty. Disbelief struck him that a month's wages was less than one passage fare. He had not spent but a few dollars on the way and yet he was seven dollars short. For the first time he felt the injustice of the Chinese Exclusion Act. It angered him to be charged the five dollars every three months for the privilege of staying in this new land of freedom—because he had yellow skin. American freedom, indeed!

He looked into the stern eyes of the captain's face, half-covered with a red beard and moustache. "I work?" Haoli's voice faltered, embarrassing him.

"You look like a strong one. I'll take you on if you swab the deck each morning before anyone is up. You agree?"

"Oh yes, and most grateful." He concentrated on pronouncing the English words correctly. "I go to San Francisco to find my sister. She might be slave girl in den," Haoli could not stop the words before they fell from his tongue.

"You may be a heathen, but your heart's as right as any Christian. I'd do the same." The captain accepted what money Haoli had for passage, allowed him to board, and gave him directions where to bunk.

As he reached the birth in the belly of the ship, he slipped his hand into his pocket. Empty except for the *Act* paid receipt, and his last three silver dollars. He tied the coins together with a strip of cloth from his queue tie so they would not jingle in his pocket. Others would not be aware he carried any valuables.

Puffing black smoke, The *Kitty Ann* eased away from the dock and headed down the Willamette to meet the Columbia River and its deathtrap of sandbars at the Pacific. Safely across the bar, it steamed along the rugged coast of Oregon.

Each morning, just as dawn lit the eastern sky and spread across the waters, Haoli rose from his bed in the bowels of the ship and scrubbed the decks. "Cleaner than they've been since this freighter was first launched," the captain had praised his work. As Haoli sailed on the *Kitty Ann* that first week in November, 1882, he worried about what lay ahead in *Dai Fou*?

Chapter 5

A picture of Haoli with graying hair hung in a gilded frame on the wall. Another displayed Jie's husband, Pai Number Two. As she often did, Molly looked in the drawer beside the bed to study a daguerreotype of her great-grandmother, Lein-Hua. "Nanai," Molly looked over to Jie, who she called 'Nanai', the Chinese word for grandmother, "Tell me again about your mother." ...

The heavy November fog rolled in, covering the Chinese village in San Francisco under its haze. Sir Zhifer sat in his bantam office, counting the day's receipts. Chimes alerted him that a customer had arrived at the front door. He smoothed his golden dragon-embroidered black robe, positioned his long queue down the center of his back and rubbed his hands together. "Ahh, the night starts." Greed lit his eyes as he entered the main lounge, divided from the lobby by a heavy red tapestry. It displayed dragons in a floral scene, and reached from ceiling to floor. The curtain wrapped across the front of the lounge and along the sidewall hiding doorways to Sir Zhifer's office, the dorms, and the stairway down to the den.

After spying through her peeping window, smaller than her face, Madame Kay opened the door, "Welcome," she bowed slightly greeting the stranger and allowed him to enter.

The anteroom was empty except for Madame Kay, who stood in front of a black-mahogany counter. Tall for a Chinese woman, her hair was piled high and held in a knob by pearl pins with beaded-strings that dangled as she moved. Her red, ankle-length *qipao* gown fit snugly. Two hanging lampshades muted the light, allowing an indistinct view of the gigantic dragon painted on the crimson wall behind her. Small black tables topped with jade vases of various sizes stood about. A heavy fragrance of jasmine caught the breath.

Also hearing the chimes, four Chinese girls, just beyond childhood, entered the lounge from behind the tapestry. They took their places, silently facing Sir Zhifer. Their haunted eyes now stared at the floor. Hands hung at their sides, one fidgeted, the others stood motionless. The long and narrow room had no windows. Four ceiling lanterns of red rice-paper stretched over black metal frames with black silk tassels, matched the two in the foyer, offered only a dim light. It reflected off polished, black ornamental dragons standing next to red cushioned chairs. Colossal pillows, also used for sitting, dotted the room. Plush red carpet dimpled under foot.

The customer Madame Kay let into the room stood uncertain at the door. Dressed in a gray suit with a green and red pinstriped vest that stretched across his wide stomach, he cleared his throat. An assortment of decorative chains dangled from his neck, and dirty black boots seemed to shorten his legs. Sensuous lips puckered his red face, as though seeking a rich morsel of food. He doffed his homburg and paid Madame Kay the price for service. She led him across the lobby and behind the curtain. He appeared unaware of his surroundings until his eyes focused on the girls.

They instantly put on inviting smiles and posed seductively. Except for one, whose eyes stared at her feet. Sir Zhifer watched her, his brows narrowed. Madame Kay presented the man, or mark, to Sir Zhifer. Then turning her back to the man she scowled at the unsmiling girl and disappeared, returning to her post in the front foyer.

The mark scanned the first one with a quick eye. A scrawny wee thing, Lein-Hua struck no provocative pose, but looked hard-eyed at him. With an uninterested glance, he dismissed her.

The second girl, Sua, a head shorter than the others, stroked her long black hair with slender fingers then swept her hand downward, fanning over her budding breast.

A third girl, made no eye contact with the mark, but absently stroked her stomach and breasts. The eyes of the man passed over her to rest on the fourth in the line.

This girl, Mei, stood almost proud, small breasts thrust out, hands on hips. Slowly, sensuously she bent a knee, showing a length of slim leg through the slit in her skirt. A flash of tawny thigh caught the stumpy man's eye. She slipped a graceful hand from hip to stomach and still lower. The customer's avid eyes followed every movement as her fingers danced in a slow fondling motion at the pit of her skirt.

Decision made, the mark's lips curled in a wicked grin, as he signaled Sir Zhifer of his duel choice of Sua and Mei.

Sir Zhifer's broad smile revealed gold-filled teeth. He was proud of both girls. This was worth twice the fee. The grinning customer paid Zhifer the added fee then followed him with the girls behind them, to the end of the dark lounge to the hidden stairway masked by the curtain.

Small wisps of sandalwood incense teased nostrils, becoming stronger down the narrow wooden stairway. Steps groaned under the weight of each man's foot as they descended to the den. The girls' footsteps made no noise.

In a room at the bottom of the stairs, perhaps fifteen men slouched idly with girls in various poses, taking turns puffing on the several community opium pipes. Zhifer ignored them, lit a bowl at an empty bunk, and offered a pipe to the new mark, who grabbed it with fleshy fingers. Zhifer took his leave.

Sua and Mei squeezed onto the divan beside him and began teasing the mark with their bodies. They would take part in the pipe before leading him to a crib at the end of the room. The cribs were just large enough for a single bed mat and a nightstand holding a candle, an opium bowl, and pipe. The doors of lattice woven bamboo draped with brocade silk filtered the already gloomy light from the den. Cribs not in use were noticeable by the silk curtain that drooped up over a hook.

Lein-Hua stumbled to the dim side of the lounge and joined several other girls sitting on pillows. She had watched the man's response to the girls, swallowed and turned to hide disgust at her friends' gestures. The bowl of rice she'd eaten earlier churned in her stomach.

Sir Zhifer returned to the lounge, marched to where Lein-Hua cringed on a large velvet cushion and yanked her up. He slapped her left cheek. Head lolling, she stifled a cry, and caught her balance as Zhifer yanked her toward him. The slap stung, but no tears flowed. Lein-Hua had learned to tolerate such treatment. She braced for the next slap, which came immediately.

"You be nice *baac baac chai*, every man's wife," Zhifer growled in a stern, controlled tone. He glared a warning at the other girls before releasing her with a shove and exiting the room.

None of the other girls offered sympathy. They kept to themselves staring silently. Experience had taught them he might return.

When the chimes rang again, Sir Zhifer greeted the next mark being presented by Madame Kay with a bow, and grinned. He straightened, and with a quick sweep of his arm towards the girls, welcomed him to take his pick from the line-up. Lein-Hua regained her poise. Under the watchful eyes of Sir Zhifer and the new mark, the girls arranged themselves in suggestive stances. Almost gagging with the effort Lein-Hua drew slender fingers along her leg and slipped them under the edge of her slit skirt, resting them on her exposed thigh.

He chose the taller girl on Lein-Hua's right who had smiled, blowing a kiss his way. Sir Zhifer led the mark with his choice down to the opium den, set up the pipes, and left them.

When Zhifer returned to the dim lounge, he headed directly to Lein-Hua. Again, he grabbed the girl this time by the hair, and dragged her face within inches of his own. "Be good *baac baac chai*" he threatened. "Smile!" He let go of her with a sudden force, causing the frail girl to stumble to the floor. He stomped from the lounge to his office.

At the next ringing, Lein-Hua's suggestive gestures caused a man with a dirty beard and a limp to choose her and awarded her Sir Zhifer's slant-eyed approval. Relief swept over her. She had avoided another beating.

In the opium den Lein-Hua forced herself to giggle at the mark's boorish jokes as they shared the opium pipe. She glanced at the doorways of the dreaded cribs over her shoulder. His rough hands groped at her under her thin gown, then slithered across undeveloped breasts and down her firm, young stomach.

"Be slow." Lein-Hua gently pushed the man's hand away. "Let opium work. You get much pleasure." She gave him an innocent smile. "Happy mind helps body." She had used nearly all the English words she knew.

The dirty beard moved as one large glob when he talked. Lein-Hua's stomach churned. She was sure to lose her supper. The time came for her to take the man to a crib. Her hand froze as she unhooked the silk curtain. The man, limping as he followed her, lost his balance and fell into her as she held the curtain. She gasped but quickly pushed him back into an upright position. With his next step he entered the room and managed to fall onto the bed. She dropped the curtain over the door behind her.

The girls slaved throughout the night, returning to the lounge after each mark left. Finally, alone and exhausted in the dorm room behind the lounge, Lein-Hua cleansed herself at the washbasin. As if trying to scrub off detestable handprints and the night's events, she rubbed the brush's course bristles against tender skin, unaware of the pain she inflicted on herself. Finished with her bathing, she still felt the horrible hands.

Lying on the thin straw mat, Lein-Hua tried to recall her life back in China. Her mother's gentle face was slowly fading from her memory. But she could not forget the feel of her father's hand as he pushed her toward the tong who escorted her from her family's hut in Chiang-Men.

Dawn's light shone through the tiny window across the dorm from her bunk as she slipped into deep sleep. If only she could sleep forever...never face another night.

Chapter 6

"While Lein-Hua and her friends worked in the awful dens, Haoli was on the ship on his way to Dai Fou to search for his sister, Yue." Jie took a deep breath and signed before beginning her story...

In late November '82, the *Kitty Ann* tied up at the dock in San Francisco just after dawn in fog so dense Haoli could see nothing of the city above him. Foghorns groaned their warnings in the bay. Haoli shook hands with the captain, thanked him again, and then moved down the gangplank.

Where should he go? Where *were* these opium dens and houses of harlotry? He would simply have to walk the streets until he came upon another Chinese who could tell him, one who spoke his dialect or a bit of English.

His stomach churned, signaling he'd had nothing to eat since the night before. He walked on, not wanting to spend his money on food, not a single coin. No matter, he'd gone hungry before and his belly did not groan as yet.

He was near Yue, his bones told him, his heart told him. Soon he would find her, though it would be like finding a gold coin in the mud of a rice paddy. He trudged on.

Tendrils of fog twisted between buildings as Haoli plodded along, leaving the bay behind, having no idea where to find the Chinese section. A few vendors unlocked doors and opened shutters. He found himself on Bay Street and finally met a Chinese man sweeping horse dung into a basket.

"How do I find our clans?" he asked. The man must have been from a different province than Haoli because he simply looked blank.

Using gestures Haoli made him understand he was looking for other Chinese. The man pointed beyond him, extending three fingers, motioned, then waved to his left. Haoli decided it meant to go three blocks in that direction and then turn. He walked through a wilderness of brick and wooden buildings. No shops were open yet, no one was about. He was not used to the salty sea air, it pinched his nose but he maintained a good pace.

He climbed a hill and wandered from one street to another. Most were lined with pretentious homes, interspersed by smaller houses and vacant spaces.

A slight breeze blew wisps of fog along the street, he followed it to the right. The residences gave way to more merchant shops. Shivering, he followed Broadway Street to Columbus Avenue. A shawl-wrapped woman and young boy in knickers crossed the intersection, the boy hurrying to keep up with his mother's longer strides.

Haoli approached another countryman he saw sweeping the sidewalk in front of a small gift shop. Hong Haoli bowed respectfully before him. "Friend, I am from Chiang-Men and work on the railroad far to the north. I am new here."

The man appeared skeptical as though to say, "Railroad indeed, I do not believe you," but answered politely. "Where do you want to go?"

Thrilled the man understood him, Haoli answered, "To our native district. Where do I find it?"

"Go on this street, we Chinese are allowed," the man pointed the way and recited as if he directed the way many times.

"Thank you, you are most kind," Haoli bowed and started off in the given direction. The man's words, 'we Chinese are allowed,' twisted through his mind as he strode onward.

Finally, Haoli saw familiar Chinese buildings with the flare of the Far East. Relieved he had found the right direction, he ambled into what could have been the center of any village in China. He gazed at the scene for a few minutes, absorbing the picture.

Now nearing noon, he rubbed his hand across his stomach. Its rumbling brought him back to the present and his mission of finding his sister. Unsure where to start, his stride slowed down Columbus Avenue and turned onto Grant Avenue. Familiar aromas drew him into Noodle House, a small eatery.

An old man sat at one table, head in hands, his thin gray beard hanging down his chest. As if asleep, he did not move. Across the room, a mother slapped a boy's hands for reaching in front of her for more noodles. The boy jerked his hand back, then asked politely for it. They took no notice of Haoli.

His eyes adjusted to the dingy light as he came to an open doorway, exposing a kitchen. A tiny plump Chinese woman bent over a sink, her back to him, washing vegetables. He tapped three times on the doorframe with his knuckles.

When she turned, he bowed and smiled. "I need work," and giving her no chance to answer added, "I am Hong Haoli and I just came from the north and am hungry. Can you help please?"

The woman wiped her hands on her apron, took a few steps toward him and shouted in Mandarin, "Father, come and see what we have here."

Surprised to hear his native tongue, Haoli glanced around but saw no one. No one answered her. No one came.

"Father, come and see." The woman called again, still eyeing Haoli.

"I see," answered a voice from behind racks of noodles hanging to dry in the far corner of the kitchen. "What do you want?" A short man limped into sight.

Haoli bowed in respect then introduced himself as a hard worker having just arrived in town, and hungry.

The man returned Haoli's bow. "Mama, fix our friend a plate of food. Then put him to some chores."

He faced Haoli and introduced himself as Mr. Chang, and the woman as his wife. "Help out for the price of your meal. If you do a good job maybe we can make a deal for further employment."

"Thank you, I will work hard for you." Haoli bowed again as good manners demanded. After he completed his formal thanks, Mrs. Chang placed a bowl of noodles topped with greens on a small table near the doorway.

"Eat. Then wash dishes." She pointed at a sink overflowing with pots and pans.

Haoli bowed, thanked her, and sat down at the table. The hot meal tasted of home and brought memories. He had not realized how lonely and hungry he had become.

The woman watched him for a moment, then went back to the vegetables.

With his belly satisfied, Haoli found pleasure in scrubbing the pots. He rubbed them hard until the copper shone, rinsed, dried and hung them from hooks under the cupboard. He scanned the room, retrieved a mop from the corner closet, and began mopping the floor. When he finished, the woman pointed to the pile of vegetables, "Can you cook?"

Haoli shrugged, without answering he retrieved a large pot from its hook.

Mrs. Chang laughed, took the pot from him and pointed towards the new customers sitting down to an empty table. "Mr. Chang's gimpy leg will appreciate relief from waiting tables. You go, take their order and pour them some tea."

Haoli accepted this challenge and went to greet the waiting patrons. He came back with two lunch orders with extra noodles. He returned to the tables and took another order. He repeated this chore as the restaurant filled. Later Mrs. Chang set a dish of rice and crab in sauce for him at the little table. Thankful, he ate with relish between the customers.

Haoli served patrons and washed dishes as time allowed. It was past ten o'clock by the time the last diners left. Together he and Mrs. Chang gave the kitchen a final cleaning.

Mr. Chang had retired earlier. When the kitchen shone, Mrs. Chang offered Haoli the attic room if he chose to stay.

He agreed and climbed the narrow stairs.

The room was small and sparsely furnished with one wooden chair at a small table holding a cup of cold tea, and a half-burnt, unlit candle. A straw mat lay in the corner under a tiny window too high for Haoli to look out. Adequate for him; he hadn't expected such accommodations. He stretched out on the mat. Four walls and a roof over him made the surroundings so unfamiliar he did not close his eyes for a long time.

Haoli roused from deep sleep by the hazy light breaking through the window. Refreshed, he stretched and rose in one easy motion. After taking care of nature in the community privy behind the building, he entered the kitchen.

Mrs. Chang had the stove heating as she mixed eggs and bean sprouts for breakfast. She turned toward him and nodded.

Embarrassed he had overslept, Haoli apologized for his laziness and set to work.

Diving into the chores she gave him, he glanced through the kitchen window, noting how the fog still shrouded the morning. He was used to waking to brilliant sunlight, chilling air, and the scent of pines mixed with smoke from campfires. Haoli wondered if he could get used to the ocean and the city. And, how long would he be here?

After the morning rush, Haoli and Mrs. Chang rested with a cup of tea at the little table. Mrs. Chang studied his face. "Something important weighs your mind?"

Haoli hesitated, and licked his dry lips. "My burden is a mission for my mother." He stared down at the floor, then spoke again. "I *must* find my sister. She may be here in San Francisco."

"You have family here? Most women are not allowed now. I came with Mr. Chang, long before the law forbade families. What does her husband do?"

"No, no husband." His eyes remained downcast as he spoke. "My father...sold...sold her...Yue...to a tong. Mama fears he brought her here to the dens." He looked up into Mrs. Chang's face then averted his eyes. Swallowing, he continued.

45

"Yue, is to turn thirteen next birthday. She is not strong. My mother's heart, and mine, both grieve. I must find her."

"You work through the evening meal then go seek her."

"I have no idea where to look."

Hearing the conversation, Mr. Chang came from behind the noodle racks. "There are many places. Rich brothels, humble dens, cribs like cages along the alleys. Begin looking at these cribs because you can see the girls, reaching to entice you."

Mrs. Chang stood and turned to walk away. Her voice rose, reminding him of his mother's when she reprimanded a child. "Deadly disease—makes you go crazy in head. Do not go into them."

"I will only look," Haoli promised. "Thank you. I will pursue my mission tonight. Every night, until I find her."

"You will need help." Mr. Chang stated. "I will see if I know someone who can assist." He left without further explanation.

At the end of the evening Mr. Chang returned to the kitchen. As Haoli polished the last cooking pot, Mr. Chang told Haoli where he could find the alley-cribs.

Haoli changed into ragged clothes Mrs. Chang gave him, "To prevent devilish men from sizing you for robbery."

He patiently searched alleyways and streets which reeked of garbage, opium, sour incense, and foul body odors. He wrinkled his nose at the stench.

Finally he found cribs, cages four feet wide and six feet deep with barred doors or heavy screens. They lined both sides of one alley. Cooing girls reached out hands, seeking marks or men customers.

An addict screamed, clawing at a wall as if digging a hole to escape. Haoli took to the opposite side of the alley. A man swore from inside a crib. A girl cried out. Thumping sounds joined by screams. Was someone beating a girl? Haoli quickened his pace.

Three drunkards slumped against a building as if dead. An empty wine bottle lay between the legs of one. Haoli crossed a street and entered another alley. More cribs lined it, like the one he had just left, the scene much the same.

"Lookee two bits. Doee six bits. Much pleasure. So good for you." A female voice blended with other screams and cooings.

Haoli ignored them all. Every few feet he called, "Yue. Hong Yue." Once a girl answered to the name—but was not his sister.

Careful to ask the right questions as Mr. Chang suggested, he narrowed his search each night. Sometimes he did not return until early morning.

He learned his way around town, met people from working at the eatery and soon became well trusted in the Celestial community as winter set in. But, where was Yue?

One evening in April, 1883, several months after Haoli began work at the Noodle House, a hefty Jewish man sat at a table in the far corner. He struggled to fit his fat body onto a chair and relaxed letting his belly expand under his navy linen suit. A gold watch chain hung from his vest pocket. He set his Panama on the chair beside him, picked up the teacup, and sipped the hot brew Mrs. Chang had set before him.

"Mr. Ableman." Mrs. Chang whispered the words as reverently as if Confucius himself had entered. "Very rich. Owns much land next to Chinatown. Has many friends in politics."

Mr. Chang shuffled to Mr. Ableman's table, sat down and poured more tea into the man's cup. Chang folded his hands and waited for Mr. Ableman to speak.

Haoli could not hear their conversation, but noticed Mr. Chang seemed to be doing most of the talking. Mr. Ableman fanned his flushed face with a napkin. He watched Haoli as he worked with no pretense of hiding his interest.

With a pasted smile Haoli set plates of noodles before two men at a nearby table waiting for their dinners. While taking more orders, his ears tuned to listen to what Mr. Chang and the huge man were saying, albeit beyond understanding over the clatter, he did hear his own name more than once.

As Haoli stood at the kitchen counter during a lull, Mr. Ableman beckoned to him with one crooked finger, akin to an insect twitching an antenna.

"Go." Mrs. Chang hissed from behind Haoli shoving her finger in his back.

Haoli bowed gently from the waist as he came to the table and looked expectantly at Mr. Chang.

"Hong Haoli," Mr. Chang introduced the two. "This is Mr. Ableman. He has interest in your sister."

Cold dread swept though Haoli's body as if he had fallen into the depth of the ocean. No words came. Finally, remembering his manners, Haoli bowed his head a bit lower and spoke, "How so, sir?"

Mr. Chang had disappeared silently from his chair.

"I wish to help you find her. Little slaves girls are not wanted in *my* town."

Ableman's words stabbed Haoli's ears. He jerked his head up to stare into the man's eyes, seeking truth. The spirits were good after all.

He swallowed air. "Help me?" Haoli questioned.

"Chang tells me you are searching in the alleyway cribs. She will not be there. Good tongs supply rich brothels."

Again, Haoli stiffened. "I cannot afford to go to them." He tried to control his shock at the news, he wiped at his forehead with the hem of his apron and added, "I ask. I call out her name. But no one knows anything to tell me of her."

Mr. Ableman reached into a pocket of his coat, brought out a handful of shiny gold double-eagle coins, and dropped them on the table. "Use these to pay for a new suit and search the finer brothels." He drew a breath before continuing as though speaking took all his energy. "When you find her, let Chang know. Do not try to free her. It will be too dangerous. I will strategize her release." He scooped up the coins and dropped them onto Haoli's serving tray.

With these enigmatic words, Mr. Ableman glanced toward the kitchen, "Bring what Mrs. Chang has prepared for me. She knows my favorite."

Feeling as though he'd been hit on the head with something heavy that had rattled his brain, Haoli went to the kitchen, picked up a plate of food, and returned to the table, setting a dish of lobster tail in curry sauce before the big man. He bowed politely and retreated to the kitchen. He would sort out his thoughts about Mr. Ableman—later.

Chapter 7

"My father was a determined man, he did not give up," Jie continued telling the story as it played out in her mind's eye, exactly as he had told her...

Two days later Haoli stretched his arms out straight from his shoulders as the tailor measured him for a white man's suit of clothes. When finished, he waited outside the shop in noon's sunshine and watched people promenading up and down the street. Haoli especially watched for any Chinese men dressed as Americans. Occasionally one passed by, easily spotted among the silk robes or tunics and baggy trousers.

Ha! Here came just what he searched for, apparently a *rich* Chinese merchant. Haoli observed the man's walk, then practiced imitating it. He took long strides, holding his head high and copied putting his right hand in his pocket, his left holding an ivory-headed cane. Both items added a casual look of importance. Soon he felt the part of someone with power.

He strode into a jewelry shop and, using one of the golden eagles Mr. Ableman had given him, purchased a gold chain with a fob the size of a two-bit piece, stamped with a Chinese symbol of promise. He pocketed his change from the twenty-dollar coin, vowing to himself that someday he would buy a gold watch for the chain. But for now, the fob would weigh against the chain's end giving him the wealthy look he desired.

The next afternoon he returned to the tailors and found the man had included a starched white shirt and a gray bow tie with black polka dots. The charcoal wool suit fit perfectly, with a satin vest in vivid mulberry. The coat nipped at the waist, reached to his knees. He attached the chain to the right length so it hung emphasizing a look of wealth.

Tomorrow night! Yes, tomorrow night I will go find Yue. His mind's eye could see her safe with him—soon.

On his way back to Chang's eatery a chilling thought like the cold of an intense Idaho winter, washed over Haoli. He would never find Yue! He brushed off the impression and told himself he was just worrying. Since he began working for Mr. and Mrs. Chang over nine months ago he had never let his meditations be so negative. He would not let them start now.

One July evening he stood outside of the Golden Dragon brothel. Pale ruby light from a glass-enshrined candle reflected on silver chimes. Haoli jingled them. He saw the outline of a face peering at him from glass not large enough for it. He reached for the chime again as a middle-aged Chinese woman opened the door. Her stare made Haoli uncomfortable. She motioned him to enter.

The bleary room glowed red from dim lampshades. A dragon painted on the wall behind the woman appeared lifelike and looked as if it would devour him in one gulp. The woman, dressed in a red silk *qipao* did not speak, only smiled. The provocative one-piece dress snuggled over her curves. Embarrassed, Haoli kept his eyes at her high neckline with the frog closures as he handed her the amount of money she requested. Muffled noises drew his attention from behind a heavy tapestry.

A Chinese man dressed in a long black robe embroidered with gold-threaded dragons came from behind the curtain. The woman in the *qipao* retreated behind the counter near the door the man had come through.

No need to explain his presence, the procurer beckoned Haoli inside and snapped his fingers. Behind the curtain, five young girls stood in a line.

They were young, no more than, thirteen years old or younger, like Yue, the last time he saw her. Haoli sucked in his breath. *Yue would be about their age.* Hoping he looked as if he were studying them as it to make a choice, he blew out a gulp of air.

The girls struck seductive poses, each extending underdeveloped breasts and giving sly, inviting smiles. Except one, her smile was pasted on, and eyes infinite sad.

Haoli pointed to her.

"Lein-Hua?" Sir Zhifer showed surprise in his eyes, as he picked up an opium pipe from a corner table. "This way."

He led Haoli across the room into the darkness, separated by the tapestry. A doorway molded into the wall, hidden so well one would not know it was there without searching for it. Haoli did not let his face show his surprise.

The door led to a dusky stairway. Steps creaked under Zhifer and Haoli's weight as they descended. The girl followed them. Haoli held his breath, trying not to take in the stench. Sir Zhifer held aside a red silk curtain blazed with stylized white chrysanthemums, allowing his new mark and little wench to enter the smoky den.

The room contained perhaps twenty men and girls, all in various stages of stupor, reclining on divans that looked like large boxes topped with thin mattresses, some with pillows. Bantam tables topped with opium bowls standing between the bunks lent the only walkway between them.

The air reeked of opium, liquor, heady perfume, incense, and body odors. Haoli exhaled. He kept from making a face like a child would in a barnyard. None acknowledged the newcomers.

"Come," the girl spoke her first word and led Haoli to a huge cushioned divan. As she sat, the sleeves of her gown fell back revealing childish arms.

Sir Zhifer filled the opium bowl and handed the pipe to Haoli, at the same time giving Lein-Hua a threatening look.

Haoli waited to place the pipe in his mouth until after the pimp retreated up the stairs. Pretending to draw in a breath, he drawled from the side of his mouth. "I do not wish happy pipe. Take me to your crib."

"Not dare go so soon." The girl whispered in his dialect, almost under her breath. "Sir Zhifer watches through spy hole to see...smoke before...." Her voice trailed off as though she could not use the word for the act to follow. "He makes much money."

Understanding, Haoli drew several breaths, without inhaling deep into his lungs he paused between each puff. He handed the pipe to the girl, who also smoked with shallow draughts.

After a time, with her mouth pinched up, Lein-Hua rose and took Haoli's hand, and led him to the end of the room and opened a crib's lattice door. She dropped the curtain closing them inside.

This one was not like the filthy cribs in the alleys, but an alcove with a soft mattress. They sat down on it side by side. Lein-Hua began to open her tunic.

"No. Don't." Haoli stopped her fingers. "I wish to ask you questions."

A tiny sigh escaped Lein-Hua's lips, her eyes widened. She stared at him.

"Have you met a girl named Hong Yue? From Chiang-Men?"

Lein-Hua drew back a fraction, her eyes wary in the dim light of the glass globes outside the crib.

"Perhaps," she replied cautiously.

Haoli's heart seemed to stop. Did he want to know more? He felt as though something had crushed his chest.

"My sister. Hong Yue. Sold from our home in Chiang-Men. More than a year ago. I have traveled many thousand miles to seek her. Is she here?"

"No." Lein-Hua shook her head. A tear spilled from her eye and slid over the bridge of her nose. Haoli wiped it away.

"She was kind. Older than I."

He finally managed to whisper. "There may be many Yues? Are you sure this Yue could be my sister?"

"She told me she had six brothers and sisters. She is oldest girl. She had several older brothers, but loved the eldest, best. We shared much about our families back home. We talk to remember them." The girl became quiet, looking away from him.

"His name? Do you know his name?" Haoli urged her and closed his eyes afraid to hear what she might say, yet hoping.

"Haoli, her *shyong*. That is the name she always said. The brother, she loved most in all the world."

I have found Yue! He wanted to shout it. I found her! Mama, I found her!

Heavy footsteps came from across the lounge area interrupting his joy. A sharp rap on the crib doorframe and a crisp, "Time up" brought fear into Lein-Hua's eyes.

"He beat me if take too long," she whispered.

"Sir Zhifer." Haoli imitated Mr. Ableman to his best ability. "I do not like to be interrupted. I will pay you for each minute." A thought came that almost made him smile. "Do not bother me again. I have much power with the authorities." The story slipped from his tongue as though he were an experienced liar.

"Yes sir. Sorry Sir." Zhifer retreated. Footsteps rapidly crossed the den and ascended the stairs.

"Now," Haoli whispered to the girl slave, trying not to sound frantic. "We will become acquainted. You must tell me all you know of my sister. I will return soon and you can tell me then."

As they got up to leave Lein-Hua grinned for the first time. She led the way from the den, up the stairway, pointed to his exit and disappeared through the lounge.

A week passed. Haoli had trouble keeping his mind on his work at the café. Mr. Ableman found the news interesting that Yue might have been located. Haoli cautioned that he did not see Yue, but was sure he would the next time. He was sure of it.

The next Sunday after he finished shining the kitchen and hung his apron, he called out a goodbye to Mrs. Chang, dashed to his room to change into his new suit of clothes, and left for the den.

Like before, Sir Zhifer led him into the lounge behind the curtain where the girls posed. At first Haoli was disappointed not to see Yue among them. Or Lein-Hua.

Sir Zhifer stood waiting for the mark to make his choice. Haoli knew he must select one to keep his purpose secret. He chose the shortest, thinking her too young to be here. He'd give her rest from routine visitors.

Again in the bunkroom, Haoli played at inhaling from the pipe. He did not ask the girl about Yue. It could be dangerous to talk with too many people. When in the privacy of her bunk, he talked of things in China and how he missed their home country. He encouraged the girl named Sua to tell him about her home and how she came to be here in the den. Her story sickened him. He puked in an alleyway on his way home.

Haoli did not return the next week. Mr. Ableman agreed that the pimp and Madame Kay might become suspicious if he returned too soon. He waited until the following week. This time he was able to choose the first girl again.

In the crib Haoli removed most his clothing and lay beside Lein-Hua. Deep sadness shadowed her eyes. At first, she was hesitant to talk when Haoli encouraged her to answer his questions.

He encircled her with both arms and felt her press against him, accepting his comfort. "Go on. What else? Is she here?"

The girl lay without speaking still for several moments, then whispered, "It was two, maybe three high moons ago."

Despair crushed Haoli's spirit. He murmured, "If only I'd found this place a few months earlier. If only...tell me," He coaxed her.

Lein-Hua stopped speaking again as quickly as she had started. She had never dared to talk about it before, but now she mouthed, "I was frightened."

"What happened?" Haoli held his breath, feeling his heart race.

Her voice shaking, Lein-Hua told him all she remembered of that night. "Sua and I finished our duties in the cribs and were crossing the main hall upstairs on the way to our dorm when thud sounds came from Sir Zhifer's room, as if a struggle, stopped us. We thought we were last to leave. We crouched between two cushions in the empty lounge. We didn't make a noise." She stopped speaking again and listened for any sounds outside the crib.

Then she whispered, "It wasn't a man fight. I heard a slap. A girl screamed. More slaps. More screams." Lein-Hua covered her face with her hands. Sobbing, she continued. "I was so scared. Some men...like to...hurt us."

Haoli closed his eyes, trying to fight away the picture Lein-Hua's words framed.

"Just as we braved to leave our hiding place, I heard another loud slap. Another mournful screech, louder this time. Then a last thump and crash—like someone fell and a table or chair broke. Noises mixed so fast we cowered back in the corner. Like blind girls we stared into the darkness of the lounge. The only light came from Sir Zhifer's room.

"'Stupid whore!' I heard his angry voice. 'No time for babies. Let her lie there'." Then a man with hurried footsteps stomped past our hiding place. Sua and I stayed hidden, listening to the voices. I do not know many English words.

"Then I saw Yue. A man carried her past us. She did not move. Her arms dangled down. Head hung sideways. As they moved into the hall light, her glassy eyes stared at me. I saw blood from her nose and mouth. We stayed hidden for a long time, peeking out to see when it was safe. When we heard no more noise we dashed to our dorm."

Haoli wiped Lein-Hua's tears and then his own with a handkerchief. "We both grieve." His mind whirled. What can I tell Mama? I can never smile again. Why have I wasted nearly a year searching? She was so close. Why didn't I feel her presence this past year? Now, too late. But, not too late to help this sobbing girl? Perhaps there was something he could do. He would talk again with Mr. Ableman.

"I will come again. Do not fear, I will help you." Haoli felt this promise deep in his being. He must rescue this girl. And the others.

Sir Zhifer swung the door open. "Time is up. Go now." His glare dared the mark to disobey.

Haoli scrambled off the bedding and as if just dressing, he grabbed at his pants reached for his discarded suit jacket. Lein-Hua dashed past Zhifer. "I am done. You have good whore girl." He faced Zhifer directly, hoping the girl escaped without mishap.

Lein-Hua ran from the crib, up the narrow stairway and across the lounge and to the dorm, she shared with over a dozen other girls. She dropped onto her mat and curled into a ball, trying to understand what had transpired.

Caught not performing her duties, she was certain Sir Zhifer would beat her. Would he kill her, like he did Yue? She could not think further, could not swallow her fear. What would happen? Surely, Sir Zhifer would come for her. Any minute. Her eyes would not shut.

He did not come.

Later, Madame Kay entered the dorm. Lein-Hua, still sitting on her mat with her arms around her knees drawn up under her chin, tightened her grip without noticeable movement. Slowly she lifted her face to see Madame Kay glaring down at her.

"Lein-Hua, stay in dorm. No more work tonight," Madame spit the words, turned abruptly, and left the room.

Many hours later Sua and Mei entered the dorm, eyebrows raised and grins smeared their faces.

"What did you do to Sir Zhifer?" Sua asked.

"What do you mean?" asked Lein-Hua.

"He so happy," Mei whirled in a circle dancing, arm raised, hand clenched, she imitated waving paper money.

Lein-Hua caught her breath. "Happy? Dancing?" She repeated the words. "Mark must be generous to Sir Zhifer," she tried to sort out the puzzle.

"Lucky girl," Sua whispered from the corner washbasin as she poured water into it.

Lein-Hua nodded. She lay down, pulled the cover over her frazzled body, and wished for relief. She determined not to worry.

Always on Sunday evenings at ten o'clock, Haoli came to Lein-Hua's rescue. She anticipated his visits. Instead of the lineup, Zhifer would call for her at the dorm and escort her to the same crib where Haoli would be waiting. When alone they shared the opium pipe, smoking just enough to enjoy themselves and let the rest burn away, emptying the bowl while they talked softly of the things outside the brothel's walls.

Haoli told stories in English and insisted she master the language of this new land. She easily learned more words at his coaching. He never used her body as other men did, although he always undressed them both in case Zhifer intruded.

Like a clock timing his visits, Haoli stayed until the incense burned out. Sometimes he stayed longer into the night. Spending Mr. Ableman's money for extra time did not haunt Haoli. He had to trust Mr. Ableman's plan but he wished the days would move faster.

Snuggled against Haoli's side, his arms holding her close, she listened as he described the emerald mountains against a lapis sky.

She found herself daring to dream of it, and if she could raise a family of her own, and of neighbors—who were friends.

Chapter 8

"The hot '83 August sun gave way to September's brisk air and cooler nights." Jie brushed her hand across her face. "Father now owned two more suits of clothes, one brown, one gray, with fedoras to match. He easily adapted the ways of an elite man. Sir Zhifer thought him to be rich and allowed him privileges no other mark had. Haoli enjoyed the acting." Jie seemed to enjoy telling this part. Molly poured tea for them both and urged her nanai to tell more...

Lein-Hua's fear of Zhifer drove away the dreams Haoli inspired on his visits. Once again hearing heavy stomping she huddled in the far corner of the crib's bed, trembling as if hiding, her thin silk gown pulled over her knees, arms wrapped about them.

Haoli placed a gentle kiss on the frightened girl's forehead. He stroked her hair, took her hand, inviting her to slide over next to him on the bunk. Holding her in his arms, he soothed away her panic. "Do not worry precious one. I will save you soon from this life."

"I know." She snuggled against him, not sure what he meant. She would do anything he asked her, he was different from the other men who came to the den. But how could he ever free her?

"Halt! Police!" a male voice shouted from the den area. "Halt. Stop where you are!"

Men struggled off the lounges, cursing. They pushed prostitutes out of the way. Girls screamed. Some hid. Some vanished. Frantic marks bounded from cribs, some still pulling on their trousers.

"You are all under arrest!" The authoritative voice boasted again, "Halt where you are!"

The den darkened as candles were blown out. Marks scrambled from the raid unsuccessfully. Police were everywhere. They appeared as if out of the walls, grabbing and cuffing the johns.

In the crib, with a finger extended over his mouth, Hong Haoli signaled Lein-Hua to be quiet and motioned her to stay. "Be ready to go," he whispered in her ear. "This is the day we leave."

She stiffened, stared into his face, seeking reassurance. They crept from the crib, hid in the shadows and listened. Holding her hand, he led her to the last crib. Inside, he pushed on a portion of the wall and exposed a hidden door no higher than his waist, exactly like Mr. Ableman had described. He guided her through it. "Wait for me. Do not move." He patted her hand to encourage her. "*Ping an.* You'll be *safe* here. *Ping an,*" He repeated "safe" in Mandarin again to make sure the girl understood. Then he stepped back though the opening, closing the door behind him.

In the blackness, Lein-Hua squatted on bare heels, wrapped her arms about her knees and winced as the cold musky air touched exposed shoulders. She shivered, teeth chattered. The sound banged in her head. Afraid someone would hear she clinched her jaws to stop the clicking.

A man yelled, pushing a girl out a crib doorway. "Stupid wench." She fell to the floor and crawled behind an upturned bunk. The john tumbled to the floor cursing, struggling with his clothes.

More police filled the room from every direction, shouting "Halt!" and grabbing whomever they could, as marks labored to escape.

Close to the crib entrance, Haoli stood behind a support beam and watched the commotion. He drew a deep breath. The raid was playing out just as Mr. Ableman had predicted. A hefty man launched a chair across the room. A policeman ducked. The chair missed its target by inches. From behind Haoli, a cop knocked the man to the floor and handcuffed him. Another chair landed next to Haoli's hiding place and broke apart as it crashed to the floor. His eyes searched the room for Sua, and other girls he knew.

Half naked, cursing, men still tried to escape. Girls screamed, ducking, running. One policeman caught Zhifer's leg in a mid-air kick and flipped him to the floor. Seeing it, Haoli grinned and watched as chains locked onto Zhifer's wrists and ankles, yoking him to other captives.

Finally, Haoli spotted Sua squatting behind the upturned bunk. Then he caught sight of Mei under a bench. He reached Mei first and took her by the arm. "Come." He ordered. He motioned to Sua. She recognized him and struggled to cross over to them. Without a word both followed him to the end of the dark room. He hurried them into the last crib.

With expert hands he opened the secret door in the wall. They bent to step through it. He closed the door behind them, ran his hand against the doorframe until his fingers found the cold metal bolt and shoved it, locking the exit.

Lein-Hua heard the click of the lock and held her breath. She strained her ears for any sound. Feeling someone touch her shoulder she shuddered, but silenced a scream when she heard Haoli's voice whisper, "It is I." She sighed in relief.

He took her hand and placed it in that of another.

Who was holding her hand? She gripped it and trailed behind Haoli who led her by her other one. With a quick tug, Haoli signaled the way through the blackness. She struggled to breathe, the stale incense and underground mustiness choking her.

The tunnel's dirt floor was cold and damp under her bare feet. Twice, someone passed them, running from behind, knocking them aside. They must have entered the tunnel from another crib, the thought raced through Lein-Hua's mind as she caught her balance. They sprinted for several minutes stumbling along the way. The only sounds were the padding of their feet on the dirt and their own racing breaths. Finally, she saw a speck of light a short distance away.

Haoli stopped.

As her eyes adjusted to the light, Lein-Hua saw it was Mei who held her hand. Then she saw that Mei held Sua's. They squeezed fingers but said nothing.

"Stay here." Haoli patted Lein-Hua's hand as he let go of it. "I'll check the street." He climbed a makeshift wooden ladder nailed to the side of the tunnel wall. A door at the top admitted light. It had been left open by who ever had rushed past them.

From the top rung, Haoli peeked through the crack to assure no one was about. Satisfied, he fully opened the door of the crawlspace into a cramped hallway. He saw stairs at one end and a door on the other. Haoli jarred the door cautiously and peered from the building. Seeing no one in the alley, he went back to signal the girls to come.

Outside, dawn approached and the foggy air felt damp and chilly. "Stay close, we must move fast," he cautioned and led them down the alley towards Columbus Avenue. By their expressions he could tell that none of them recognized the area. "You are safe with me. Come." He crossed Columbus and into the next alleyway.

The aroma of baking bread tempted appetites, but he kept moving. He did not see where the bakery might be located, but the sweet scents grew fainter as they crept further down the alley and crossed Pacific Street into another alley, leaving the more populated area of Chinatown. At Sansome

Street, a milk wagon pulled by a swayback gray mare clattered by. The driver paid no attention as Haoli guided the trio into the back door of a small mercantile shop.

Haoli greeted the clerk with a nod and escorted the girls into a room at the back of the store. There he retrieved a carpetbag from a closet and handed it to Lein-Hua. He pointed to a washbowl and two pitchers of water. "I will wait for you, come when you are ready." He smiled and left the room, closing the door behind him.

Lein-Hua pulled garments from the bag and shared them with her friends. A smile spread across her face replacing the gloom in her dark eyes.

After splash-bathing at the bowl, and dressing, Sua was the first to show off a blue dress trimmed with lace. The garment fit perfectly. "Like American girl." She admired herself in the small mirror mounted on the back of the door from which Haoli had disappeared.

"Ohhh." Mei tucked a white blouse into the waistband of a tan skirt, pleated in front and back.

Lein-Hua liked the fit of her straight navy gingham dress with yellow and white daisies. "Feels strange." She looked back at her image in the looking-glass.

Quietly each donned cotton stockings and tied shoes that came above their ankles, pinching toes that were usually bare or in satin slippers.

A small bag contained hairpins and combs. They snickered as they tried to subdue their straight black hair into styles seen on American women. Sua settled pulling her hair up and letting it flow from a ribbon anchoring it at the back of her head. Mei let her hair fall straight again and pinned on a floppy bonnet, tying it under her chin. The others also placed bonnets on their heads.

"I feel peculiar." Mei's face sobered, fear clouded her eyes. "What will happen to us now? Do you think we are safe from Sir Zhifer?"

"Haoli will keep us from harm." Lein-Hua assured them, hiding her own fears. "I know it."

"I believe it is so," Sua turned to Mei. "Haoli *is* different. He means us no evil."

Lein-Hua picked up the carpetbag and stuffed the extra clothing back into it. As she picked up the nightshift that Sua had worn in the escape she stopped, looked at Sua who shook her head sideways. "Right. We will not need these." She crumpled the shirt into a ball with her own gown and Mei's thin robe and piled the unwanted garments on a chair. Mei placed the unused hairpins and ribbons back in the small pouch and handed it to Lein-Hua to add to the carpetbag.

"Are we ready to show our new selves?" Lein-Hua asked as she tied the bag and picked it up by the strap. She positioned it on her shoulder and faced the others.

Sua and Mei nodded their agreement. Mei stiffened as Lein-Hua knocked softly, turned the doorknob and cracked the door open.

She found Haoli waiting for them in the mercantile near a table displaying shirts, matching the fresh one he wore. "Good. You are all like pretty red roses in a field of daisies." He handed each girl a handkerchief, a safety pin, and a few coins including a double eagle for each.

All three held out the items and looked into Haoli's face, confused.

"For just in case." He answered the unasked questions. "Fold the hankie about the money, twist it tight so they make no noise and pin it to the inside of your garments.

Without hesitation, Lein-Hua and Sua did as directed. Mei stared at the coins in her hand.

Haoli saw her hesitation. "What's wrong?"

"I...ahh...I had a coin once. A mark gave it to me—said I was good to him. Zhifer found it. He beat me. Said I stole it. I could not walk for many days."

"It is safe, Mei," Haoli assured her. "You are forever protected from him now. Please, hurry. Hide the money. It will provide for you if anything should separate us."

"Now you are scaring me." Lein-Hua felt the hidden lump against her skin. "Do you think we will get lost?"

"No. You all are safe. Hurry. We must be on our way."

Mei nodded and fixed her treasure as directed.

The store clerk held three overcoats and offered them to the girls.

Haoli signaled his approval.

The clerk smiled as each accepted the gift.

"I have never had such a wrap." Lein-Hua caressed the sleeve gently as if petting a kitten.

"Now we must go. Stay close to me and do as I do." He took the carpetbag from Lein-Hua then picked up a smaller bag with his own clothes rolled in a tight bundle, and some food Mrs. Chang had supplied. "We must hurry." They left through the back door of the shop.

No one was on the street to notice the Chinese foursome.

Chapter 9

"Auntie Sua told me how scared they all were when they saw the huge ship. It was so much like the one they had arrived on from China to America. Auntie said they were all relieved to learn from my father as they boarded that all the girls in the den were also going to safe places." Jie shivered, sometimes telling the stories was too much for her, but she looked into Molly's eyes and stressed, "Do not forget what I tell you, it is important to your heritage." ...

As they neared the harbor, shivers ran down Lein-Hua's back. Heavy October fog rolled in off the Bay, concealing building tops. She could only see a few feet ahead of her. The eerie echo of a foghorn bellowed, as if calling to them. She and the other two followed Haoli to an undersized shack near a dock, stretching onto the water like a floating roadway before disappearing into the mist.

A ship nestled against the dock with ropes the size of elephant trunks looped about the wharf posts. Waves slapped at its hull. Crewmembers were busy loading massive crates onto the ship. Their work was nearly finished, as the last few boxes landed aboard and the crane's ropes fell into a pile around them.

Mei gasped.

Lein-Hua squeezed Mei's hand to let her know she understood—the sight of the ship revived memories of their hideous arrival in this country.

Suspicious frowns covered the girls' faces. "This is a cargo ship," Haoli told them. "It will take us to Portland, in

Oregon, where we will board the train to your new home in the Idaho Territory. Trust me." He pointed to the pier.

Understanding his gesture, Lein-Hua took the lead. Tugging her coat tightly around her against the wind, she trudged down the pier. Mei and Sua followed, both holding onto their bonnets with one hand, and coats with the other. Haoli came behind them toting the carpetbags.

At the ship's gangway, Lein-Hua hesitated at the wet plank. A fat man stepped out from behind a shadow and startled her. Her foot slipped, but she caught her balance. Haoli rushed to her side and grabbed her arm.

The man wore a dark American style suit that draped over his paunchy stomach. Fingering a gold chain connected to his pocket, he stared at the four Chinese. He checked the time on his pocketwatch.

Lein-Hua noticed the stranger nodded at Haoli who returned the greeting, smiled and pointed at her. She arched an eyebrow and glanced back at the foreigner. "Who is he?" she whispered and retreated behind him.

"A friend." Haoli's answer was quick. "*Yo.*" He said in Mandarin. "*It is all right.*" He took her hand and led her up the ramp. Still holding their bonnets, the other girls hurried with brisk steps to keep up.

The ship's captain stood on the deck near the gangplank. He shook Haoli's hand. "We have everything ready for you. Mr. Ableman there," he nodded toward the fat man below, "made all your arrangements. I hope you and your *sisters* find your quarters comfortable. We're not used to taking passengers."

All eyes followed the captain's glance toward the dock. Lein-Hua saw that Haoli understood the commander's meaning and relaxed some, glancing at the other girls.

"Oscar, my first-mate here, will show you to your cabin." He excused himself and climbed the steep metal steps to the bridge.

Haoli greeted Oscar with a bow, then a quick pump of a handshake. The first mate reached for the carpetbag Lein-Hua now carried. She flinched and jerked the bag close to her side.

Oscar drew back his hand and allowed her to keep it. He turned to lead the way to the cabin prepared for the young women.

The cabin, built atop the deck, looked out of place surrounded by cargo crates. Inside, the threesome found cots with mattresses and blankets. Three stools at a small table crowded the rest of the room. A pot of hot tea, cups, and a bowl of fresh biscuits were on the table.

Lein-Hua set her tote on the floor next to the first cot, pulled out a chair, sat down, and reached for a teacup and the pot. She sighed from deep in her chest, poured tea into the three cups, and took a biscuit.

Mei licked her lips. "S*hyr yu, I am hungry.*" She took a chair and helped herself to the delicacies.

Sua joined them, "I did not realize how famished I was until smelling the food." She spoke with her mouth full in their tongue.

The three swallowed biscuits and tea without conversing. Stomachs satisfied, and bodies exhausted, they chose places, settled onto the bedding, and slept as the ship left the bay and entered the open sea.

During the voyage to Portland, Lein-Hua and the girls kept to themselves. The cabin hid them from the crewmen, some of whom reminded her of marks they'd been forced to service.

"I never thought I'd miss the privy behind the den. I hate using this chamber pot." Lein-Hua complained and placed the pot outside the door in a small crate as Haoli had instructed, his face reddened as he did so. She dropped the crate's lid and dashed back inside the cabin, leaning against the closed door.

"It is better than the crude accommodations for the men." Sua laughed at Lein-Hua, "I saw yesterday on my walk." Her body shuddered. "At least Oscar empties it often, and returns it with fresh seawater in the bottom."

Mei lay quietly, curled on her bedding, her stomach rolling with each motion of the ship. She ate little. Crusts of bread and sips of tea seemed to stabilize the agitation best. Her dreams took her back to the voyage to America, in the bottom of a ship. Dark. Cold. Drugged. Tied to the bunk. Lying in filth. She awoke, but could not shut the horror of her last voyage from her mind.

The youngest, Sua, however, was more adventurous. From the railing just outside the cabin, she watched the sea. She clutched the new overcoat tightly around her as the wind whipped against her thin body. She leaned against the baluster. Dolphins leaped and played along the ship's portside. Fascinated by them, Sua ran to the cabin. "Lein-Hua, Mei, come see. Fishes." Not waiting for them, she ran back to the railing.

"Not I." Mei groaned from her bed. "I can't look at the water."

Lein-Hua grabbed her coat and joined Sua. Both girls watched a dozen dolphins dive in and out of the blue water. "They dance." Lein-Hua words faded away in the wind.

The show over, Lein-Hua now noticed several crewmembers not far from where she stood had also watched the dolphins. Embarrassed, she retreated quick, to hide inside the cabin. She enjoyed making Mei sit up and smile with the news about the dolphins.

Late afternoon of the third day, Oscar stood at the rail with Haoli, Sua and Lein-Hua. "Look." Oscar pointed out a whale's fluke before it vanished into the ocean. "He will come up again just keep watching the surface."

Haoli repeated his words in Mandarin for the girls' understanding.

Patiently the three stared at the water and soon saw the fluke appear only long enough to splash as it sunk out of sight. They watched the smooth water anticipating another appearance of the whale when Sua saw a perfect circle of tiny bubbles floating to the top. Hundreds of them. Pointing to the area with the bubbles she shouted, "There he is."

The whale nosed up out of the water and dove back down, crossing through the froth. His tail slapped the rise as it completed the dive.

"He is feeding," Oscar explained. "He swims in a fast circle to rush small fish together. They are entrapped in his spinning funnel. Then the whale dives into them gulping as many minnows as he can catch."

Mesmerized by the story, Lein-Hua could not wait to tell Mei. As soon as the show ended, she hurried back to the cabin.

Mid-afternoon on the fourth day Sua rushed to the cabin and shouted, "We land, soon." She flopped on the floor next to Mei's cot. "Haoli says to get ready to leave the ship and that the Captain thinks it is best we stay in here until we are told it is safe to come out. We are approaching the dangerous sand bars in the throat of the Columbia River. The waters will be rough."

"Oh," Mei groaned, "I cannot think of it." The others tried to comfort her.

The girls rode out the passage, white knuckles clutching protruding boards on the walls of their cabin. When the ship settled from the awful swaying, Sua opened the door to the cabin. She saw Haoli and Oscar coming, waved and went out to them. She spoke with the two men and ran back to the cabin. Leaving the door open behind her she announced, "Haoli said we are at the Portland docks on the Willamette River. Where is that, Lein-Hua?"

"Ah, I do not know. I have not heard of it. We must pack?" Lein-Hua retrieved the carpetbag from the corner.

Just as she tied the bag shut, Haoli knocked on the cabin's doorframe. "Ready to go?" He asked. "We disembark soon." He stood looking into Lein-Hua's eyes then added, "I must warn you. We may run into trouble along the way. Not like here on the ship, the crew was warned to show you respect."

The crewmen worked with automated energy unloading cargo as they passed by to the gangplank. A few waved goodbye. Sua returned the gesture, smiling to ones she had met on her ventures.

Light rain drizzled. Haoli's words came back to Lein-Hua as she set foot on the dock. *We may run into trouble*. What did Haoli mean?

Chapter 10

"Where am I? My father's house? No. No now, it belongs to my son, Wong Mack. Mack, now in his seventies, walks bent with a cane, but manages the household well. I have lived here my entire life. My father, Haoli, was a wise man, he had his descendents in mind when he built this house. Let's see, now besides me, and Mack," she ticked a finger for each name, "my grandson Haoli Number Two, his wife Lilly, and their three children, Mandy, Bobby and baby Timothy." She stretched again and glanced out the window, the Sunday church folks had left. "This younger generation of the family acts more American than Chinese. Old customs are disappearing." Jie sighed. "So am I, just wasting away into a pile of bones that scarcely make a bulge under my blankets." She always felt a chill in spite of the summer's temperature, and pulled the covers up on her shoulders. "I always wonder what my mother felt in her escape to Idaho." ...

At the Portland's Oregon Railway and Navigation station, they did not enter the building with the other passengers, but boarded a train from the rail yard. "This way," Haoli led the three through two coaches sporting leather cushioned seats on each side of a narrow aisle, then into an empty dining car with two tables by the window across from a long counter lined with leather-backed stools. It was void of any odors except cleaning soaps. He saw Lein-Hua wrinkle her nose and grinned at her. Sounds of metal banging against metal came from the hidden kitchen area. Haoli guided them through the dinner's car, plus a Pullman coach containing several private sleeper rooms.

Past the coach, in the last car they found bare wooden benches against each sidewall. Two more benches filled the middle of the coach, backs together facing the ones on the sidewalls. Black smoke puffed into the crowded area from the wood-burning locomotive in front of them. Haoli guided the trio to the last vacant bench on the left side. Each took a seat.

On the bench across from them hunched a cripple-jointed man with a straggly gray beard hanging to his chest. He coughed into a snotty red handkerchief. Haoli sat next to him. Knowing that being Chinese his presence not welcomed, he left a space between him and the old man.

Lein-Hua muffled a cough under the collar of her coat and pulled the brim of her bonnet further down as if to hide, as the clanging bell announced the trip to be underway soon.

A flaxen-haired lady with rosy cheeks boarded last. Her eyes darted about the cramped coach as she followed the colored porter carrying her baggage. The only space available was between the old man and Haoli. The porter placed her tote next to it and left. She fought to balance herself as she glanced around, as if looking for a better seat.

Obviously a lady of high fashion, Haoli thought, porters never come in here, odd she is traveling third class. He noticed the woman's distressed expression and scooted closer to the old man, who again spit into his rag. With a sigh of resignation, the woman gathered the edge of her lavender bombazine gown close to her petite frame and sat on the bench's edge next to Haoli. Overtaken by the smoke, she pulled the end of her white velvet shawl over her nose and mouth. She sat straight, as if a board was attached to her back.

Maybe she is escaping from something, too, Haoli thought, or she is a widow going back home in the east. Or maybe, a kept woman of a wealthy merchant, now freed? Haoli could not help but enjoy the fragrance of her perfume as it vied with the smoke. Maybe violets, he reflected.

From under the wide brim of her boater, she studied the Chinese girls across the aisle on the middle bench. Lein-Hua and Sua stole glimpses at her. Catching their eyes, the lady turned away and gazed out the window across from her on the other side.

We must be the first Chinese she has ever seen, Haoli thought. Are we so odd? We have same bodies, minds, and hearts. Only our skin and eyes are different. I fear she would be even more uncomfortable if I were wearing a traditional tunic of silk brocade patterned diagonally with frog fasteners. Immediately he was glad he had chosen American clothes for their journey. At least we look like casual travelers.

Passengers stuffed carpetbags and straw suitcases under their seats and settled back for the two-day ride. With bells ringing, the dragon puffed from its underbelly and jerked forward. As the locomotive's engine roared, thick wood smoke wormed its way though cracks around the windows and drifted in clouds throughout the car, leaving soot on every surface. The smoke thickened in the coach as they pulled away from the station.

"Tickets. Tickets," called the conductor as he entered the coach.

Lein-Hua caught her breath. They had no tickets. They'd be put off the train. She stared at Haoli with wide eyes, but he did not move.

The old man hacked into his rag, then handed his ticket to the conductor, who punched it and gave it back to him. The lady pulled her ticket from her left sleeve and handed it to the conductor. When he returned it to her, she held it in her hand for a time before stuffing it back inside her blouse cuff. Ignoring the Chinese man, the conductor turned around and stood before Lein-Hua, waiting for response. She froze, knuckles white in her lap, she stole a glance at Haoli while the Conductor stared at her.

"Ah, here." Haoli drew the conductor's attention, gestured toward the three with an envelope, and handed it to him. "For my sisters and me." The lady arched an eyebrow, then looked down to her lap and adjusted the lump in her sleeve.

The conductor eyed the Chinese man wearing a dark blue suit, accepted the envelope, opened it finding four tickets, and punched them. He started to hand them back to Haoli, but instead, dropped them on the floor. Scattering they fell at Haoli's feet as the conductor walked away.

Lein-Hua stared at Haoli. Where had he gotten tickets? When? And the clothes? Only now, did she ponder at this miracle he'd performed. Escaping Zhifer. The ship. And, now this train. She did not even consider the phenomenon of the forgotten money inside her blouse. Disgusted at the soot settling on every inch of her, she brushed off her shoulder, leaving a black smudge. I must look like a blackbird she thought, and then worried if it would wash out of the new clothes. A Chinese laundry could do it. But, would there be one in this far-off Idaho?

Haoli smiled at her and spoke in Mandarin. "Rest, we have a long journey. Remember I told you about the mountains with trees too tall to see the tops, and the sky-blue lakes? We are going there now. To Idaho. You will like it. I promise." He handed her a paper package he retrieved from his carpetbag, "Here. Eat."

She unwrapped broken rice cakes and pieces of dried fish. Grateful, she took some and handed the wrapper to Sua and Mei. She tasted the familiar bits, prepared like the ones they ate on the ship, conscious that the American lady watched her, she swallowed.

The man had stopped coughing to listen to the foreign tongue and frowned at the Chinese girls in American clothing, but said nothing.

The locomotive steamed its way along the Oregon side of the Columbia River. Moving at a steady pace, heavy smoke puffed into the coach behind it. Lein-Hua watched out the filmy window across from her, past Haoli's head. She no longer could see the tall snow-covered mountain. Mount Hood, Haoli had told her its name the first time she saw it.

Soon high rocky cliffs with trees scattered along their ridges came into view. This is not yet Idaho, she thought. The trees are not tall enough. I can still see their tops. Later, she noticed a huge waterfall splashing down a tall bluff. Pointing it out to Mei and Sua, she turned her head, keeping her eye on the falling water as long it was visible as the train continued rocking and clanging forward, leaving it behind them.

Enjoying the scenery Lein-Hua was in deep thought when all of a sudden the coach turned black. She sat up straight. She blinked her eyes, but could not see anything, not even the hand which she held up to her face. The blackness engulfed her being. She heard Mei panting next to her. Before she could react, the light reappeared. She heard Haoli say, "What a dark tunnel." She let out her breath, glad the danger was over.

Tired, she leaned her head against the back of the hard seat and closed her eyes. The clanging of metal against metal of the wheels rang in her ears in a rhythmical harmony interspersed with coughing passengers. Her heart pounded in her ears, she did not rest well.

Haoli tilted his head back against his seat and closed his eyes. He envisioned his favorite uncle when he first met him again in America. Uncle Hong Kai had taken a puff from his pipe, lifted his head, and released a perfect artistic smoke stream. Uncle Hong Kai had told him of several things to never forget about the railroads. "Our clansmen worked hard to build though the High Sierras. We built tall bridges, felled logs, hewed them flat-edged, and tied them together. The angles and lengths all calculated by our men of wisdom with their abacuses who were accused of only playing with beads." Uncle Kai had taken another draw, skillfully exhaled and looked Haoli in the eye. "Never forget these things."

And Haoli had not forgotten.

Uncle's voice echoed in his head. "The Irish, Swedes, and all compare us to monkeys." Haoli startled at the memory and sat straighter. He pulled his feet back under the bench, leaned back again and closed his eyes. Not the most comfortable position, but then why should he have luxury when so many of his forefathers lived such hard lives?

He returned to his musings. "It was our clans who knew how to build the impossible." Uncle Kai had said, "We contrived the Great Wall in China of stones over terrain where no man could walk upright, and we did the same for American railroads." His uncle had paused and looked him in the eye.

"Our men wove great baskets of vines and young branches, some large enough to hold several workmen. On the waist-high baskets they knotted four eyelets in the directions of the Four Winds. They etched them with befitting prayers before hand-braided ropes were tied to the eyelets. The baskets holding two or three men were lowered over the edge of a cliff to the roadbed site, sometimes hundreds of feet below."

Uncle Hong Kai dragged on his pipe and blew the graceful stream once more. "They swayed in the wind, working to chisel away rocks and earth. We set dynamite charges and swung away from the cliff with all our might. Men on top hoisted us up, away from the explosion. But many died. Others would then go down to complete the work. Sometimes baskets tore and men fell to their deaths."

Haoli opened his eyes and looked out the window He could almost feel the cool breeze on his damp skin and smell pine trees his uncle talked of instead of the locomotive's stinking smoke that choked his breath. He fought to recall each word Uncle had uttered. Then he thought about Westwood in Idaho. Recalling the roadbed dig, he left over a year-and-a-half ago, he, too, could take pride in building a railroad to span the continent.

Finally asleep, Haoli dreamed. Uncle Kai's vivid face looked up at him from the basket. Then, Uncle lit a fuse and pushed out from the cliff. Haoli heard men shouting commands as they struggled to hold the rope steady and pull against the weight in the basket. He saw a bright flash, and felt the earth shudder in a deafening blast. Then all went dark.

Haoli awoke with a jerk that nearly unseated him. His eyes flew open. He shook himself from the nightmare. He felt the lady straighten and tighten her shawl over her nose and mouth. "Excuse please," he struggled to recover from the illusion.

"Of course." Her eyes shifted first to Haoli then at the disgusting man. Then the woman's eyes settled to stare past the Chinese girls to the view out the dirty window.

He watched the man bend over and spit into his rag and realized the blasting sound had been yet another of his fits. The glare of light had been from leaving another train tunnel. He saw part of the tunnel's frame and dark entrance behind them as the train twisted around a bend following the Columbia.

The old one resettled on the bench but not before the continued hacking awoke Lein-Hua, who yawned, looked about the coach then re-closed her eyes.

Haoli observed the girls. *I need to complete this journey and keep them from harm.* He vowed to himself as if a pledge to his *jia,* his *family.* He could sleep no more, so sat listening to the metallic music of the rolling coaches.

Studying Lein-Hua's face, love filled his heart and his uncle's image pushed from his mind. He hoped helping these girls would heal the pain of losing his sister. *I will not forget the cruelties my kinsmen have suffered.* He swore to tell Hong Kai's stories of malice to the Chinese as they worked the railroad to all who would listen; and the tragedy of Ming Yun. And Yue. And, now these girls.

The Oregon Railway and Navigation paused in startup villages to take on and disembark passengers. When it stopped in Wallula, Washington, they changed trains, boarding the newest railroad, the Northern Pacific, for the first time. "My railroad," Haoli bragged as he led them through the rail yard instead of going to the station platform with the other passengers. They had only half-an-hour between trains before theirs would leave.

After settling the girls in their seats on the Northern Pacific, much like that of the Oregon Railway's, Haoli hurried from the coach and crossed the tracks to purchase white bread sweetened with molasses from a street vendor. He dashed back to sit beside Lein-Hua just as the train jerked forward. The strange sweetened bread, tested on taste buds, finally met with approval, made the three smile at each other. After eating the last of the unusual treat, the girls leaned against each other as they napped.

The conductor's booming voice awakened them. "Ainsworth. Next stop. Twenty minutes.

Once more Haoli produced the requested tickets when the conductor came through the coach. He did not have to look around to know the old man with the long beard was on this train, he heard the familiar coughing from the middle of the coach. The young lady in lavender must have left them at some hamlet while they were sleeping, unnoticed until now.

"Ainsworth. Next stop." The conductor repeated and exited the car as he finished calling out, "twenty minutes." His words hung in the smoky air.

Haoli straightened to pay full attention, realizing he did not know exactly where they were. He brushed his fingers through his hair and smiled at the girls. They also shook themselves awake and straightened their clothing.

Lein-Hua frowned. "Where are we, Haoli? What is next for us?" He noticed those about them listened to their foreign tongue.

He reached over and patted her arm. "Do not worry, little one. We have a long journey. Where the Columbia River meets the Snake River and divides the town of Ainsworth, we will have a long wait. To cross the Snake River the train will need to ferry each car across the river separately. We can stretch our legs."

"How do we ferry?" Lein-Hua smoothed her skirt and twisted her fingers together in her lap. "I do not know this word."

"Ah, ferry. A ferry is a large boat that carries loads across the river. Because the bridge is not completed, the

82

brakemen will disengage each car. The engineer will steer the locomotive onto a long barge that will float it across. Then, the ferry returns for the next coach. Each is pulled by mules onto the barge and ferried across. This is why the train does not have many cars. Once the train is guided onto tracks on the other side, and the cars hooked together again, we will be on our way.

"I do not like this idea." Lein-Hua's face soured her expression, showing concern more than her words.

Haoli put his arm around Lein-Hua and hugged her close to him, "Not to fear. We will not stay on board the train. A separate ferry will take us across. We will arrive before the train is ready to travel again. We can eat dinner. You will see where they are building the bridge from the ferry. I am told it should be finished soon."

Sua and Mei's faces brightened, but Lein-Hua's did not, "We will surely sink in the water." She shook her head and looked at her feet.

Haoli noticed the fear in her timid demeanor. Maybe I'm wrong. Maybe she is just tired, not frightened. "You will like the country we are going to, he tried to soothe her anxiety. Think of the tall trees and not of the ferry. The country is unlike the city. You will see."

"I trust you are right," Mei firmed her jaw. "You must be, or we will be no better off than before."

"*Ping an. Safe.*" Haoli smiled to assure the three the best he knew how. He dug deep into his trouser pocket and felt for the cloth wrapped coins. "Perhaps we can buy a hot meal while we are stopped."

The train slowed, steam hissed from its belly, and bells rang as it rolled to a clang-jerk clang-jerk stop. In the general hubbub of passengers preparing to leave the train, a hefty woman directed two young boys to gather their bags and not to bump an inebriated man next to them. One of the boys stared then pointed at the Chinese. "They look funny mommy." He wrinkled his face. The woman hushed him and pulled him to a seat farther away.

The conductor's voice boomed again. "Ainsworth Ferry boarding in ten minutes. Stop time about two hours on the other side." He repeated the warning as he left for the next car.

Lein-Hua started to rise with the other people. Haoli kept his seat. With a tiny wave of fingertips, he indicated she should stay.

"We wait. Never push the Whites. Let them go first. It is expected."

A well-dressed businessman who hadn't spoken to anyone during the whole trek and a drunk were the last standing in the exit aisle.

Haoli rose, picked up the baggage and motioned the girls to follow.

Chapter 11

"I realize some of my stories may horrify you and the younger grandchildren, Molly. But it is necessary to tell the truth of these things. I remember the past as vividly as if it had happened only yesterday," Jie grinned, glad that she kept the promise and did not forget. "Father had a hard time bringing home the girls—all because he was Chinese."...

From the ferry dock at North Ainsworth, Haoli and the girls faltered over a labyrinth. "Careful of your step," Haoli warned. They crossed the dozen tracks, used for connecting the coaches, watching their feet as they picked their way across to the squat brick station. As they entered the doorway, they paused at the sight of the crowded dining room. Most of the passengers from the train sat on wooden benches at three long tables, eating and visiting. Haoli saw the unfamiliar scent seemed to pinch the girls' nostrils. He winked at Mei as she sniffed the air and made a face of discontent. "The aroma is not as welcoming as noodles or fish, is it? You smell Irish stew. I know it from the rail camps. You will like it. Come." Together they stood at the end of the serving line.

At the nearest table, two small brothers from the train whined about not wanting to eat. The older boy kicked the younger under the table. His mother did not seem to notice as she shoved a spoonful of stew into her mouth. The last few travelers stood in line, in front of them, where a man on the opposite side of a table slopped the brown mixture with orange lumps from a huge kettle into tin bowls. Wisps of smoke floated from the top of an iron cook stove behind him, mixing with the tang of the stew.

The old man with the continual cough leaning on his cane limped across the room from the direction of signs pointing the way to the privy. "Let him go before you," Haoli motioned to Lein-Hua. The girls allowed the man to precede them. Sua and Mei, following Lein-Hua, stepped up in line before Haoli. After the old man was served, Lein-Hua studied the cook, as he scooped food into a bowl. He dropped a soda biscuit on top and handed it to her. She took it. "Thank you."

Each girl accepted a full bowl, picked up a spoon from the table then waited for Haoli's guidance. While holding his dish with one hand, he indicated the far corner with the other, "Over there, we can sit alone," he nodded toward the empty bench at the last table.

"Who do you think you are, chink?" A fist landed on Haoli's shoulder with a force that staggered him. He stumbled, caught his balance and faced a burly man whose contemptuous sneer twisted his fat lips. "This here's for Whites," he boomed, catching everyone's attention. "You and your wenches aren't welcome here, you see?"

Haoli held his tongue, but his insides flamed. Embarrassed for the girls, he had to keep face. He nodded to the stranger, and before he could express an apology, hard knuckles struck his jaw, then his stomach.

He fell backward, landing against the wall. His legs crumbled beneath him as he slid to the floor, the bowl and steaming contents flying.

"Ohhh," a woman screamed and jumped away to avoid hot splatter. The two boys laughed. "Hush boys," their mother shushed them. They quieted but wore big grins staring at the chinaman on the floor. Another lady gasped and another screamed and jumped away from the table. Several men got to their feet.

The attacker jerked the full serving scoop from the cook and yelled, "You hungry chink? Eat this." He dumped it on Haoli's head. A man and two women at the first table closest to the attack jumped up from their places as stew splashed on them, "yikes, euweee," one yelled scraping the food off clothes and skin.

"Yuk, what a mess," her friend brushed stew from her sleeve with her napkin gawking at the victim. Two little girls ducked under the next table by their mother's feet. She looked down at them and let them be.

Terror blanched Lein-Hua's face. "Shhhhh," Mei covered Lein-Hua's mouth with her hand and muffled her friend's scream. Together the three scrambled to the corner behind the table and crouched down, huddled like frightened bunnies spotted by a hawk.

Haoli swiped away blood and hot gravy and vegetable bits now dribbling down the side of his face, and rubbed at his chin. His face burning, he looked up wide-eyed, speechless to see the man standing over him lifting a booted-foot to kick his face.

Three men moved in behind the thug in time to stop the raised leg. A husky man in a red plaid mackinaw pulled the bully back. "He's had enough."

Readied for a new fight, "What the..." the aggressor turned to seeing who had grabbed him, "stay outta this..." but he quickly backed down when he saw the scarred face of the smallest of Haoli's three rescuers. The scar stretched from his left ear, across the jaw to his chin, giving him a savage look that matched the one in his eyes. "You're done here," the man growled. "We'll take over now. Be on your way."

"I ain't had my supper yet. That chink got in line ahead of me. He needs to learn his place."

"Then get your eats and get out," ordered the third man. His full rust-colored beard gave him the rugged appearance of a lumberjack no one would want to tangle with.

Outnumbered, the attacker held out his hand to the cook for a filled tin and a spoon. He accepted the meal, spun around on his left heel, stomped a half-dozen strides to the door and exited onto the depot platform.

Inside, the lumberjack offered Haoli a hand, "Here, let me help you up," he pulled Haoli to his feet.

"Maybe this will help," the red-bearded one gave him a wet cloth retrieved from the cook.

Unsure what to expect, Haoli kept one eye on the three men as he wiped his bleeding mouth and cleaned off the stew. Then, using his best English he said, "Thank you," keeping the towel pressed against his burnt cheek.

The men shrugged. "Sorry for the fracas, mister." The scar-faced man offered his hand in a friendly gesture. "Don't know what gets into people."

The confrontation over, other travelers turned back to their own dinners. The three protectors escorted Haoli to the table where the girls now sat hunched over their bowls, but not eating. "I'm alright. Do not worry," he spoke quietly in Mandarin, then dabbed the towel at his face again wiping off more blood.

The cook brought over a fresh bowl of stew and set it on the table before Haoli. He nodded his appreciation, picked up the spoon and took a bite. Chewing hurt, but through swelling lips he tried to smile at Lein-Hua. "Eat. We've not much time left before the train leaves." He attempted another grin, hoping to ease his own worry as the three picked up the awkward spoons with fingers used to chopsticks. Adopting a taste for this strange food would be difficult for them, he thought.

A businessman in a black broadcloth coat and a stove-pipe hat leaned over from his chair, "Glad to see no real harm done, boy. That's some language you're using there. Never heard anything like it," he glanced at the three finishing their dinners, "and these little gals understood."

Haoli did not need to guess at his *business.* The girls bent their heads with eyes focused on their bowls, but Haoli observed their fright by the tightness around their mouths and the shift in their eyes. They would know the man's profession better than he.

"My sisters," Haoli lied, his eyes glinting. He would fight if necessary and not lose this time. The man returned to his dinner.

"All aboard! Depart in ten minutes." The conductor's voice rang out in the dinning room.

The old man cleared his throat then quieted, attracting looks of disgust. He limped out of the dining area to stand on the platform leaning on his walking stick.

"Stop that you two. Your scuffling drives me mad, fighting is not good," their mother scolded as she pushed them from the room with her suitcases.

Others had finished eating, paid and also left, ignoring the Chinese as though they were invisible.

The girls waited for Haoli's next move. They joined the end of the line to pay for their meals. Haoli felt the coins in his pocket and pulled out his largest silver piece. "Thank you," he handed the coin to the man and waited for his change, but received none.

"What you waiting for, boy? Get on out of here," The depot master ordered. "It's the price you pay for causing a ruckus. Now get."

Haoli picked up his carpetbags, bowed, "thank you, most kind sir," he told the man, then turned to the girls signaling them to go. They left the depot to board the train without another word.

What next? Haoli wondered holding his side trying to ignore the pain, hoping the girls wouldn't notice.

Chapter 12

Molly found strength in her Christian faith and understood the impoverished struggles of her ancestors. Confirming the promise, she whispered to Jie, "I will never forget." She listened to Nanai's stories with conviction that the discrimination must change. She could see that her elder's body ached from age, and that she could not get about except in the wheelchair, but Molly knew nothing blocked Jie's mind or her will to remember...

The girls followed Haoli outside as the Northern Pacific whistle tooted its first warning to board. They stayed close behind him as he limped across six tracks to the coaches.

Haoli stopped. "Wait for the other travelers to embark first." When all boarded, he led them to the steps. Lein-Hua went first. Her foot slipped but she caught herself, gripping the handrail. She straightened, brushed at her coat skirt and climbed the last step into the coach. On board, each headed towards the back seats. As they jostled their way down the aisle, taking care not to bump into other passengers, a man tipped the brim of his dirty beige cap to Haoli. "Feeling better?"

Haoli recognized the red-bearded man. "Yes, much better, thank you," he attempted a warm smile through bruised lips and nodded his head. Then he spotted the scar-faced man two seats away. Haoli watched for the third rescuer amongst the travelers as he made his way to the end of the car, but did not see him. He wedged himself on to the hard bench across the aisle from where the girls found room to sit. Thick smoke already filled the car.

The same two youngsters from the depot, tugged at each other when their mother wasn't watching. The train lurched as it pulled away from the station and the smaller boy fell out of his seat. The portly woman scowled at him but said nothing as he got up and sat next to his brother, pinching the other boy's leg.

Haoli glanced about the coach. He listened for the hacking. He did not hear it. The old man must have stayed at Ainsworth. It would be good to arrive at Westwood and be off this train too.

He stretched against the hard bench, winced and clutched his stomach, hugging both arms across it. His face contorted from a spasm of pain. The humiliation of appearing weak in front of others stabbed his heart. Shamed by the attack in the diner, he averted his eyes away from the girls' and stared out the dirty window. It is too difficult not to defend my honor he admonished himself. I must not let them think me a weak man, he thought. With purpose, he uncurled his body and allowed himself to pose as if relaxing. He studied Lein-Hua's face and saw concern. "Do not worry little one, I am fine." His heart skipped a beat. His true feelings for her became apparent—he was in love with her. He leaned against the stiff wooden seat and tried to relax. He had much to think about.

Within minutes, the train lumbered away from the banks of the Snake River, leaving Ainsworth behind. The coach swayed behind the locomotive. The clickety-clacking of the wheels resembled music and carried them towards a new life.

The stale odor of unwashed passengers mingled with smoke, strong enough for Haoli to taste it. He saw that Lein-Hua, Sua, and Mei all covered their noses with coat sleeves.

The train made several stops, admitting more passengers than got off. The woman and her youngsters, who constantly squabbled with each other, got off at Bluff Wells. Arms wrapped across his ribs, Haoli observed the new travelers who had boarded. The coach still carried too many people.

The conductor came through the car and shouted, "Next stop, three hours, Well Number Seven." Haoli shut his eyes welcoming the time to sleep.

He slept most of the seventy miles to Well Number Seven, where the train stopped for water. He awoke and opened his eyes when the rocking of the coach halted. He assessed his position before moving. He had not dreamed and felt more rested. His ribs ached. He took a deep breath, which rewarded him with a sharp pain. He grimaced in silence. He noticed the girls were awake and talking in whispers.

Haoli cringed as he got to his feet. He limped across the aisle to where the girls sat. "Look," he pointed out the window. The four watched, as did most of the other passengers, as dozens of men formed a line from Well Seven's water tower, up the slope to the locomotive.

A man positioned at the tower took a bucket from a pile, filled it with water and handed it to the man next to him. The second man passed the pail to the third, while accepting another from the first man who had filled it. Water splashed as each man jerked his arms, catching and delivering the containers along the line. One after another, buckets almost flew from one hand to the next in rhythm to their singing, "Heave. Ho. Heave. Ho. Here you go."

"It's a 'jerk-water' line," the red-bearded man who had rescued Haoli explained to the onlookers. "They have to hand-haul water to the engine because they haven't piped it to the station area yet. This is called a *jerk-water* town, only a water stop for the train. Fascinating, isn't it?"

Haoli repeated to the girls in their tongue what the man said and added, "I've only observed a water brigade in action to fight fires."

A few more passengers came aboard at the Well Number Seven stop, and the coach shook and rattled again as it proceeded. A fat man appeared in the doorway, wearing wrinkled woolen pants and a crumpled white shirt, not tucked in at the waist. A too-short black tie hung askew from its proper place, his stomach bulged beneath it as he stumbled down the narrow aisle.

"He's drunk and he stinks," Haoli spoke in Mandarin.

The voice drew the drunkard's attention. His eyes settled on Mei. "Hey," his voice slurred, "I know you. You're that little whore at Zhifer's."

Mei's face blanched. She ducked her head and pulled her bonnet brim down to hide. Haoli saw her knuckles turn white as she gripped her coat button. He vaulted from his seat and stood in front of the drunk in an attempt to hide the girls from prying eyes.

Lein-Hua put her arm around Mei and pulled her close.

"My sisters," he shouted. "Not whore." His stance firm, hands raised, ready to defend the girls' honor though his size was no match against the fat man. Haoli knew his suffering muscles rendered his martial arts nearly useless, but still he positioned himself against the attacker.

The drunk slammed Haoli onto the lap of a middle-aged woman, who screamed and pushed the chinaman off her legs. Haoli hit the floor and folded into a ball. Pain shot throughout his body. He let out a low groan.

The scar-faced man pulled Haoli to his feet. "Seems you keep finding yourself in a predicament, little buddy." He helped Haoli to his seat and glared at the fat man. "That's enough. You're done here."

The drunk took a seat down the aisle from them and stared back openly at Mei.

Haoli crossed his arms over his stomach again. "Thank you again," his head bobbed his thanks. It hurt too much to smile.

The conflict over, Haoli relaxed and told the girls in Mandarin, "His soul was removed to make room for his big belly." Their eyes twinkled as they shared the joke, keeping smiles suppressed.

Haoli looked about the coach. Amazed people could so easily ignore what went on around them. *I get beat up and people go back to reading a book as though nothing happened.* Even the scar-faced man settled in his seat and snoozed. Haoli took the cue, leaned his head against the coach wall, closed his eyes and mind, and tried to sleep through his pain.

Awakened by the memorable rattle and jerking of the train, Haoli still felt the throbbing in his side. He made no movement. Through the streaked windows, dawn's light revealed mountains far off on either side of the tracks, their heights topped with trees. He quickly regarded the girls, sleeping peacefully. Good, he thought. Lein-Hua slept with her head resting against Mei, who awakened.

Mei stretched and moved Lein-Hua from her shoulder to Sua's. "Haoli, do you know a place called Spoocan Fulls?"

"Ahh, yes, Spokane Falls. Are we coming to it?"

"The conductor announced Spol-can-phalls is our next stop," she tried her best to pronounce the name as Haoli had. "Where is that, Haoli?" Mei whispered as Lein-Hua awoke and stretched her legs.

"It is not far, I think." Excitement lit his words as he recognized the landscape. "But, we may have to take a freight wagon to Idaho if the railroad is not finished. It will be rough and monotonous, but you will think you are in the Celestial Kingdom when we reach Westwood."

"It sounds like a happy place, Haoli." Lein-Hua looked into his eyes. "If we *ever* get there," she added, doubt coating her words. "Are you feeling better?"

Protecting his stomach, he tested the tenderness of his ribs, pushing gently with his fingers. It hurt. Bad. "How long did I sleep?" His face twitched when he moved.

"Many hours—four I think. We stopped in Sprague. After others got off, we ate the last of our rice cakes, but saved some for you." As she handed him the food, her heart fluttered as her hand touched his. Blushing, she looked away so no one would notice.

He nibbled a piece of the rice cake. It hurt his jaw to chew so he sucked and mashed it with his tongue then swallowed. "You did well," he said. "I do feel better now that I've rested. It is good you stayed aboard. 'A camel standing amidst a flock of sheep' is most noticeable'."

Haoli tried figuring the distance of their travel. Just less than fifty miles from Sprague to Spokane and another, maybe, thirty to Westwood—but the tickets had Rathdrum printed on them. He was not sure of this place, Rathdrum? But new jerkwater towns sprouted up along the railroad everywhere. Would the tracks be completed to Westwood? The dig had just started when he left more than eighteen months before. Not having to travel by wagon from Spokane to Westwood would save time, and be more comfortable for them all. He had to trust Mr. Ableman's plan.

At Spokane Falls the new depot building, with its fresh red paint, stood proudly atop a short incline overlooking the city. As they waited for the other passengers to disembark, Sua and Mei busied themselves re-packing the carpetbag after having washed up and changed their blouses in the public lavatory.

Left alone, Haoli took Lein-Hua's hand and leaned close to her. The words he wanted to say had tumbled in his mind since leaving Ainsworth. This feeling was new to him, an area of the heart he had never explored before. He fumbled, twisting his fingers around hers, smiled and looked into her eyes. Now fourteen, she was young in years, but hardened by her experiences. They could wait to be married. He just knew he wanted no other man to have this sweet girl.

Lein-Hua looked into his bruised face and waited for him to speak.

Finally, Haoli found his voice and whispered. "Honor me, be my wife." He stared into her dancing eyes, and saw that words caught in her throat. Her head nodded once, and she looked away from him.

In the Spokane Falls depot's waiting room, Haoli limped over to the ticket counter to ask about the *Rathdrum* destination. The Station Master dismissed the chinaman with terse, gruff replies. "Please, sir," Haoli persisted until the man gave his attention. Haoli touched the burn on his face. *Perhaps my injuries annoy him.* He pressed his query, "Can you tell me if *Rathdrum* is a new town? I do not know this place. I need to go to Westwood."

"It is the same place. Now step aside, I have customers to tend to." The man waved his hand at the chinaman as if to brush him out of the way. Haoli stepped away from the counter.

Relieved to find that Rathdrum *was* his Westwood, and indeed, they could arrive by train. He noted the date on the depot wall sign. October 27, 1883. He overheard a man telling his wife that the Northern Pacific tracks had been completed to Rathdrum in Mid-July. Holding his aching side, he moved with difficulty back to where the girls sat on a bench in the corner of the room. "I have good news. We are almost home!" Now if Mr. Ableman kept his promise to send Wong Pai a telegram announcing our arrival. And if it was delivered, Haoli worried knowing messages rarely made it to Chinatown. He sat next to Lein-Hua, grinning with excitement, "It will be good to see Idaho and to show it off to you and the girls."

As the train ran eastward, leaving Spokane behind, Lein-Hua became aware of the countryside. The mountains, visible on all sides of the wide prairie seemed to envelope her as if they were a protecting fortress. The prairie sported a colorful mixture of untamed brown grasses and harvested farmland, dotted with occasional hardwood trees enflamed with their yellow-orange autumn leaves, and tall evergreens. Smoke rose from farmhouse chimneys, twining in the late October air. Grazing cattle grouped together near them. Boulders poked up in various sizes. She watched for rice paddies but never saw them. Not like in China, this country displayed odd scenery, yet pleasing. The farms differed very little as they passed by in the window, most displayed the same split-rail fencing around red barns and smaller shanty houses. Horses, cattle, and dry land. Haoli sat next to her, holding her hand. She turned from the window and saw Mei smile at her. Lein-Hua's face flushed but she did not take her hand from his.

The scenery beyond the window slowed as the conductor entered the coach and shouted. "Idaho. Silver Lake stop. Water only." Hadn't they just left Moab only minutes ago? Maybe they did not fill the water there? It was a quick stop, wasn't it?

Haoli recognized the place he and Wong Pai had shared a meal at the rail camp. It was Mud Lake, not *Silver Lake*, like the sign read. Another name change? What else would be different? Across the coach, a woman moaned. "Why are we stopping again?" she whined.

"It won't be long now, dear." He heard a man's low voice trying to comfort her. "These short stops offer local travelers quick access to towns." Haoli reflected on their journey as he looked about at the other passengers. Not one who had began the expedition with them in Portland had come this far. They had encountered all types of people. Some friendly. But most not—not to them. The train lurched forward, jolting him from his meanderings with its clanging.

"The next stop is your new home." Haoli informed them, now familiar with the area. "It is well. I am ready to be off this rackety train."

"Will we really be home, Haoli?" Lein-Hua moved her hand from his grip and stretched.

"Really." His soft voice promised.

Mei fidgeted in her seat. "I can not wait to leave this coach." She wrinkled her nose drawing her face into a pout. "I forget what air without smoke is like."

"Me, too," Sua laughed, her expression mirroring Mei's.

Lein-Hua giggled with her friends. "This new place cannot come fast enough for me, either."

"Look!" Haoli pointed across from the bend in the tracks. "See those buildings? That's it! We are home!" His shouts drew the attention of several passengers who also turned their heads in the direction of buildings and tall trees on the hillside, south of the tracks.

As they rounded a long curve, the locomotive slowed. The conductor hollered, "Rathdrum." The familiar clacking-singing rhythm dwindled. In another minute, seeming like forever to Lein-Hua, the belching dragon stopped.

PART

TWO

1883

Chapter 13

"I used to go to the depot and pretend I saw my mother, Lein-Hua, getting off the train for her first look at Rathdrum, Auntie Sua told me about it." She stilled a moment, then making a point added, *"Do not confuse the Northern Pacific Depot with Milwaukie's still standing near the park, at the edge of town. Two different depots."*...

As Lein-Hua stepped from the last stair of the train, she reached for Haoli's extended hand. Standing on the wooden platform, she beamed as she sucked in a deep gulp of fresh air.

Morning sunshine warmed her. It seemed to welcome them all, as the three stared, devouring the sights. Lein-Hua's face widened as a true smile etched across it. Realizing she was looking at tall trees and a mountain behind them. She shifted her eyes from the mountain back to the station. A tree next to it was so tall she could not see the top from where she stood. This indeed was the place Haoli had told her about.

Her eyes glanced around, even more surprised to see Chinese men mingling within the crowd of about fifty people. The celestials moved about in the midst of duties, as though they belonged. Passengers with carpetbags or cases sat on benches, while others waited for friends or family members to arrive. All Lien-Hua noticed, of differ nationalities, conversed pleasantly with one another.

A Chinese man following a hefty white woman crossed the yard, carrying luggage into the depot. Another, with a young boy, exited the depot and strolled off towards the buildings, which appeared to be the main part of town.

Confused, Lein-Hua glanced at Haoli then at Sua and Mei. They see them, too, she thought and smiled without curving her lips—a habit she'd taught herself to keep from showing emotion.

"You are a bright flower of meditation in the wilderness. What are your thoughts?" Haoli's question brought her out of the daze.

"Did you see them?" She nodded to Haoli in the direction of the man and boy.

"Yes."

Lein-Hua blinked, making sure she was not dreaming. She noticed that Mei and Sua also stared.

"Haoli, can this really be?" asked Sua. "Can we, ah, can we, go where, ah, we want? Anywhere? Anytime?"

Haoli stepped between Sua and Mei and put his arms around both girls' shoulders. "Yes. Anywhere. Anytime." To Lein-Hua, he looked as if he hoped he was right.

"Oh," Sua and Mei breathed at the same time.

"Haoli, hey, Hong Haoli?"

Lein-Hua turned hearing Haoli's name being shouted from near the end of the waiting train where the brakeman checked the couplers and brakes between the cars.

Whirling towards the voice, Haoli hollered, "Wong Pai. Ang Li." He started to sprint to reach his friends, but the throbbing in his body stopped him in his second step. He stood still, letting them advance the length of two train cars.

Wong Pai seized Haoli's hand in a tight grip. "We looked for you in the coaches. Most glad to see you, Haoli."

The three men laughed and greeted each other like brothers reunited, as if one had been lost and the others frightened he would never be found.

"I told Pai you'd be on today's train." The thinner man grabbed Haoli's hand away from Wong Pai and pulled him into an embrace then let go quickly, as if embarrassed when he realized *girls* were watching.

Haoli let out a muffled grunt at being hugged too tightly and was relieved Ang Li let go of him.

"If you know so much, why have we checked the depot every day for the past week since the telegram came?" Wong Pai chided Ang Li.

"No matter now, Pai." Li turned his attention back to Haoli. "It's good you are here. How was the trip?"

"It was good." By habit, Haoli's hand rubbed at the pain in his left side.

Lein-Hua recognized the names as the friends who Haoli had told her about so many times. She peeked at Sua and Mei who had backed away from the men. Haoli faced the girls. Both men bowed to them.

Haoli gestured towards Mei with his hand. "This is Mei."

She smiled from under the brim of her bonnet and ducked her head again.

"And this is Sua."

Sua gave a quick bow then stepped back next to Mei.

Then he took Lein-Hua's hand and pulled her close to his side. "And, my friends, this is Lein-Hua."

Lein-Hua looked secure at Haoli's side and bent her head with a half bow.

"It is good to have you join us here," Ang Li greeted the three. "Now, where is that sister of yours?" He rubbed his hands together eager to meet the one he'd heard about while digging on the railbed not so long ago.

"She is—she is gone." Haoli hung his head and gave it a slight shake. "She died in the dens."

"No! Not so! I'm so sorry. I can not believe this sad news."

"No, not good news. But, these girls are safe now." Haoli's voice lowered. He took the carpetbag from Sua. To change the direction of the conversation, he handed the bag to Ang Li and adjusted the weight of his own valise over his shoulder to follow Wong Pai to his donkey-drawn cart.

As they had become accustomed, the girls followed Haoli. Ang Li quickly fell into step along side them in the muddy street. The recent rain left the air freshened and cooled. The morning sun kissed them, like magic sent from the ancestors. Ang Li helped Sua into the cart, smiling at her. She lowered her head, shying away.

Pai lifted Mei to the box-seat. "Did you have an agreeable trip?"

To shy to speak, Mei did not answer, but gave a nervous grin and nodded twice before settling herself next to Sua. Ang Li climbed aboard positioning himself near Lein-Hua, across from Sua and Mei.

Sensitive to Mei's mood, Haoli interrupted, "We all had a good journey, and are tired. Can't wait to get some good rest, then we can show these little ones their new town." As Haoli climbed up onto the seat next to Pai his foot slipped. Attempting to catch his balance, he fell against the sideboard landing on his ribs. He let out a low groan before relaxing next to Pai.

Wong Pai and Ang Li glanced at each other. Taking the reins, Pai chatted of happenings while Haoli was gone. Eighteen months was a long time to crowd into one twenty-some-minute ride.

Pai guided the donkey cart away from the station, down a slope turning right onto a rutted roadway. It was the main road that stretched west to Spokane Falls and northeast towards Fish Lake, now called Twin Lakes, Pai informed them. The girls and Ang Li remained silent, listening to Pai's story about Rathdrum welcoming the first NP train in July.

Haoli recognized the route leading to the old rail camp, now more defined as a road rather than the simple pathway he had walked thousands of times to the dig. In only a few minutes they had left the last of the town's houses behind as they entered a clearing of the trees toward the familiar mountain. They came to the shallow, flowing creek. A large ponderosa pine rose from the creek bank, a four-foot temple at its base. Immediately Haoli recognized the place of his cousin's grave. New red paper ribbons decorated the brick temple with clay molded at the top into a dome, all painted white. Candle flames flickered under the arch, protected from the wind. Wong Pai halted the cart, turned to Haoli and smiled.

Haoli slid down from the seat, protecting his side, approached the temple, bowed and offered a prayer. The others stayed in the cart and waited. He mounted the cart again, pulling his sore body onto the seat and wiped mud off his shoes against the edge of the cart. "It is good this spot has been marked and Ming Yun's life is honored. Too many were buried along the railbed with no regard for their existence. I could not let that happen to my cousin. I will never forget that day when the entire crew rebelled against Swartz. Thank you for showing me this."

"We did it for all Chinese, Haoli." Pai slapped the reins gently on the donkey's backside and they crossed over the bridge of smooth hewn logs.

"I have missed Storm King Mountain, and the trees," Haoli voiced his deep thoughts.

"It is called Rathdrum Mountain now," Pai informed Haoli.

"So many names changed." Haoli sighed with disappointment. The sun faded behind a cloud as he sniffed at the pine-scented air and sucked in fresh air. "But they cannot change the fresh skies, can they?" He stole a look back at the girls and smiled. "This is better than the train's smoke, is it not?"

Each girl smiled back in agreement, but did not speak— not in front of the strangers in the cart. Wong Pai and Ang Li honored their silence, without talking.

Beyond the creek, beautiful pines, tamaracks, cedars, and firs came into full view, snuggled against the base of the mountain, and towered over huts that looked to be one and two rooms. It was a Chinese town, separated from the main city, a mile away. Haoli stared at the unexpected village, "Ahh, this was our camp." Several rows of huts lined each side of the roadway, dampened from recent rain. At the end, he could see a blacksmith shop with a corral behind it, holding several horses and donkeys. He swelled with pride that so much had been accomplished in his absence.

Pai halted the cart in front of the third house on the left, jumped down from his seat and announced, "This is your new home, ladies."

"Ohhh." Lein-Hua uttered, astonished at the sight of a complete Chinese homestead. "This is wonderful," her hand flew up and covered her mouth, embarrassed she had spoken.

"It is wonderful," he repeated, reassuring the girls by his tone.

Pai pointed out Bachelor's Row, where unmarried men roomed together in several crude shacks, closer to the Mountain. At the end of the street, two more houses undergoing construction stood side by side without roofs or doors.

"I have not seen grass-roofed huts since leaving China." Lein-Hua found herself mesmerized by the sight. Finally, she noticed Sua and Mei also stared, their expressions reflected their yearnings for home when they saw the familiar huts.

Lein-Hua discovered that they were *not* the only Chinese women here, as Haoli had warned. And, there were children too. Lots of them. Some her own age—budding into teen years. But misuse had aged her into womanhood. She might have been innocent if she had come with her family as these had. Their new home, set between two ample ones both occupied by families, was an unpretentious wood-built house with a prairie-grass sod roof.

Four women with three toddlers in tow greeted the newcomers and honored them with traditional bows, which made Lein-Hua immediately comfortable. Excited, the women helped the three get settled.

Chinatown was humming with activity. Haoli's face showed his astonishment at the progress. "I feel like a newcomer to this place. It is amazing to see small children and women here. Now we have a real village. When I left only hard, working railroad men lived here in tents. Now look. It is magical. How this has happened?"

"Yes, it was magic. I will fill you in about how the families were able to come here, but let us get you settled and rested first." Pai slapped Haoli on the shoulder and led the way to where he could rest. Haoli cringed from a sharp pain at being touched; he tried to hide it from his friends.

They sat on the stoop of a small hut and talked for a time. Haoli politely listened to Pai and Li, enduring the throbbing in his side. They told Haoli about when the rail crews completed the tracks in Montana many came back to the Westwood-Rathdrum area. "Many joined the miners in the Silver Valley, across the Coeur d'Alene Mountain pass, probing the earth's crust for gold and silver." Pai paused, "Those of us who remained here in the new Rathdrum were easily employed as cooks, hotel staff, brewery and creamery personnel, farmers and blacksmiths. But," he took a deep breath, "employment with the government is the best. That is why Li and I work for this new county, building offices and such places."

"Last year in China," Pai told Haoli, "famine was destroying our people. The government finally allowed family members of to join their men here in America. Whole families could not leave before. Remember?" Pai shook his head as he spoke, "Children, or wives, or parents of the men in America, had to stay."

"I heard about the famine and family release while I worked in San Francisco. Many came on ships while I was there." Haoli thought of his family still in China—except Yue. "And my mother, is now too old to make such a trip," he added in a whisper.

"I think China found it did not assure that United States currency would be sent to back home. It worked to a point. Then the people lied about their clanships to escape to this new land." Pai paused, staring at his feet then added, "Many died trying to get here. My mother was one. But we are happy for these who live here now."

"Yes, I am please so many families are here, now."

"Pai served as the arbitrator and acquired jobs for our men," Ang Li boasted. "He even petitioned the Northern Pacific to help bring clan women and children from the coast and allow the them to reside at old rail camps. We have built our Chinatown because Pai stood firm for us!" Li stood straight with his head high as he spoke of his friend's accomplishments. "We earned the right to stay in exchange for labor, building public structures for the city. Pai gained permission to salvage scrap materials from the city's building projects."

"Good for you, Pai" Haoli approved of all he was hearing.

Pai shied from accepting honor for leading the clans' negotiations with the city's politicians. "My friend, Pai, is well known among the white men," Ang Li continued. "Some admired Pai, while others felt him a nuisance and wanted him gone. We Chinese helped complete a county jail, a courthouse and offices, a post office, started a schoolhouse, and also constructed private homes."

"Many had sent for their families in China with wages saved from the Northern Pacific and other positions," Pai explained. "The Postal Service demanded the name Westwood be replaced as too many towns carried that title. Rathdrum was chosen because it reminded an old-timer of his native home in Ireland. I would have chosen a Chinese name," he laughed at his own cleverness.

The town's new name, Rathdrum, was as strange to Haoli as were the improvements. "This is all good. I am happy to be *home!* But, I am exhausted. Let me go rest and then we will talk more." He retired after bowing his respect and thankfulness to his friends.

As Pai and Li walked from Haoli's hut, Pai told Li, "I think Haoli is hiding something and has much to tell us about his trip. He does not look so good."

"Yes," Li agreed. "He must tell us what has happened. He is holding his belly with protective hands."

While the men were talking, the women led Lein-Hua, Mei, and Sua to a hut. Left alone in it, Lein-Hua eyed her friends. "This is home. I would like a long rest." She gathered up one of the soft-looking bed covers and a mat and placed it on the floor against the furthest wall, stretched out on it, and closed her eyes.

"Good idea." Mei yawned, selected a mat, crossed the room, and laid it out.

"Me too," Sua wasted no time placing a mat closer to the door than she wanted, then repositioned it towards Mei's corner. Satisfied, she also laid down.

Later, Mei awoke to the sounds of children laughing outside. She got up and peeked out the small window above her mat. Several youngsters played tag across the street. She recognized two of the little girls that had been with the women who welcomed their arrival. Smiling, Mei watched. Nearby, two boys tossed an almost round ball. Then she realized the toy was created from a hog bladder. In China, she and her brother had a ball like it that her grandfather made.

"They look happy," Sua's voice interrupted her thoughts.

"I don't know if I ever I played like that. I am not sure. I do not think I was young for very long." Mei's face showed confusion as she struggled to recall her young years at home, in China.

"It is sad." Lein-Hua joined them at the window. "Do you think we were carefree like them? Ever?"

"No. But, my children will be. I worked in the rice paddy." Mei put her hands on the shoulders of each of her friends. "Let us go out and get acquainted."

Together the three exited the hut, squinting against blinding sunlight. Children played in the dirt street, still muddied from recent rain, and lined on both sides with nearly the same sized wooden houses sporting the grass roofs. Some displayed glass windows but most had wooden shutters that opened from the inside.

A cart with a mule hitched to it stood across from the hut, much like the one they had ridden in earlier. On the north side of the last building, a corral housed several mules, donkeys, and horses. Down a sloping hillside chickens scratched in yellowing grass near a pigpen. The late *Shi-yue,* or October, breeze stirred awareness of the farm animals. Mei wrinkled her nose at the farm odors, but Sua took in a deep breath. "Do you smell that? It is like home." She turned to Lein-Hua, who covered her nose with her sleeve.

"Yes, not like the city and dens," Lein-Hua added, immediately sorry she had mentioned it.

Mei shook the San Francisco memories away and announced she, too, liked the animals' odors. "And, no smoke like the train."

"Look mama," a little boy called as he pointed to the trio. The woman advanced toward the new comers to greet them. Several others followed. A toddler lifted his arms up to Lein-Hua wanting to be picked up. She hesitated to oblige him.

"He likes you." One of the women encouraged her to pick up the child. "He is my son, Zharg Bin, and I am Zharg Chyo." Chyo bowed politely to the three girls.

Surprised at hearing her native dialect she answered, "I am Lein-Hua," and bent down to scoop up the toddler after returning the bow. She hugged him close to her and drank in the sweet baby smell of the child, so reminiscent of her baby brother in China. She had not thought about her clan for a long time. She took in another deep breath. The thought of her family warmed her.

Feelings of home billowed in her mind she fought back tears. "I am so happy to be here." She handed the child over to his mother at his insistence, then introduced Mei and Sua, who in turn bowed greetings.

"We are glad to have you with us. Did you rest well?" Zharg Chyo put the child down, "Go play, Bin." The toddler scampered away.

"Oh yes, we slept much." As she talked Lein-Hua noticed that Mei and Sua also made friends instantly with other children and their mothers. "This is going to be a good place."

Lein-Hua grinned at her friends. A true smile shaped her face now, no longer afraid to show her pleasure.

When Haoli spotted the crowd, he knew it could only be the three girls gaining so much attention. He had given up trying to sleep, his discomfort too great to lie still. He had watched anxiously for the girls to appear.

He shuffled over to the gathering, holding his ribs. His presence quieted the chatter. "I see you are getting to know your neighbors," he bowed to the women. His statement was directed to no certain person. He bowed again as Pai and Li joined the group. Straightening, he rubbed his hands together, and beamed first at Lein-Hua then to Sua and Mei. "I have asked Lein-Hua to become my wife. She has not said so, but I know she will agree this is a fine plan." He ended with a wide grin.

The women turned to Lein-Hua and all congratulated her in unison. She shifted her eyes downward, too shy to say anything.

Mei and Sua not too surprised, kept silent. Both watched Lein-Hua with interest as her secret was made public. She still looked down, but smiled.

After hearing the announcement, Ang-Li chided Haoli in a whisper. "Marking your territory like an old panda bear, my friend? I hope you have left the good ones for the rest of us."

"Please come and share suppertime with us. We prepared a special meal for your homecoming." Zharg Chyo picked up Bin and led the way to her home where a feast table is ready.

Chapter 14

"My father told me how it pleased him to find Wong Pai and Ang Li so favored by the city authorities. Their favorite place to visit and catch up on old news was sitting on the bank of the creek near the tall pine towering over Ming Yun's temple. Father said he felt Yun's spirit joined them."...

Sitting at the creek bank, Ang Li shivered in the early November chill. "Mr. Winter is promising his cold weather early this year."

"You cold, Li?" Pai pulled his own coat tighter around himself. "Do you not recall winter?"

"I remember. I remember every minute. Digging through snow. Freezing winds. I do not forget." Li turned to Haoli. "You missed much fun with us." Li slapped his leg at his joke. "But this is only November. The chill is coming fast, it will be worse."

"I was sorry to leave. I did not have a happy time in San Francisco. I had my own terrors. Yue died. The horrors she lived—and the others." Haoli looked up at the pine tree as if it would give him answers to his troubles.

"Ahhh." Pai and Li agreed in unison understanding Haoli's statement. They sat in silence for several minutes. Then Haoli told of his adventures in San Francisco and of the train ride home.

After listening to Haoli's story, Li wiped a tear from his face and waved his goodbyes. He left at a jog, saying he wanted to go see what Sua was doing.

"I think he fancies Sua." Haoli nodded his head towards the path of Li's leave-taking.

"Aye," Wong Pai agreed.

"I am curious," Haoli nodded toward the people, "I did not think so many women would be here. I told the three girls they would probably be the only ones. How has this happened?"

"Different ones came various ways, arranged before the new law was approved. Zharg Chen and Chyo came here with their family, saying Chyo was his children's *teacher* not their mother. Wang Fu's daughter Bo came to be with Fu after her mother fell ill in China. Chan's wife came with Bo, I am not sure what story they gave the government. Others arrived in a group, as allowed when our homeland relaxed the rules for them to leave. Many came as *picture brides,* to join their husbands here. They traveled on the Northern Pacific free, before the last spike was celebrated. Many settled along the way in other rail camps. The railroad saw the need for the men to have wives to keep them happy. With the tracks about to be completed, railroad management realized that they needed to rely on our kinsmen for maintenance." Pai relaxed, glad his friend was now *home* too.

Haoli's story had also bothered Pai. He slipped the shoulder strap of his leather pouch he wore over his head, loosened the drawstrings, and removed a hard leather liner containing a dozen marshal arts weapons. The flat star-shaped metal objects had razor-sharp pointed tips. "Come, too much sad talk, let us throw the *shurikens*." He tipped the liner to slide the *shurikens* halfway out and inserted his index finger in the center holes as he removed them, balancing the spiked stars with his thumb. He held a stack of a dozen of the weapons, careful not to cut his hand. He let Haoli examine them.

"You made these? They have perfect balance."

"Yes, at Zharg Chen's blacksmith forge." Pai got up, paced off a distance from a tamarack, turned and sunk three of the star weapons into the tree so fast it seemed as one.

"You are good," Haoli praised his friend's aim then tossed the one Pai had handed him. It missed the tree, landing in the bushes. A distant train whistle moaned its arrival, drowning out Haoli's voice. He waited and repeated his approval. "You *are* good."

Wong Pai nodded his thanks then laughed at Haoli's aim in the bushes. "No, no. Like this." Pai held his hand so that Haoli could fully view how his index and next two fingers formed a guide for the star. "See how my little finger gives more support and my thumb holds the blade in place?"

Haoli inspected Pai's grip on the shuriken. Then he placed one in his hand in the same manner.

"One." Both raised their arms.

"Two." They flicked their wrists into position.

"And three." Each man tossed a star at the tree.

Wong Pai's blade stuck in the center mark. Haoli's swished beyond the tree and bounced off a nearby stump, then into the brushes. Wong Pai let out a hearty laugh. Haoli shook his head and chuckled as they retrieved the weapons, the movement caused a sharp pain in his ribs but he did not let it diminish his pleasure.

Pai motioned with one hand. "Look, Haoli, hold it as though it is a swallow's egg so as not to break it, lest you cut your hand. When you throw it, let your wrist snap forward as your arm straightens in front of your stomach. I can pitch several shurikens in rapid succession by cupping them in my left hand like a stack of coins and pass them to my right so as soon as one is released I have another ready to go." He took two steps to the right and let half a dozen stars fly. All hit the target almost on top of each other.

Haoli let out the breath he'd been holding as his friend demonstrated the martial art technique. "I see. You are an expert."

"I tossed best in my group back home. These are generally used for throwing and sometimes to stab or slash an opponent's arteries."

"Holding the sharp points makes me nervous," Haoli admitted, gripping the star between finger and thumb.

"It has been a long time since I felt that way, but I know the feeling. I have handled them so often. I can make blades from a variety of items. I have used nails, knives, coins and other flat plates of metal objects. But I have never used them as weapons, only for target play. Wang Fu warns, 'Habits are cobwebs at first; cables at last.' I take joy keeping myself in practice. It is an art that may escape our generation." He finished the lesson and went to collect the stars out of the tree. "I will teach my sons someday."

Pai and Haoli sat against the tree. Only the flow of water pouring over rocks in the stream made sound until the sudden flutter of a grouse a short distance away in the woods. Pai broke the silence that followed. "You should have seen it, Haoli." He stretched and lowered his voice in a serious note. "We were at the end of the rail line in Montana, tenting near Gold Creek, where rails from the east and west met. The crews from the east came into sight. We all dropped our shovels and picks and cheered. They did the same. Everyone started running to the other's crew line. Such chaos. Cheering. Backslapping. Bowing. The Irish, Swedes, Finns and all, hugged, hooting and hollering. Even some of *us* hugged. We were so happy to have the line finished."

Haoli resettled himself against the tree. "I can see it from your descriptions. Tell me more."

Ang Li rejoined them reporting that the girls were busy cooking and Sua seemed not to notice him. As if fitting for their conversation, they heard the Northern Pacific blow its whistle. "There's the 4 o'clock," Li raised his voice to be heard as the sound blasted a final time.

Pai informed him, "I was just telling Haoli of our joining the tracks in Montana."

"Ah, a good time, that was. Continue, Pai."

"We Chinese had brought our rails further than the eastside thought we would. The whites were angry with us. Saying we Chinese worked faster than a bunch of jackrabbits chased by wolves," Pai added, disgust in his voice.

"How dare they compare us to animals. Always animals with them!" Ang Li picked up a good-sized rock, jumped to his feet and tossed it hard into the water causing a splash that made the men leap away from the tree on the bank.

"I know, Li," Pai tried to comfort his friend. "Maybe it helped drive us to do the work faster. They supposed we would meet the east team in the Idaho Territory. Not into Montana like we did. Haoli, our men worked a miracle getting across the rough terrain of the Panhandle. We dug through the highest mountains I ever saw. And, built trestles over rivers and valleys. Leveled the roughest of land, so the trains could glide across."

Li sat again on the bank where the others had returned, still heated at the memory and took over the story. "We crossed the Pend d'Oreille River at Sandpoint, following the north shoreline of the huge lake to Hope, then to Clark's Fork where we crossed the river again then into Montana. Montana. It felt like the top of the world. Above the mountains," Li added thoughtfully.

"Yes," Pai agreed. "None of us knew we had crossed the territorial line 'til Swartz celebrated with his whiskey bottle one night. We could always tell good news," Pai chuckled. "That's when he would fall into his bottle. The next morning while Swartz lay in his bunk, we worked a full day—that was a great day. No boss man with his whip and cursing. We all put in a longer, harder workday. Added a couple extra miles than usual, we did.

"You should have seen Swartz then, Haoli. All smiles he was." He grinned at using the Irish slang. "I think he finally learned to quit cracking his whip over us. Found we worked best without all his hooting and name-calling. Maybe that is why we made it so far into Montana. No one knows. But we did it, Haoli. *We* did it." Pai stated with purpose as he tossed a shuriken, hitting the tree dead center.

"Pai, you have flawless aim." Haoli admired his friend's toss. "What else happened?"

Pai shrugged and went on to tell about the last spike driven near Gold Creek in Montana, a few miles east of the Drummond camp.

"In mid-August the crew had left 1200 feet for the last four rails to be laid in the celebration of the final connection. It was September 8, 1883. Two locomotives arrived, one from the

117

east and the other from the west. What a sight, Haoli! Coaches were loaded with important people, including President Ulysses S. Grant. After long-winded speeches, 300 men—all whites—quickly laid the last track from both ends, joining the East and West of the continent."

"Hundreds of people came," Li emphasized, his anger still biting as he recalled the day. "But our crew was only allowed to watch from the ridge by our camp. You can see for yourself in the pictures at the county courthouse what I am saying is true. All the Irish, Finns, Swedes and French are shown in the newspaper. And, they only permitted one of our kinsmen to be photographed—made him wear a white man's suit...and hide his pigtail. *We* built this railroad. Our blood spilled for it." Li rose and paced down the bank a few steps, then quickly returned and sat down by his friends.

"You had a rough time of it, Li." Haoli pointed up at a squirrel in the pine tree watching them. "I'm sorry I could not be here with you." He walked over to where his star landed and picked it up.

Pai sat silent for a few minutes, staring at the shuriken stuck in the tree. Then heedfully he added, "Know why they had the whites lay the last rails? I heard the boss telling the Governor. He did not know I understood his English. It was because when the Continental Rail connected with their gold spike, they had four Chinese carry the last rail hanging from ropes on their shoulders. A cameraman watched, ready to signal his assistant to snap the shutter. He shouted 'shoot!' for the perfect picture to be taken. Well, when our kinsman heard the word 'Shoot,' a word well known to us, they dropped the rail and ran."

"Everyone roared with laughter." Li spat the words. "Whites make fun of us. Always."

"But better the joke was on them at our last spike." Pai patted Li's arm. "They hooked telegraph wires to an iron spike partially driven into a tie. It was wired into the national telegraph system. The instant Northern Pacific's president, Villard, and President Grant would hit the spike, the outside world would learn that the deed was done." Pai paused with a chuckle. "But that did not happen, did it Li?" He laughed and slapped at a mosquito on his arm.

"What happened?" Haoli asked.

"Both failed to hit the spike!" Li clapped his hands above his head.

"But their mauls vibrated the wires and sent the message." Pai explained grinning. "People cheered. Mistakenly. And, a rail man had to finish the deed."

"That is a good one, Pai. I did miss the fun." Haoli laughed.

After a loud chortle together, the three calmed catching their breath then sat quietly, watching the sun sink behind the crest of the mountain. A doe jumped the creek, startled at the men then bounced away, disappearing into the forest. A breeze stirred, chilling them. Haoli rubbed his arm, "Brrrr."

They heard the six o'clock train's whistle announcing its arrival. Realizing they had been gone a long time, Haoli picked up a shuriken. He gave it a toss. It stuck next to Pai's still in the tree's center.

"Good," Pai congratulated him with a bow of honor. They got to their feet, gathered the stars and headed back to Chinatown.

Pai led the way. "Everything changed in Westwood when the railroad came, Haoli. When you left in '82, the Idaho Territorial Legislature announced Westwood would replace Seneacquoteen as county seat." Pai shivered, "Let's hurry, it's getting cold."

"Seneacquoteen?" Haoli repeated as they jogged down the pathway. "I do not remember that place."

"It is up north. The famous ferry crossing on the Pend d'Oreille River at Seneacquoteen. Until the bridge was built over calmer waters at nearby Priest River. When Westwood got a United States Post Office, they ordered the town's name change. Too many Westwoods, Rathdrum was chosen. You know now about that mix up, right? That's when things really leaped around here."

"How do you mean, Pai?" Haoli was not sure he understood.

"People came. White people. Thousands. They came from Spokane Falls. From the West coast. From the East. Those who had had enough of big cities. And, others looking for gold and farmlands. So many people Haoli. So many."

"Is that when you built our Chinatown at the old camp location?"

"Yes, and Chinese men sent for their families, too. And more men came searching for gold, being told large nuggets just waited to be gathered."

"Did you dig for gold too?"

"Yes, along with most of our kin, we began digging for gold on Storm King, ahh, I mean Rathdrum Mountain," he corrected himself.

"Yes." Pai agreed. "And we took jobs building businesses, houses, and government offices. All had to be built with speed. Who else, but our people to do the work? But, we do not trust the whites. We continued to dig. We made tunnels under our homes and to the mineshafts. I'll show you sometime soon."

"In Montana," Pai took the conversation back to what he had been saying, "Ang Li and I knew we would come back to Rathdrum. We liked this countryside. Wang Fu agreed with us. We could find work here, after the railroad. And, Haoli, we knew you would return here someday—with your sister..." Pai's voice trailed off with a sad note.

"Yes, that was always my plan. I, too, knew this place would become my home. I regret I cannot share it with Yue."

The three walked without speaking until they reached the cabins. Finally, Haoli broke the silence saying, "We must see how the girls are doing." They headed to the hut where Lein-Hua, Sua and Mei were preparing the evening meal.

Haoli became starry-eye when Lein-Hua came to mind. As his pace quickened, his limp seemed to straighten.

Chapter 15

"My mother's friend, Zharg Chyo, organized several of the clan women to plan the wedding. The women held their first meeting at the Zharg's home, the largest in Chinatown. The ladies included Chyo's eldest daughter, young Jaoi almost thirteen, nearly as old as the brides to be, and the age of Sua, Lein-Hua now fourteen and Mei, fifteen. They would all be old maids in China, Auntie said."...

The first December snow of the season floated lazily to the earth. Lein-Hua's eyes sparkled as she watched from Zharg Chyo's window while waiting for the other women to arrive for planning the wedding. Pointing her index finger on the window, she traced a single large flake as it floated to the ground. She could not tell where it landed on the swelling whiteness. She realized she had not seen snow in four years. Since China, as a child of nine. Thrilled, she chose another flake and idly followed it with her finger against the windowpane. December. 1883. It seemed this place had been her home, forever, not just the few months she'd been in Idaho.

Pai and Mei had requested permission of the elders to get married in the New Year's holiday, also. The weddings, it was decided, would be a duel ceremony with special highlights for both couples.

Wang Bo knocked on the slightly opened door. Lein-Hua greeted her, "welcomed" she gave a quick bow, and took Bo's coat to the bedroom. She left the door ajar, a custom of courtesy when expecting company. Bo rubbed her forearm and shivered off the cold draft but said nothing, displaying good manners.

"Hello," Chyo greeted Bo coming from the kitchen. "This is going to be the grandest of events. Everyone in uptown Rathdrum will receive an invitation." As her excitement grew, her words spilled faster.

"We will have the weddings then our Lunar New Year's ceremony. Fireworks, parades, and feasts—it will be magnificent." Chyo explained her newest plan as several more ladies entered her home for the gathering.

"Wong Pai is friendly with important people from working with them on building government projects. Mayor McGuire, Judge Henry Melder, and Sheriff Ryan, they will all want to come to his wedding," Chyo assured the ladies.

"And don't forget Charles Wesley Wood," Bo put in. "Pai says he's been here for over twenty years, was first to build a cabin here when he rode for the Pony Express. He still owns half the town." Pausing, she thought out loud, "Can one man own half a town?" Bo glanced at Mei, noting every time someone mentioned Wong Pai, she ducked her head and grinned, turning red-faced.

"Yes, I hear he can, and does." Chyo's voice brought Bo's attention back to the conversation. "We can introduce the Americans to a traditional Chinese celebration. It will show them we are a people of beliefs and customs with a heritage. They will learn we are from a respectful country." Chyo's words accelerated again as she described her plans while dusting rice cakes with ginger.

"Let's see, this is December, '83, year of the Sheep." She ticked her fingers as she figured out the time zodiac for 1884. The new year coming will be of the Monkey." She stood up and shouted, "That's perfect. It is a year of intellect and good influences to others. But, we must also be watchful. It is also a year for easy discouragement and confusion. We must plan carefully to please the ancestors."

Around the room, heads nodded in agreement.

Sua refilled teacups while Wang Bo, Chan's wife, and other women decided on details.

122

"The red silk arrived yesterday at Brownson's Mercantile." Chyo placed a box overflowing with material imprinted with chrysanthemums on the low table in the middle of the room. "It is so beautiful, better than we saw in the catalog."

Chyo draped the smooth fabric from her fingers as she unfolded it. "We will use it for our brides and also trim the maidens' dresses. Each dress must be designed most special for our first weddings in Rathdrum." Her words now ran from her tongue.

Bo and Mei were first to reach out and touch the fabric with graceful fingers, as if petting a fragile bird feather. Lein-Hua and the women all leaned from the edge of their chairs to admire the silk. Ooohs and aahhhs filled the room as they appreciated the cloth.

Overjoyed, Lein-Hua was speechless at the thought of her wedding. She welcomed toddler Bin to her lap and snuggled her face into his hair. The boy had captured Lein-Hua's heart from the first day she arrived in Rathdrum, when he stretched his chubby arms to her.

Lein-Hua held Bin on her lap while his mother buzzed around them with her measuring stick to make sure she had ordered enough silk.

"I can fold flowers from silk." Mei fingered the material. "We can use them with the paper lanterns to decorate. My mother taught me in China—when I was...." The abrupt memory surprised her, and bounced off her tongue before she could stop it. "Awk," Mei cried out, "I, ah, think I still know how to crimp them. It seems years ago...when I was young." Suddenly not sure, she folded her hands in her lap and sat silent, looking down.

Lein-Hua watched Mei, realizing childhood recollections rarely existed for herself and her friend. The dens had stolen their memories, erased their youth.

"Silk flowers will be perfect." Chyo tried to comfort her. "I'll make sure you have plenty of the silk to practice with." She patted Mei's hand and quoted the ancestors' proverb, "'you cannot prevent the birds of sorrow from flying over your head, but you can prevent them from building nests in your hair'."

"We can dress up our candles with silk bows, too," Wang Bo suggested. The sad atmosphere broken, their attention returned to the planning.

The large floating snowflakes gave way to finer, faster plunging ones. Near Bachelor Row, under the lean-to of the blacksmith shop, Haoli, Pai and Li worked with others led by Wang Fu cutting and peeling scrub-pine poles to build sedan chairs.

Two peeled poles were laid horizontally. Willow branches tied with leather straps crisscrossed the poles linking them as one, leaving an arms-length at both ends for handles.

Four poles placed vertically on top this base created the frame for a dome. The front side facing the parallel poles was left open for a doorway. Window frames on both sides also left exposed to view the rider behind curtains. Under the dome on the base, they built a seat. A pillow would offer comfort for the occupant.

When completed, the roof of the dome would arch to a point at the center.

The sedan chairs had to be the best ever, especially the one for Haoli's bride. She would have the most festive sedan. His hand trembled in his excitement. He could not hew the sedan handles like the elder man showed him. Over and over he whittled but his knife only scarred what he wanted to smooth.

"Let me show you again." Wang Fu took the knife from Haoli and skillfully fixed the cuttings, turning them into perfect handle knobs.

Haoli watched Fu's gnarled hands work the wood. "How do you do that? I will never be able to accomplish such fine work."

"You will, but grooms are always nervous," Fu teased the younger man, now healed from the beatings he had endured on his trip, thanks to Fu's needles. "We will fashion the finest sedans for the brides. You will see."

Tying the flat board section onto the finished carrying poles proved to be the easy part. Building the upright enclosure with the seat, windows, and pointed roof was more difficult.

Haoli and Ang Li stood on boxes to reach the top. They held the corners in place while Wong Pai tied them as Wang Fu directed.

Zharg Chen, Chyo's husband, had traded Brownson his best rooster for a gallon of whitewash. He boiled beets saved from his garden, thickened the juice and added it to the whitewash until it shone bright red, the symbolic color of happiness. He used it to paint the sedan chair.

Chyo had supplied the men with silk tassels and bows the women made to decorate the sedans.

Wang Fu then demonstrated to the young men how to place the silk coverlet over the sedan. They added the bows and tassels creating a mysterious hide-a-way for the bride. As each sedan was completed, it was stored in a shed on Bachelors Row.

December gave way to January '84, as the snow deepened. February approached, the Chinese Lunar New Year. The men decided it best to postpone the Lunar Year celebration until after the nuptials in the springtime, when the weather would be warmer for the parade.

A snowstorm prevented outside work other than daily chores. The men gathered at Wang Fu's house where he taught the young men how to wind firecrackers. Fu laid out a square of red rice paper and tapped a bit of black gunpowder mixed with a white powder from a bottle onto the paper. He dropped a long piece of wet string on the powders, rolled it, letting the mixture coat it. Then he angled it across the length of the paper, leaving it longer off the paper on one side. Pulling up opposite corners making the powder gather in the middle, he then rolled the paper, tucking in the edges.

"Make sure you fold in the sides without spilling the powders." Fu's fingers worked the paper as he spoke. "And keep the string end hanging out, for the fuse." When he finished creasing the last edge under, he dabbed it with wetted fingers and patted it tight to make the rice paper glue to itself. He looked at the group. "See." He held up his firecracker, just larger than an expensive cigar. "You can make them any size, depending on how you want it to explode, for noise or smoke effects." Fu grinned knowingly at his students. "You do it now," he challenged the group.

Chyo and Bo's homemaking lessons also were received well by the girls. Lein-Hua, felt elevated as part of the community and enjoyed the attention. She and Sua favored cooking and sewing.

"I enjoy making the house fresh, giving it a good scrubbing." Mei confided in Lein-Hua, "I dream of keeping house for Wong Pai," as they both dusted the furniture and swept the loose wood-plank floors the two giggled at the secret.

"Wang Bo you are an expert seamstress." Chyo admired her work. "The dragon and lion costumes you created from scrap fabrics are so colorful, perfect for our parade."

"Father, fashioned the head frames from sticks and papier-mâché, see." She held it up for Chyo to have a close look at Wang Fu's craftsmanship. "Our ladies helped paint them black with red, white, and a mix of multi shades of oranges, yellows and greens. We added tassels of feathers and pompoms see how they jiggle when the head shakes." The dragon and lion bodices fit together easily from strips of fabrics stitched together in long flowing runners to drape over the men. "The men's trousers will be sewn of colorful fabrics to form the illusion of the intended parade animals." I'm so excited Bo patted the fabric to lay straight. They completed three lions and one dragon costume and had the men store them with the sedan chairs. "The brides can not be allowed to see them completed until the celebrations began." Bo loved the secrets.

The ladies gathered again at Zharg Chyo's house two months later in March to use the oven. "Chyo you have the best cook stove in Chinatown. So many only have open fire pits for cooking and heating. Thank you for letting us come here to prepare the food," Wang Bo put her coat on a hook as she greeted her friend. Bo greeted Mei and Lein-Hua as she washed her hands. Together they patted bits of dough into tiny *Dan gau* cakes shaped like peaches for the wedding and Lunar feasts ahead.

"We will pack them in ice and store them the root cellar to keep the cakes fresh for later," Chyo showed the girls how. "Our men worked hard to build the underground cellar. It keeps ice chunks cut from Twin Lakes throughout the summer."

"It is good we postponed our Lunar New Year's party. February is so cold our dragon would freeze." Bo laughed at her statement repeating, "A frozen dragon?"

"Yes, April is a better time. After the spring rains." Chyo washed the flour off her hands so she could tend to Bin. "This will be our finest celebration since coming to America. Too bad so many families have moved away. And the whites, too. Be glad we still have nearly five-hundred clansmen. It will be a great time."

"Sua is late today. I wonder where she is." Chyo looked to Bo and Lein-Hua.

"I think I know." Lein-Hua glanced at her friends. "She is with Ang Li."

"Ahh." Bo put her cake on the pan and picked up a towel to wipe up. "I saw them last evening down by the creek. Alone."

"Ohhh." Chyo came back into the room holding Bin, setting him at the table with a piece of rice cake. She heard enough of the conversation to pique her interest. "How so?"

Bin nibbled the cake and flirted with Lein-Hua in his baby-babbling way.

"I took a walk. I wasn't spying. I just, ahh, I just happen to notice the two, ahh, off by themselves." Bo took more dough and worked it with quick fingers. "They always shy from each other. I did not think they were getting along so fine. Young love is good."

"It is good." Chyo agreed. "Do you think she will tell us about him?"

Sua rushed through the half-open door. She dropped her coat over the back of a kitchen chair and burst, "He is so special. I, I, love him...." She let her body drop onto the chair.

Everyone stared at her.

Lein-Hua smiled and finally said, "So, exactly when are you going to tell us everything?"

"He says we should wed." Sua giggled at the sound of her words. "Soon."

Lein-Hua, took Sua's hand. "And you? Do you think so too?"

"Ohhh yes." She pulled her arm from Lein-Hua, jumped to her feet, and closed her eyes. "Oh yes, I think so too."

Opening her eyes, she saw the ladies standing in a semicircle grinning at her. "What?"

They all laughed and hugged Sua, and each other.

"A triple wedding." Chyo was first to speak and embraced Sua again. "We knew Mei and Pai agreed to combine their wedding, but now, you and Li too? This is even better. I must get Fu and Chen to ask the men to wind more firecrackers. We will need many to show all the happiness."

"The cakes." Bo shouted and rushed to retrieve the last pan from the oven. "This is going to be the best time for all of us. I cannot wait."

Chapter 16

"My wedding was not as spectacular as mothers and her friends. My Pai, Pai Number Two, and I married without all the traditions as there were not many Chinese living here then." Jie began telling Molly...

Only two days before the April ceremonies, Mei and Lein-Hua met again at Chyo's home. Bin toddled over to Lein-Hua as she entered. "I must go to the mercantile, Chyo smiled at her son in Lein-Hua arms. I think he wants to stay here with you."

"Yes, you will be faster without his help, I will care for him."

"Good. It's a bright sunny day. I'll leave the door open for you. The fresh breeze will energize you as you work." Chyo wrapped her shawl around her shoulders and waved goodbye as she hurried out.

As she worked, Lein-Hua watched Bin draw circles on the table with stubby fingers covered in rice flour. She picked up the bowl of sweet sauce she was making for the chicken baking in the oven. "Today I cannot think about my wedding." She whipped the mixture faster.

"I know." Mei tapped her spoon on the table, unaware of the rhythm she made. "Wong Pai and I both are anxious too. I am not sure I want all the traditional details." The spoon bounced faster. "We both missed out on the customary proposal with not having family here to do the bargaining." An unexpected tear dropped from Mei's eye. She wiped it.

Lein-Hua noticed. Understanding, she touched Mei's hand, "Whatever happened to us before no longer is in my memory. Remember this!"

"I want to forget." Mei turned away.

Lein-Hua took the pan of chicken from the oven, placed it on the table next to the bowl of sauce. In silence, they coated the chicken with the sweet sauce and arranged the pieces on a platter.

Mei looked at Lein-Hua with blurry eyes. "Now we face our wedding nights but we have already been defiled."

"You must forget. '*Ye clean.*' *It is in the past,*" Lein-Hua repeated in English. She slammed her fist on the table. "We have a new life. A good life." She searched Mei's face. The word *defiled* stuck in her mind.

When the girls prepared supper, the young men practiced their dragon and lion dances behind Bachelors' Row. Wang Fu, Zharg Chen, and Chan directed the inexperienced ones until gracefulness flowed from the twisting and rotation of their waists and shoulders.

Fu explained the desired costumes' movements. "The dragon is always feline in natural form. He must march to the music like a playful cat." Fu tossed his arms in the air, his feet danced as he spoke. "The three lions must step in unison to the loud music and firecrackers, which will scare away any evil spirits. This will allow good luck to follow the newlyweds. The power of the dragon offers protection."

The practice continued until the elders were satisfied they had taught the dancers to perfection.

At the urging of Alfred Potter, a large property owner in Rathdrum, Attorney C.L. Heitman filed court papers to allow the Chinese to obtain legal marriage documents. In court, Heitman argued that since the Governor decreed the county seat be moved from Seneacquoteen to Rathdrum, would not the State Territory have to recognize new laws enforced by the new Kootenai County? Would they include rulings over Chinese, who still are not recognized as citizens?

Judge Melder ruled on behalf of the Chinese over the protestors, including James Orenstein and others, who debated the case. Pai praised the judge as a man of justice.

"Acquiring the legal wedding licenses is the last thing to be done." Chyo smiled her approval of all the arrangements. "Everything is ready. I am sure of it."

"Yes, we are making history for our clans to have American papers," her husband, Chen hugged her.

The day before the weddings Zharg Chen and Chyo prepared to install the bridal beds. The grooms chose them as the "good luck man and woman" because they had a large family of five children. Chen and Chyo stood on the front stoop of the house built for the newlyweds before a crowd of neighbors outside, the Zhargs faced each other and bowed. The crowd outside cheered as a few firecrackers sounded at the side of the house.

The Zhargs crossed the threshold, bowed again at the bedroom door, and entered. Slowly each moved to opposite sides of the bed and pushed it into a new position, for a new beginning. As tradition required, Chyo smoothed the coverlet and scattered dates and peanuts covered with red paper and some small apples on the bedding. Coins wrapped in red paper were also tossed among the treats.

Together, they exited the room, went to the front door, stood aside and invited the waiting children inside. With hands folded the children filed into the bedroom and formed a line around the bed.

Zharg Chen was last to enter the room. The wide-eyed children watched as he raised his arms above his head. Some giggled. When Chen dropped his arms, the children climbed atop the bed. Laughing and singing they quickly gathered up the treasures as they jumped around on the bed. Adults had entered the room to watch the *scramble of the fertility*, an omen assuring many children to the couple.

The game over, Wang Bo shooed the last toddler clutching an apple in his hand out of the room to join the others and go to the next cabin.

Completing the third fertility entertainment in the last cabin, Chyo straightened the bedcovers. "This is well," she told Bo and Chan's wife.

"Yes. It is good joy. Our brides will be blessed with many children. Now we must tell Lein-Hua, Mei, and Sua of the success."

The next morning, Chyo, Bo, and Chan's wife along with some of the other women, gathered at Zharg's with the three brides for the "hair dressings." After bathing in water infused with citrus juices to *cleanse evil influences*, the brides dressed in new underclothes.

Lein-Hua sniffed her forearm, inhaling the fragrance from her bath. She liked how she smelled and blushed as she thought of Haoli, and if he would approve. The women helped the brides into their gowns.

Chyo and Bo styled each girl's hair. Winding it high and fastening with pearl pins. As they worked, they chatted and giggled with excitement about the future.

While the ladies went about the business of the *hair dressings*, at Chyo's home, the men were involved with *capping* the grooms at Wang Fu's home.

Freshly bathed, Haoli dressed in a new floor-length black garment. Wang Fu, chosen to replace his father, faced Haoli and placed a black cap on the groom. It was decorated with red paper trimmed to look like cypress leaves, because they did not have real ones to use. Then Fu draped a red silk sash tied in a large bow with a silk ball attached at his chest, all signifying happiness.

At the same time, Chan and Chen tended to Wong Pai and Ang Li in a similar fashion, as custom dictated.

Their sashes in place, each groom stepped into new red shoes. Then they all knelt near the door, before altar tablets representing Heaven and Earth and the Ancestors.

After praying, Fu, Chan, and Chen removed the silk balls from the grooms' sashes, strolled outside to the waiting bridal sedan chairs and hung the balls above the seats in the sedans.

Beads of sweat formed on Haoli's forehead as he followed the elders to his sedan. Hearing the first firecrackers, he flinched. Loud gongs, cymbals, and drums began a rhythm, marking the start of the cavalcade.

Head held high, Haoli prepared to lead the procession, holding now three-years-old, Zharg Bin's hand. Pai and Li followed with Bin's two older brothers. The boys represented an omen of promised future sons.

The elders, then the friends carrying the bridal sedans followed the grooms, with the boys. The musicians stepped into the lineup, trailed by the dancing lions and the long dragon. Children twirled streamers on sticks and men tossed firecrackers. The celebration underway, they marched to the bridal house followed by all the clans.

Hearing the procession, the good luck women, Chyo, Bo and Chan's wife, finished the bride's dressings. Chyo smiled to reassure Lein-Hua as she fastened the last button.

The red *qipao's* full-length skirt and quilted jacket, sewn from the silk they had admired months before, fit perfectly. Chyo attached a tiny mirror to the jacket lapel and kissed Lein-Hua. "This mirror will reflect away any evil influences. Do not remove it until you are safely seated upon the marriage bed."

The gongs and drums sounded closer as Chyo attached a red and white beaded veil to Lein-Hua's high-styled hair. It hid her face. She moved her head slightly to feel the beads shake across her nose and chin. She giggled. Bo and Chan's wife readied Mei and Sua in the same manner. Together, the three slipped their feet into new red shoes placed next to the doorway.

"Come," Chyo led her charge by the hand. They peeked out the opened door to see the parade approach.

"Oh!" Lein-Hua gasped as she took in the sight. "This is all for us? If only mama could see me." She squeezed Chyo's hand.

Chyo glanced at Lein-Hua and asked, "Are you ready, little one?"

"Yes. I think so, but I am unworthy."

"No, do not say that. Do not think it. You *are* special."

Lein-Hua nodded her understanding, and tried to relax.

The parade stopped, with the first sedan parallel to the house door. Two men rolled a red tapestry from the sedan to the house, handed Chyo three *ang pau,* red packets of paper money from the grooms.

Chyo accepted the *ang paus*. She and Bo stood on each side of the covered pathway. Lein-Hua stepped onto the red carpet, her shoes not allowed to touch the ground.

Bo held a parasol over the bride and Chyo tossed rice as they approached the sedan. The music drummed, while cheers and firecrackers intensified as she entered the sedan and sat down.

A *shai-tse,* or sieve, to strain out evil, hung next to a metallic mirror. It also offered protection from evil influence over the bride. As the men hoisted the sedan onto their shoulders, Lein-Hua balanced herself with her hand against the window frame. They went forward only a few feet until the next sedan was even with the carpet.

After Mei and Sua were aboard their sedans, music and cheering accented the beginning of the bridal parade.

Lein-Hua peeked past her veil, out the silk covered sedan window. Happiness overwhelmed her. She set her mind to concentrate on Chyo's remark. "This is the life you deserve." She could not swallow. What lay ahead?

Chapter 17

"Auntie told me what my mother shared with her about her wedding day. Such lucky brides, to experience Chinese traditions, don't you think? When you marry, Molly, you should have such a wedding." Nanai looked star'ry-eyed at her granddaughter...

As the parade began, several firecrackers exploded close by, causing Lein-Hua to shudder. She determined not to cry and reflected on her future. She caressed the tiny mirror attached to the breast of her *qipao's* jacket and stared ahead.

The sedan swayed with each step of its carriers. She let go of the mirror and grabbed again at the window frame, tightening her grip, knuckles white. The rhythmic music told Lein-Hua that Mei and Sua, each in their bridal sedans were behind, as were the dancing dragon and lions, but she could not see them. A tight smile creased her face.

Holding little Bin's hand, Haoli, followed by Pai and Li with his brothers, they led the procession through Chinatown, toward the wedding pagoda at the edge of their village.

As they passed the newly constructed pagoda, Lein-Hua was amazed by its strength. The roof, held up by cross beams atop tall-carved pillars, straddled a polished wooden floor. On the white painted pillars, red silk flowers and lanterns made the pagoda appear red, for happiness. "So pretty," Lein-Hua lips formed the words without sound. Down the roadway, towards the creek's bridge, Lein-Hua realized the next time she saw the pagoda—she would be a married woman.

At Ming Yun's gravesite under the ponderosa, Haoli stopped to pay homage to the temple. This did not surprise Lein-Hua. For the first time since boarding the sedan, she relaxed watching her betrothed tie fresh red paper ribbons on the temple and light the candle.

Lein-Hua saw Haoli returned to his place. With slow, thoughtful steps, the parade moved forward. "Where are we going?" Lein-Hua worried. "Not across the bridge. Not to the Whites?" She resolved to trust Haoli, letting her grasp loosen though she had to steady herself as the men rocked the sedan to the music and manage the rough road.

Through the veil, she saw they were climbing the hill to Main Street in Rathdrum. From the bend in the roadway, she could see hundreds of town folks gathered along the street.

Some waved and cheered. Some danced, keeping time with the drums. In front of Orenstein's Saloon, a man yelled curses. A shiver ran down Lein-Hua's back. She pushed her body tight against the seat, trying to hide.

The mayor and Sheriff Ryan fell into step along side the sedan. Lein-Hua blushed and kept her face hidden behind the silk-covered windows. Behind the beaded veil, she secretly wished the wedding vows were fulfilled.

Parading up Main Street, Lein-Hua recognized the attorney standing next to Mr. Potter. She did not know the other man, but had heard Haoli say Charles Wood had a handlebar mustache like Mr. Brownson's but longer. She did not like being scrutinized by the men, even with the veil hiding her face.

As the procession passed the end of Main Street into the Northern Pacific depot yard, travelers came out of the depot to the platform and cheered. Looping around the building and crossing the tracks, the dragon and the three lions pranced to the delight of the spectators. Then the celestial parade curved, marching back down Main Street, and then back to Chinatown with the townsfolk's joining them.

Halting in front of the wedding pagoda, the men lowered the three sedans to the ground. Relieved to finally be motionless, Lein-Hua folded her hands in her lap. She watched the grooms pray, give packets of red paper money to the temple gods on both sides of the pagoda, and light the three candles.

Lein-Hua, concentrating on her poise, stiffened when the sedan's curtain opened exposing her to the crowd. She licked her lips, gave a timorous smile to her friends standing behind Chyo, who held the edge of the curtain in one hand, and extended the other to her. Bo winked at her over Chyo's shoulder.

Accepting the gesture, Lein-Hua stepped from the sedan onto red carpet to look up into Haoli's shining face. The veil hid Lein-Hua's expression as Chyo placed her hand in Haoli's. He led the way to the front of the wedding pagoda.

Together they climbed the pagoda's two steps and stood on the polished floor. The other two couples followed. They all turned to face the onlookers. Wang Fu blessed them, bowed and stood to the left. At the altar, each paid respect to heaven and earth, to the ancestors, and to the kitchen god, *Tsao-Chun*. The three grooms drank a traditional cup of tea with two red dates in the bottom prepared by the parent stand-ins. The simple ceremony completed before the pagoda altar, the brides and grooms bowed to each other.

Lein-Hua's crimson face behind the veil deepened as she realized she was now a married woman. She watched the other brides make their own promises.

Bowed heads cemented the vows.

The aroma of fish mixing with rice and noodles aroused Lein-Hua's hunger. From behind her veil, she noticed the feast tables lined the east side of the street, now piled high with foods.

Red floral arrangements and candles decorated the tables, matching the pagoda. Red paper lanterns hung overhead from doorposts. She saw Mei's roses dotted the table, placed next to platters of whole fish, or *yu*, an indication of "plenty and a wish for abundance." Chyo had told her. The *yu* tempted her appetite. She inhaled deeper, taking in the aroma.

Among the guests, Brownson, Nogle, and their wives, along with Al Potter and Charley Wood, crowded shoulder to shoulder in the narrow street. Children, both whites and Chinese dashed about the gathering, playing together. Firecrackers popped as the couples joined hands, faced the assembly, and waved their thanks. The attorney raised his cup high and nodded to Pai, who smiled back.

The chosen parents led the three couples to the feast table and began serving them. Friends and guests followed, helping themselves, signaling the public the recognition of the unions.

"We have neither red Peking duck nor lobsters to denote the traditional joy and celebration omen, but instead we will serve mallard ducks and crawdads in red sauce. That will do to complete the custom." Chyo had explained earlier. It did look delicious.

Eating with the veil in front of her mouth proved difficult. Lein-Hua watched as Sua tried to take a bite and giggled.

To indicate wealth, shark fin soup was traditional. With no sharks in the local waters, sunfish soup replicated it. Chyo had agreed the small fishes seemed all fins and would be a fine substitute. Lein-Hua held the veil away from her lips with the tip of one finger while she sipped soup from her spoon. It tasted sweet. She liked the flavor of the crawdads and took another bite.

The peach-shaped cakes with a sticky coating sent wishes for fertility and a sweet life. She had a difficult time keeping the beads from touching the gummy bun. She only took one bite and gave up, leaving it on her plate. A selection of bite-sized sweet treats wrapped in wontons, symbolized a desire for many children, proved easier to eat.

With the meal under way and most of the guests eating, the mayor elbowed his way to the head of the table. He raised his hands for silence, determined to give a speech. All he managed was to offer his congratulations before the music started again, muffling his voice.

Haoli chuckled at the mayor's attempt to speak and nudged Pai's arm, "People with virtue must speak out; people who speak are not all virtuous."

Pai and the others snickered at his joke.

Lein-Hua enjoyed the comic antics of the mayor who didn't understand Mandarin, and watched as he sat down, defeated.

The music and firecrackers continued. Relentless, loud blasting clamored among the merrymakers. The dancing dragon and lions twisted through the spectators as the musicians followed. Chinese children, twirling streamers, joined them.

Jimmy Orenstein ran up to the dragon and reached for the tail. The last man under the costume was quick to keep the tail away from the boy, teasing him as they moved down the street. Many children, both Chinese and whites joined the fun. None of the children managed to catch the skillful dragon.

Jimmy Orenstein and Denny Barton collapsed on the wooden sidewalk laughing so hard their stomachs hurt. Denny's face glowed as red as his hair. The Zharg brothers joined them. Lein-Hua saw the mixture of Chinese and white children playing together for the first time. She smiled at seeing them mingle.

When most of the guests finished eating, one lion danced up to the couples still seated at the table of honor. The musicians started a new song in rhythm. "It is time for the *choy cheng,* or eating of the green," Wang Fu announced. "The lion pretends to eat vegetable greens with a *hung bao* attached. The *hung bao i*s a red envelope with *lay see,* or money is enclosed," he explained to the guests' understood the custom.

The audience cheered as the lion approached the pagoda where the *choy cheng* hung. Carefully doing his three-star dance to ward off any others who may want to eat his green, the lion approached his prize. He sniffed at the greens, testing to make sure they were safe, not a firecracker or other dangerous trap. Then cautiously, he danced before the *snake* of martial arts weapons placed on the ground in front of the *choy cheng.* "How can he keep from stepping on the shurikens with his huge feet?" Lein-Hua held her breath. Satisfied the green-treat was safe, the lion took it in his mouth and pretended to chew it, tossing his head and throwing pieces of vegetable leaves first to the left, then to the right and finally out in front of him, to spread prosperity in all directions. As the music changed to the high dance, the lion raised his head to show he was happy to consume his award. Lein-Hua laughed allowed, then remembered her manners and kept quiet.

Unknown to the viewers, the man inside the costume removed the *lay see* from its *hung bao* envelope and put the money in his shirt pocket careful not to drop it, which would mean bad luck to the newlyweds. He would give it to the grooms later.

After the *choy cheng* dance was over, Haoli took Lein-Hua's hand. "Come let us visit with the guests." The others newlyweds joined them. The over-filled street allowed her no room to step. She hugged close against Haoli for the first time. The music and dancing continued for several hours. Children played, twirling streamers as they chased after the dragon and lions.

Lein-Hua admired the cotton dresses and hairstyles the white women wore. No one pointed because of skin color. Secretly, she wished it would always be this way. She shook herself out of the daydream to pay attention to Haoli saying, "You are most beautiful." The compliment surprised her, "Thank you," she whispered back to him.

Mayor McGuire took another opportunity to gain attention. "This is a wonderful time for everyone here today," he began. "Our Chinese friends have treated us, allowing us to share in their traditional celebration."

Haoli poked Wong Pai with his elbow, getting Pai's attention. "He speaks as if we Chinese could vote for him in the next election."

Both laughed, along with other celestials who heard the Mandarin joke.

Al Potter interrupted the mayor by taking his hand and shaking it with a congratulatory nod and indicated his chair. McGuire sat, not seeming to notice he'd been taken off his pedestal. Brownson and Nogle cheered the loudest when the mayor stopped talking.

The wedding celebration advanced into the evening when Zharg Chen and Chyo led Haoli and Lein-Hua to their bridal home and into the bedroom, as Wang Fu and Bo, did the same with Pai and Mei, and the Chans with Li and Sua.

Knowing Haoli guessed her uneasiness, Lein-Hua was glad her veil hid her face from him. He teased her, flipping the end of the dangling beads with his fingertip, and sniggered. Haoli and Lein-Hua sat upon the bed while friends came to taunt them and joked with the couple for what seemed hours into the night.

Exhausted, Lein-Hua leaned against Haoli's shoulder, which brought more comments from the well-wishers as they passed through the room. She felt him shake his arm flanking hers and quickened to sit upright.

Chyo just stepped into the room and saw it. Quickly she shooed the guests out of the bridal bedroom, and shut the door behind them. She helped Lein-Hua remove her headdress and veil and then left the couple to themselves.

"You are exquisite, my tired little one." Haoli voiced softly and filled with love. He reached for her hand and wrapped his arm around her shoulders.

"I cannot be." She peeked at him without turning her face up towards him. "I am scarred from the damage to my soul—before you." A tear fell from her worried eye. Shame pressed her lips together as her body began to shake.

"Nonsense!" He hugged her closer to him, and with his hand he turned her by the chin so she looked directly at him. "You are my new bride. Remember this! Always I will love you. Today we begin our life together. I'll have it no other way."

"You are good to me." She smiled at him. "Forever you will be in my heart."

Haoli inched off the bed, "I will be right back." He returned with a large serving spoon from the kitchen.

Lein-Hua wide eyes displayed her curiosity.

Seeing it, he offered an explanation. "We must protect our gifts." Haoli laid the dozens of red paper-wrapped coins and a leather sack on the edge of the bed. She yawned as she watched. Taking his foot, he tapped the floorboards until he felt the loose one. He pried the board up, revealing the earth under it. Digging a hole about a foot deep with the spoon, he placed the coins in the bag and laid it in the hole. He covered it with the dirt, then replaced the board, leaving no signs it had been removed. The task completed he slid back into bed taking his bride in his arms.

Lein-Hua wondered, again, if Mei and Sua felt as she did, exhausted, and self-conscious from being the center of the day's ceremony. She put the thought away and slipped into Haoli's arms.

Chapter 18

"In the middle of April, 1884, with the two-week wedding ceremony over, the celebration gave way to preparations for the Chinese Lunar New Year. Remember, Lunar Year is traditionally in February." Jie shivered, "Too cold for parades, so it was planned to be after the weddings. I've been telling you my stories for a long time, haven't I?"

"Yes, almost two weeks now," Molly agreed, "but I am not tired of hearing about your family. I hope you are not exhausted from my visit. I must go back to law school at the end of the week. I will miss our talks, Nanai. I am writing what you tell so everyone will someday know what our clans experienced. It was not always happy times for them."

"Good," Jie patted Molly's hand, then reached for her teacup and took a sip...

Lein-Hua fed the three chickens Haoli had presented to her the morning after the wedding. She loved watching the red hens. It pleased her to find three eggs in the grass. She thanked the hens for providing them food. "You three are real ladies," she told them as they took turns pecking at the corn she held in her hand. Then hearing Haoli calling her name, she tossed the last of the grain to the ground and went back to the house.

At fourteen and now a bride, Lein-Hua had vague memories from her childhood of the dragons and parades at Lunar New Year's in China. She scolded herself for not recalling more. "Am I so old that I cannot remember? Why is my mind empty of these things?" she confided to Chyo who directed the celebration. Lein-Hua enjoyed learning the homeland traditions, things she should know. She put her troubling thoughts aside as she helped Chyo and Bo add decorations to those left over from the weddings. They added multi-colored lanterns to the wedding's red ones. Floral displays and brightly painted banners emblazoned with happy greetings in Chinese symbols hung from buildings and on streamers across the street.

Zharg Chyo instructed the others in the customary preparations. "All must pay off debts to allow a new beginning." She also warned the children, "Put on your best behavior to avoid bad luck."

The next week each family thoroughly cleaned house for the Lunar New Year. "For the symbolical sweeping away all traces of misfortune," Chyo quoted from their heritage. After the scrubbings, they applied new coats of red paint on the outside doors and window frames and decorated them with red paper flowers for prosperity. Lein-Hua again searched her memories, wondering if her mother had cleaned and painted. She could not recall.

In the evening Lein-Hua and Sua enjoyed sewing new tunics for their husbands. "Help me," Mei begged, "I cannot make the needle and threads obey my fingers like you two."

Lein-Hua teased Mei, saying she must learn the stitches to be a good wife, as she demonstrated how to weave the needle, making a long seam line. They giggled together as they worked on the garments.

The second week after the weddings, May 1st, was the first day of the Lunar ceremony. Everyone took pleasure in donning new clothes, denoting the discard of last year's misfortunes. Lein-Hua liked how Haoli looked in his new tunic. Adult friends gave *hung bao* gifts of red paper-packets of money to confirm importance of their friendship to each other. Tables were again in Chinatown's center street, laden with special feast dishes prepared with fresh rice-flour cakes and fruits for the promised good luck and prosperity.

The noon sun warmed the day. The long dragon and the three lions again filled the streets with a long trail of people joining their procession, frolicking to the beating of gongs and drums accompanying the flute and cymbals. Children paraded in the festival, carrying lanterns of various shapes and patterns, lit with candles. After sharing in the feast, they danced into the evening. Musicians took turns entertaining into the evening.

Fireworks frightening off evil spirits, exploded from midnight until dawn.

In traditional style, the partying persisted for another two weeks. The continued bursting of firecrackers littered Chinatown with paper debris. During the Lunar celebrations, Jimmy Orenstein found a string of unexploded firecrackers near the creek. He showed it off to his friend, Denny, before hiding the treasure in the hayloft in his dad's barn.

George Mudgget, who had been the wagon master of the supply train for the rail camps, now worked as barkeeper at the Silver Bar uptown. His gimpy leg still bothered him and he often wondered if the Chinese medicine would have given him relief. He limped his way over to the table of card-playing customers and poured more whiskey into emptied glasses.

The group of drinking men grew rowdy as they picked up newly dealt hands and placed bets. "Stupid chinks," one grumbled. "I can't sleep with their racket. It's been weeks, now. We outta make 'em stop!"

"How ya gonna do that?" another with too much whiskey in his belly butted in. "Just how ya gonna shaddup a whole town of yeller-skins? Huh? Just tell me that?" His tongue slurred his words. "Ya know ole McGuire is protecting those monkeys. Just in case, he doesn't want lose a vote or two in the next election over them. Wake up, it's your turn to discard."

Mudgget moved away from the table and went behind the bar to perch on his stool. He preferred to stay out of the line of fire of these fellows. Serving their drinks was as close to them as he wanted to be when they were liquored up. He poured himself another watered-down shot and picked up the newest issue of the Silver Blade News. He found where he had left off and started reading, ignoring the drunks' on-going complaining.

"We can fix 'em, don't worry 'bout how." The first man swallowed the last of his whiskey and tossed an ace of spades on the table. "Who's with me? Huh?" He nearly fell off his chair as he turned to the men drinking at a table behind him. "You there." He pointed at the Irishman who used to ramrod coolies' rail workers. "You wanna help shaddup those chinks?"

The Irishman emptied his glass and slammed it on the table. "I'm with yer al'right. I'm tired of all their racket. What'll we do?"

"Meet tomorrow at dusk. At the train depot. Mount yer best ride and bring yer guns. We'll show'm how to party."

"Sounds good to me," someone else yelled. "Who else is coming?" The card game folded, and the men stuffed winnings into their pockets.

From around the room drunks cheered their agreement. "I'll be for home 'n get'n some sleep," another shouted, "I wanna be 'wake for this party." He slurped the last of his drink and headed out the door.

Soon the bar stood quiet, emptied of everyone except Mudgget, who wiped up the messes with a dirty rag. Half looped himself, he was too tired to pay much attention to the boisterous night customers. "They are always full of talk 'round here." He mumbled as he wiped the last table. "Means nothing, anyhow." He locked the door, turned out the lights and went upstairs to his room.

The next day, as the sun set behind the mountain, half-a-dozen mounted rowdies met at the west end of the tracks at the depot. Travelers waiting for the train paid no attention to them. As the locomotive pulled away, its clanging-clickity-clacking muffled the hoots and hollers as men kicked horses into action. In a cloud of dust, they rode toward Chinatown.

At the bridge, one kicked his booted foot out and knocked over the temple-shrine by the tall pine. The plaster arch crumbled as it hit the ground. Laughing and shooting his gun in the air, he led the group toward Chinatown. Riders yelling and shooting wildly rode toward the unsuspecting village.

Wong Pai sat on Wang Fu's porch, chair tipped balancing on the back legs as he leaned against the wall his feet perched up the front railing. Pai could view most of the houses from where he sat. Chatting with Fu in the evenings and watching the antics of neighboring children as they played tag was a favorite part of Pai's day. "Yeah," he cheered as little Bin tagged his older sister. Their figures became less identifiable in the setting twilight when Chyo called them in for supper. With the little ones inside, Pai listened to the creek bubbling behind the row of huts. "Someday Fu, my sons will play on evenings like this."

"Yes, you will be blessed with many sons."

A roar of pounding hoofs, whooping and gunfire stopped the two's conversation. Wong Pai jumped up from his chair and shouted, "What goes on here?"

Wang Fu joined Pai in the street. "Ayaaaah." Fu grabbed his head in both hands. Horrified, he witnessed the destruction of the temple. Other men who had been doing chores ran to Fu, too.

"Get inside!" Wong Pai yelled running back to Fu's porch, then he grabbed the supper triangle hanging from the corner post. Banging on it, he hurried down the street ahead of the riders, yelling "Take cover! Trouble coming. Take cover!"

Hearing the alarm and the approaching intruders, men shooed crying children into houses, grabbed clubs, knives, and machetes to face whoever was coming. Women closed window shutters and fastened door bolts.

Ang Li made his way behind huts to Bachelors' Row where he mounted a donkey and under cover of the trees rode to get Sheriff Ryan. Hong Haoli, Chan and other men joined

147

Wong Pai and Wang Fu in the street. The men up-sided two donkey carts to provide a barrier.

The women stuffed flour sacks with food, in case they needed to hide, then ushered children discreetly out back doors and ran to the safe-houses, which had hidden tunnel entrances. Together, families exited the safe-houses, through the tunnels, to the woods on the mountain. Under the covering of thick brush and trees, they climbed the hillside to the old mining pit dug into the mountainside.

In the mining shelter Lein-Hua hugged Bin and helped Mei and Bo calm the children. From behind bushes at the edge of the hillside Chyo, Sua and Chan's wife spied down on the village.

Below them, they watched as drunken men on horseback spotted the over-turned carts in the street and came to a stop. "Let's get 'em," one yelled whacking his horse into a gallop. The others followed. Reaching the blockade, they encircled it like Indians attacking a wagon train, shooting and yelling curses.

"They are like the whale. Feeding upon the minnows," Sua gasped. "Our men have no chance against these devils." She burst into tears and covered her face with her hands.

Chyo put an arm around Sua and pulled her close, keeping eyes on the scene below, she could not, *not* watch.

One of the riders grabbed a lighted lantern off a doorpost. He threw it against a porch. It burst into flames, immediately igniting the house. Satisfied with his destruction, he shot into the burning home. In moments the houses on the east side of the street were ablaze. Fire burst through roofs, destroying everything in its path. Each home became easy fuel, spreading to the huts on the next street.

Seeing his home in flames, Wong Pai grabbed his shuriken pouch hanging at his side. He did not notice one of the stars had sliced his finger as he emptied the tote. He tossed four shurikens at the rider who had thrown the lantern. The shurikens, well aimed, ripped into the man's arm and shoulder.

He fell from his horse, screaming for help, unable to get to his feet. Blood spurted from his arm, shoulder, and chest.

Before Pai released his fifth weapon, a second rider landed a lasso around Pai's chest pinning his arms and pulled him to the ground. The roughneck kicked his horse into a full run, dragging Wong Pai.

"Yeehaaw," a rider yelled shooting his gun, turned his mount to join the chase of the others chasing after the one dragging the chinaman. They headed south through Chinatown. Seeing the raiders leaving, toward the pagoda at the other end of town, several Chinese gathered buckets and ran to the creek.

At the pagoda, built for the weddings, the riders stopped. "This will do," the leader shouted and dismounted, grabbing the rope he pulled Pai to him.

Wong Pai's limp body, covered in dirt, lay still at his feet.

The man picked Pai's head up by his queue. "Hey, this here's the coolie who's been so chummy with da mayor."

"Yeah, he's the one. Let's teach 'em."

"How can ya tell 'em apart? These yeller slant-eyed dogs all look alike," shouted another getting off his horse.

"It's him, all right! And I've 'ad enuf of him for sure. Always sticking his nose in our business. Trying to change our laws to side with the chinks. Thinks he has rights. Let's give him his last rights."

"Look, there's a good place." The one with the rope pointed and tugged Pai over to the pagoda. Without hesitating he looped his rope over the brace beam and tightened it.

Another cowboy slipped the rope from the chinaman's chest to his neck. Together in one quick hoist, they left Wong Pai swinging from the heart of the temple where just days ago, he had pledged his love to his bride. Sobering at what they had done, the men rode out of Chinatown, turning towards Twin Lakes.

Wailing as he ran to the pagoda, Haoli hurried to cut the rope and caught his beloved friend's body in his arms. He crumbled to the floor. Wong Pai's lifeless corpse in his lap.

Zharg Chen joined Haoli. Together they wept.

149

After the raiders left Chinatown, the sheriff arrived with a small posse, including Wood and Potter. Ang Li came behind, trotting on Pai's donkey. Sheriff Ryan dismounted near the wounded man, lying in the street. His face had deep cuts and part of his right ear was missing. He inspected the sliced up shirt sleeve coated in bright blood.

"Looks like…he's been…shredded?" Sliding off his saddle, Potter asked, "Machete do this?"

"Shurikens." Chen smirked his approval of Pai's last effort.

"You two deal with him." The sheriff pointed to Potter and Wood. Back in the saddle, Sheriff Ryan, followed by Brownson, Nogle, and four others, slowed as they passed the pagoda. "We'll get them," he looked Haoli in the eye. "See which way they rode out?"

"That way!" Fu pointed toward Twin Lakes.

A bucket brigade was already in action from the creek to the burning homes. They managed to prevent the flames from jumping the street but could not stop the homes already on fire, turning them into smoldering shells. Chan and two bachelors were found dead, shot from flying bullets.

With the immediate danger now past, the women and children returned to the village through the woods. Some crumbled to the street and wept at seeing the destruction of their homes and village.

In shock, Mei and a few others trudged to the pagoda-temple to pray and tell the ancestors of their distress. Approaching the pagoda, the women found men gathered in front of it.

Wang Fu ran to them. "Mei, I'm so sorry. Please don't go any nearer. It is horrible. Sua take her back. Please turn away, Mei!"

His pleading did no good. Mei pushed away from Sua's side and ran forward, screaming. "Pai. Pai. No! No! Pai!" Mei lifted her beloved's face in her hands, screamed and fainted.

Chapter 19

"Wong Pai would have been my father-in-law, you know."
Jie's eyes watered, displaying the grief she felt at the injustice.
Molly took her hand, "Tell me about it, Nanai, and do not
leave anything out, so my journal will be complete."...

In the pagoda, four coffins rested on two stools about a foot high, heads positioned to face towards the homes and destruction behind them. Incense and white candles burned at the foot of the coffins of Wong Pai, Chan, and the two bachelors.

Friends brought gifts of food and paper money, placing them at the heads of the unsealed coffins. Fu chanted as he broke the combs of each of the deceased men. Ceremoniously he put one piece of the comb in the owner's coffin and gave the other half to the wives and friends of the bachelors.

Both Mei and Chan's wife dressed in white. Neither put on jewelry or decorative items. Women honored the dead by sitting on the right side of the deceased. They wailed and cried during the mourning period, displaying their respect and loyalty to the families.

At night, Haoli, Li and male friends took turns sitting next to the altar, guarding the corpses. "It is tradition that the "guards" engaged in friendly gambling." Fu produced a deck of Chinese cards, without numbers but dots instead, they look more like dominos than cards. "To keep awake during our vigil." He dealt the cards. "It will lessen your grief." He smiled at Haoli as he handed him a card.

Haoli did not return the smile but nodded to his mentor friend.

Through the night they gambled and chanted prayers, accompanied by men playing flutes, to help ease the passage of the deceased's spirits into the heavens.

By day, working in silence the men constructed four sedans to transport their dead comrades to the new Pinegrove Cemetery east of Rathdrum.

The heat of Haoli's anger flowed through his muscles as he tied rawhide stripes across the poles, to carry the coffin with the shrouded body of his friend. Instead of a dome as the bridal sedans, these would have a simple arch of willow branches, draped with white cloth, to fit over the coffin.

Haoli's mind whirled. "First Ming Yun died and now Wong Pai, Chan, and the two bachelors were dead." He tightened a strap as he pondered aloud. "We did not plan to die so soon in this new life." His meditations sapped his strength as he secured another line to the poles, tears blurring his vision. Then he helped Zharg Chen bend the willow branches to create the arch over the bed.

"To keep away prying eyes," Chen whispered as they worked.

Haoli and Chen knotted them in place while Ang Li held them. It was the sixth day since the raid.

"When we finish here, I will go gather the bones of Ming Yun." Haoli wiped his brow and tied the last knot.

"That will please the ancestors," Chen agreed. "Want me to come too?"

"Yes. I do not feel sturdy today." With his left palm, Haoli rubbed his right forearm's hard muscle.

"I know. You are not yourself. These are hard times for us all." Chen picked up one of the white linens and draped it over the arch to decorate and honor the deceased that would be under it. "This is the last one. Our chore is nearly finished."

"Only one more sedan to build. The widow's." Haoli wiped his face against his sleeve again. "They will ride together for support of each other."

"It will be fashioned as the weddings sedans are, but not as high." Wang Fu gave the instructions from where he sat watching them. "And Bo is making a straw-filled leather pillow seat for Mei and Chan's widow."

After completing the sedans, Haoli and Li took shovels to their burnt homes and dug up the buried treasures hidden under the floors. They searched for Pai's stash to give to Mei after the funerals. After finding Pai's hidden coins, they marched to the pine on the creek bank. "We must stop the demons and give Ming Yun and his spirit a proper resting place, too. I promised the ancestors this when we were forced to bury him here." Haoli set to digging for his cousin's bones, tears filling his eyes.

On the seventh morning, the five-hundred-some Far Easterners filled the street, all dressed in white apparel. Soft wailings drifted with the breeze. They encircled the pagoda, several times.

"Blessings from the deceased are bestowed upon pallbearers, so many have volunteered to do the bidding." Fu informed Haoli, Li, and Chen. "I have picked out good men to serve." He pointed to the two lines of men standing next to the coffins in the pagoda as they joined the inner circle, covering their noses to smother the odor, they were the last to arrive, showing their close friendship to the deceased.

A prayer chant began and all turned around, facing away from the coffins.

The pallbearers nailed the coffins shut. "For the separation of the dead from the living," Wang Fu's voice raised above the hammering.

Chen's son, Bin, twisted his head to peek when he heard the hammering.

"No. Do not look." Chen put his hand on the boy's head and guided his gaze away. "To watch the sealing is unlucky." Chastised, Bin obeyed his father.

Hearing the banging of nails, it was hard for Haoli not to peek, too. He did not blame little Bin, but did not turn to look. He chanted louder to relieve his own pain.

The sun bore down and the breeze was warm against his damp skin, making him hotter. He fought the desire to wipe his face again with his sleeve. It would not be proper to move.

Finally, the hammering stopped. The chanting changed to a humming. Flutes played softly. The pallbearers pasted pieces of torn yellow and white papers on the coffins to protect the bodies from malignant spirits. Haoli felt the last of his energy drain from his body as if the spirits left him empty. He was glad to hear the command to turn and face the coffins.

The pallbearers in ceremony loaded their burdens under the arches of the five sedans. Picks and shovels were placed beside the coffins on each sedan.

The team carrying the widow's sedan waited outside the home of Wang Fu.

Four friends with Haoli at the lead headed to Wang Fu's hut. They waited quietly, heads bowed. On cue, Haoli approached the hut, tapped on the door and waited.

Wang Bo opened the door. Mei and Chan's widow, dressed in fine white silk brocades, exited. Haoli bowed, then took both women by an arm, escorted them to the sedan and helped them aboard. Mei placed her hand on her nauseous stomach and winced. Chan's wife patted her on the shoulder, but did not speak.

Haoli stepped away from the widows and faced his friends. Together they led the sedan back to the pagoda. He held his arm high. Silence fell over the crowd and he announced in their native tongue, "We have shown the whites how we live. Now we let them see how we die—with dignity."

In unison, the pallbearers stooped, picked up the handles and with a smooth swift motion hoisted the sedans to their shoulders. Mourning and weeping broke out in a loud chorus as Haoli returned to his lead position next to Wang Fu, the elder. Deafening cries commenced, as the procession started. The sedans swayed to the rhythm of men's steps. Bobbing white arches filled the roadway. The wails grew louder, more sorrowful, and grief-stricken.

When the cavalcade came to the creek, they stopped. Wang Fu looked skyward and announced, "Wong Pai, Chan, Friends, and Ming Yun, hear me now. We are about to cross this body of water. Do not be afraid. Your souls shall cross with you." With the formal declaration he again stepped back to his lead position and marched across the bridge. All followed. The mourners' cries and music increased in volume.

Riding Welch ponies on a nearby farm, sons of the first homesteaders, Jimmy Orenstein and Denny Barton, heard the commotion of the mourners. They cantered out to the road to check out the noise.

Seeing the funeral train, Jimmy hollered, "Look at that," pointing toward the sea of white-garmented Chinese moving toward the town.

They headed their mounts toward town at a gallop. No one was on the street. Jimmy aimed his pony towards his dad's saloon. He jumped down from the saddle with Denny at his heels and burst through the swinging doors. "They're coming!" he puffed for breath. "The Chinas are coming."

"What in the world do you think you're doing?" His father bellowed when his son enter the forbidden room. "You know...." His words were cut off by someone over-talking him, "Let the boy speak, can't you see something is up?"

Orenstein, forgot his own rule and allowed the boys to report what they had witnessed. As soon as the boys stopped talking, men rushed for the door, emptying the saloon.

"Hush," someone yelled. "Listen."

The mourning hums and chants floated towards them with what seemed a warning in the rhythmic beat of eerie drums. More folks from the mercantile and other shops joined the saloon's gang out in the street. Together they hurried down the slope of McCartney Street to get a better view.

Word spread among the town people that the Chinese were coming—to bury their dead. Folks stood along the street and stared. Some pointed and whispered. Others shouted, cursing the yellow-skins. A woman holding a baby wept silently, hugging the child to cover her face.

Like an exhibition, the Chinese marched passed the gathering crowd of whites. They crossed the railroad tracks and turned east on Main Street towards the cemetery. Haoli deliberately had led the funeral train through the main part of town.

Pinegrove Cemetery lay peaceful, protected under pine and fir trees, an acre of land surrounded by a new-whitewashed fence. Road cuts crossed through the tall pines. Only a few grave markers stood near the north fence line.

Orenstein, leading a self-appointed committee, hurried to get ahead of the funeral train at the closed gate under a new hand-painted sign, *Pinegrove Cemetery*. Like vigilantes, they flaunted rifles and gun belts, standing behind Orenstein blocking the gate. Among them were Brownson, Nogle and others, including the mayor and a man with his arm in a sling and the right side of his face and ear swathed in bandages?

As Haoli arrived at the gate, Orenstein shouted in a voice of authority, "Halt where you are chinaboy. You'll not defile our dead with your yellow-heathen-kind."

"But we made arrangements for burial today. We paid the fee." Haoli kept his voice steady, not showing his feeling of betrayal. "We must bury our own, to rest with the ancestors. We paid the fee." He repeated his voice stronger than he felt. "We agreed to dig the graves." Haoli felt the warmth of his body raise, not from the day's heat. He did not understand why the men blocked his way.

"You heard me. No coolies are gonna be planted in here." Shouts from behind him reinforced Orenstein's words. The man with the wounded arm cocked his rifle.

Haoli had no time to reply. The protestors' noise stopped short as a surrey trotted up to them. The driver's rugged face, softened by graying dark hair, frowned as he guided his horse between the Chinese and the men at the gate. "What goes on here, Orenstein?"

"We don't want any of them heathens buried here, Mr. Potter."

"I knew you'd be up to no good." Alfred Potter shouted at the men blocking the gate, and then turned towards Haoli from his seat. "This is my land. I laid my infant son to rest here and let the Nicholls widow bury her man here. Then a few others came and I established this field with its patch of trees as a formal cemetery."

"Yeah, well it's for Christian folks. Whites Only! We don't want their kind here," shouted Orenstein.

"Quiet." Potter ordered Orenstein. "I'm talking to this man." He turned his attention back to Haoli. "This is all my land. While I don't agree with these men I think it best if you bury your kin over there." He pointed to the field beyond the fenced cemetery. "That's mine too. Dig your graves there." Potter spun around in his seat so he looked down at the mayor with a hard stare. "These men *will* stop their huffing. Right McGuire?"

"Ah, all right," Mayor McGuire agreed. "Long as they keep out of our way. Right boys?"

The band of men mumbled agreement.

Haoli turned to his people and spoke loudly in Mandarin, "Follow me."

Potter clicked his tongue at his mare, taking the surrey to the open field beyond the cemetery fence. The noon sun bore down. The breeze stirring the treetops brought some relief from the day's heat and the odor of death.

Potter let out his breath and wiped a brow with a sleeve. His graying hair fell back to its natural twist on his forehead. Controlling McGuire and Orenstein sometimes proved difficult but was a challenge he enjoyed.

Haoli took up his lead position and followed Potter who pulled up at the edge of the fence and pointed. Haoli nodded and kept moving in the direction Mr. Potter indicated. The mourners followed. The grassy field soon filled with the white-clad mourners. The pallbearers placed the sedans in a row and took up the digging tools. The people sat on the ground and wailed.

As the digging continued, Haoli thought about Orenstein. Then as if he was working on the railroad, he chanted the words in singsong fashion, "'Maybe he has feathers where his spine should be'." The proverb brought a slight grin to his lips. Others joined in the chant for a few rounds.

Pai would have liked this, Haoli thought, glancing over to where Mei and Chan's widow sat. He noticed Mei seemed so pale. Then he saw his own bride standing near Mei and smiled at her. Lein-Hua nodded. Her eyes returned to Mei.

Once the coffins were lowered into the graves, the pallbearers stood at the head of the gravesites to guard over the burial. The families performed a ritual of burning paper money, clothing and food to send with their loved ones into the next world.

Mei held her nauseous stomach. She watched as the clans came in small groups to the foot of the graves, then departed silently to return to Chinatown. She wished she could go, too, and lie down.

The traditional mourning continued into July. Every seventh day they repeated the prayers and music vigil, fulfilling the forty-nine-day custom burial. The men filled the days with rebuilding burnt homes. The women sewed new clothes, linens and fashioned pottery for the new houses. They never neglected their mourning ritual.

At the last prayer night, Mei felt ill as the ceremony continued. She shamed herself for thinking she wanted privacy, to be in her room at Wang Bo's curled up on the bed. She slipped her hand down over her abdomen. She concentrated on the words Wang Fu chanted, trying to make her stomach settle, and not embarrass herself with sickness. After the ceremonies, she was thankful friends helped her walk home. She shooed them away, "I need to rest." Shortly after closing the door, she disgorged, leaving her belly as empty as her heart—she finally slept.

Chapter 20

"Where was I? Oh yes, the hot summer of 1884 parched the land. Father said no rain fell after the funerals in mid-June. The fields and the forests dry as tinder. A terrible time for the town," Jie shuddered at the memory—or was it the chill in the room? "The Northern Pacific chartered a new line from Rathdrum to Coeur d'Alene and up into the Silver Valley. Hundreds of our Chinese men, and as many of the bogies hired on, leaving Rathdrum. Mining, in Silver Valley and in Montana, became the newest ambition for the workers after the Northern Pacific was completed. Gossip spread that a mining company ore-scout, Noah Kellogg, searching for gold struck a rich silver vein under the turf where his jackass munched grass. More rumors followed that gold and silver were abundant. Some told that fist-sized nuggets lay on top of the ground on mountainsides—all lies," Jie giggled at her own cleverness...

Chinese men worked claims that whites had given up, as they were not allowed to file for ownership. The Chinese worked diligently only to be killed for their pokes. "What else bad can happen to our clansmen," Haoli wailed as he learned of friends who had met this fate. "We must bring our friends home and give them proper burials."

Several times he and Chen fetched bodies back to Rathdrum for interment, in Al Potter's field next to Pinegrove Cemetery's fence. As they placed each body in a grave, Haoli renewed the vow to Uncle Kai to *never forget*.

One late September day, Haoli and Chen returned from Silver Valley to Rathdrum with three coffins in the back of their wagon. They recognized several white boys playing ball near the railroad tracks behind Orenstein's saloon. They waved to them and hollered, "Hello there."

The boys returned the greetings and went on with their game as the Chinese men passed by.

The oldest boy, Peter, complained, holding the ball over the other boys' heads. "I wish we had something new to do. It's boring here."

"I have something," Jimmy Orenstein volunteered.

"What could you possibly have that's new? You're just a kid."

"Well I do. I have firecrackers." Jimmy reached up and pinched Peter's arm.

"Ouch," he dropped the ball. "You don't really have any crackers. And try that again, I'll tear your arm off."

Ignoring the threat, Jimmy stomped his foot. "Yes, I do...I do so."

"Prove it." Peter shoved Jimmy, knocking him on the ground.

"I can go get 'em."

"Okay. We'll wait right here."

Jimmy got up and brushed dirt off his pants, then mounted his pony and cantered home. "I'll show 'em, girl," He kicked Beauty into a gallop. In a few minutes they arrived at his farm.

In front of the barn, he slid from the saddle. Climbing the ladder to the loft, he retrieved his treasure hidden in the hay and tucked it under his shirt. He jumped on Beauty and in record time, made his way back to town where the older boys waited.

"You don't have anything," Peter accused Jimmy as he got off his pony and tied her to a post.

"Oh yeah?" Jimmy turned to face the taller boy, unfastened the top two buttons of his shirt, and pulled out the string of red firecrackers. He held them up, exposing a dozen firecrackers, each bigger than a cigar.

"Whoa. This is great." Peter snatched the string away from Jimmy. "Let's blow 'em."

"I don't think that's a good idea, Peter. I feel a wind stirring," Denny Barton protested.

"Ah, don't be such a baby. It won't take long to pop 'em." Peter got his matches from the saddlebags he stored for lighting the occasional tobacco he stole from his father's pouch. Kneeling, he laid the strip of firecrackers out on the ground along side the rail tracks and scratched a match against the rail. It blew out in the wind.

A second one sparked into a flame, nearly burning his fingers. Peter touched the fire to the string-fuse, dropped it, and hollered, "Run!"

The boys dashed away and turned with hands over ears.

The fuse shriveled and hissed as it reached the first firecracker.

Nothing happened.

"You stole a bunch of duds," Peter yelled at Jimmy.

"I didn't steal 'em. I found them, and it's not my fault they didn't pop." Jimmy ran to Beauty, climbed on, and rode home.

The wind came in wild gusts, blowing strong. In minutes, it was pushing hard against Jimmy. He tightened his grip on Beauty's saddle horn. At the barn, Jimmy could not open the door against the swirling winds. "Come on girl, we need to get out of this windstorm." He led her through the small door on the far side, removed the saddle, and brushed her.

"Awe, they won't light with this wind kicking up," Peter declared after striking two more matches. "I'm going home, this storm is coming fast." He and the other boys left, forgetting about exploding the firecrackers.

Wind flurries ripped shingles off buildings as they headed for shelter. The Brownson's mercantile sign fell to the ground, shattering as it landed. Storekeepers scrambled to get their horses and riggings to the safety of the blacksmith's new barn at the far end of Main Street. Barton's buckboard and stud overturned. The horse fought to stand, but became tangled in the harness. The gale twisted the cart sideways, dragging the horse some ten-feet, before several men up-righted it and rescued the horse.

A train, heading east sounded its whistle as it chugged down the tracks. No one paid any attention.

Folks hustled to get belongings off porches and streets. Unnoticed, several "pops" sounded near the tracks as the train left town. Fire flared in the weeds near the rails, fed by the wind. The back wall of Orenstein's saloon ignited. In minutes, the wind spread the fire in a wild blazing ball. It quickly consumed two more stores. Frenzied, men tied wet hankies over their faces like bandits and attempted to fight the fires.

The wind carried the smoke to the north, augmenting over Chinatown and the mountain. "Grab buckets, let's go help, Haoli hollered to the others as they gathered.

"Why should we help them?" the brother of one of the deceased bachelors demanded. "They killed my brother. They treat us with disgust. Like animals. Help? Why?" He spit on the ground.

"Because, *we* are not like *them*. And, what if the fire spreads to our homes? Get all the buckets you can carry. Let's go." Chen was quick to put the brother into action and together they picked up several pails women brought to them.

The Chinese jogged to Main Street and began a water brigade, filling and passing buckets from the Main Street pump. Whites came and joined the line, bringing more buckets. Together they fought the spreading inferno. The wind hindered their efforts, scattering the fires to more buildings.

Men tossed water on nearby structures not yet enflamed. Hot, and tired, they drank from the buckets and splashed water on themselves to cool off. The battle against the raging fires continued into the night. Lightening lit the sky periodically, but no rain came. Each breath was smoke filled, even through the damp handkerchiefs about their faces.

At a nearby farmhouse, women gathered to make sandwiches and coffee for the fire-fighting men. Boys transported the food to the men fighting the fires. The efforts did not stop the intensity of the fires. The night wore on. Exhausted, men continued working, trying to save buildings from the flames.

The next morning the town glowed as hot coals through smoke-filled blackened streets. The first rain since early June poured down, finishing the firefighting efforts of the past twenty-four hours. Stinking smoke filled the damp air, making breathing difficult.

Mid-morning, Frederick Post, strolled along with Potter and McGuire through the disaster area, all shaking heads. Post had traveled from Post Falls with a group of folks, who, seeing the smoke across the Prairie came to help and stayed to lend a hand afterwards. Already, clean-up work was in process where ashes had cooled.

From the surrey, Alfred Potter and Mayor McGuire counted fifty-five buildings and homes along with several wagons in the streets destroyed in the downtown district. They chatted briefly with attorneys Herren and Heitman who were sifting through the ashes of their offices. They found Mr. Yost squatting in the street, head in his hands, in front of what used to be his newspaper. The café, the barbershop, and Silver Bar—all gone. Timbers still sent up smoke from the Wright Hotel and other structures.

"It was a no-good chinaman," Orenstein boasted from behind his makeshift bar, "that's who started the fire."

"You're crazy. Sparks from the train caused it," Nogle with too much moonshine in his belly shouted from his perch on the stoop.

"Y'all got it wrong," another put in, "It was a bunch of kids. Wasn't your boy out there where it started?" He looked deliberately into Orenstein's hard eyes.

"Nah, it started in the kitchen of the Silver Bar. But we'll never know the truth of it, maybe it was a Chinese?" Brownson slammed his empty cup on the table and got up, leaving the rest to ponder.

"The city's population has dropped from over 7000 people to less than 800. Maybe less, we'll have to wait for a good count by the mayor." Herren scratched his head. "Instead of rebuilding, many business owners left to go to the mines. Those who stayed are constructing with bricks."

Heitman was quick to agree. "The hanging of Wong Pai alarmed the Chinese residents. Most vacated already, many are following the new rails to the mining in Silver Valley. Can't blame them."

"Aye," Herren got up from bending over his papers. "Haoli tells me Zharg Chen and others left, drifting along the rails into Montana. He says Butte is a booming mining town and a popular place for the clans."

"I think only about a dozen Chinese families remain here in Rathdrum. Haoli and Li gained employment with the county, erecting replacement buildings, but that won't last long." Heitman shook his head.

Lein-Hua stood waving, wishing friends well as they moved out of sight. She turned to Haoli, "Should we leave Rathdrum too?"

Haoli shook his head, "No, this is where we belong, I will not go."

"Vacant lands lay everywhere, for sale at cheap prices, but not available to Chinese." Haoli tossed his hat against the wall. "A Methodist church group bought the land next to where I want to set up a laundry. It's a good location, at the edge of town next to the creek, southwest of Chinatown. We have used the acreage as a shortcut to the town for years." Each time Haoli crossed it, his dream of owning it grew stronger.

"I've learned the ways of the law from Pai's attorney friends and Mr. Potter." Haoli told Ang Li as they discussed their plans. "Under the law, Mr. Herren told me, we must have approval before we can do business."

"The congregation will build on their lot in the near future. We will help," Li suggested, "they will learn to trust us."

Haoli liked this idea. "Money needs to be raised before their church can be erected. I want the Americans to get along with us again. We need peace in order to stay here and do business with them."

Haoli and Ang Li decided when their employment with the county ended they would open a laundry in the spring. "With our brides and Mei, we will have plenty of help," Li's excitement grew.

Chapter 21

"Let me back up here," Jie thought for a moment, then continued. "It was soon after Wong Pai's funeral when Wang Bo discovered Mei's secret— that she was carrying Pai's child. In the midst of the tragedy of Pai's death and its aftermath, Mei's pregnancy was a glimmer of happiness. At their insistence, Mei moved into Lein-Hua and Haoli's home."...

Wang Bo came to Lein-Hua's for tea a few months after the big funeral. "I'm worried for Mei," Bo confided in Lein-Hua, as Mei napped in her room. "Her condition has weakened a great deal. I think she needs bed rest, more than I have witnessed with other expectant mothers."

Lein-Hua's hand stroked her stomach, covering her own worries.

Mei stayed in bed as the cold weather set in. Winter brought extreme temperatures with snowstorms that left drifts too high for horses to plow through without a cleared pathway. During a storm just after the American Christmas holiday Wong Mei gave birth to a son. She named him Pai Number Two, his father's namesake.

Wang Bo reminded the new mother and friends. "This is the end of 1884, the Year of the Monkey. The child would be of great intelligence and able to influence people. He would be an enthusiastic achiever," she smiled at Mei.

"Like his father," Mei took courage for her son in the zodiac sign.

The excited Bo told the newborn's visitors, her father Fu, Ang Li, and Sua she was determined to keep Chinese customs alive that Zharg Chyo had taught them. "We will have a party to celebrate the birth. We'll invite the few clans left here and serve red eggs and ginger-flavored treats for a long life to the child."

Wang Fu bit his lip holding back his excitement and became serious, "We will be careful not to pop too many firecrackers. We do not want to make the whites angry, *again.*"

Ang Li nodded his agreement.

Little Pai was a strong baby and Mei proved to be a wonderful mother. Lein-Hua and Sua, and their husbands acted as extended families to Mei and her son. The months dragged by until Lein-Hua's baby would be born.

One evening as they readied for the night's sleep Lein-Hua confided in Haoli. "Sua feels left out. I am so sorry for her. She wants a child so much. I can tell the way she cuddles little Pai. I think she envies Mei, and me too."

"Do not borrow trouble." Haoli slipped his nightshirt over his head.

"Sua said she loves the children calling her *Auntie*, and she is glad Jaoi and the younger children think of her as family." Lein-Hua picked up her hairbrush and pulled it through her hair. "Sua hopes young Pai and our babe will call her Auntie, too. Sua hugged little Pai so tight she made him squirm and cry." Lein-Hua brushed her hair faster. "She tends the babe as if he is her own. I think her spirit is empty."

"She and Ang Li will have children. I am sure of it." Haoli's words fell on his wife's heavy heart. He took the hairbrush from her hand and stoked her hair with it.

"I am not so sure. She should be with child now. She was so young, the youngest of all in the dens."

"Do not speak of it!" Haoli's mood peaked. "Do not think of those days. I cannot bear it—for you—for Sua—for Yue. None of you should have been there. Do not speak of it again." His voice carried a sour warning. He tossed the brush onto the bed.

"I apologize. I will do as you say." Lein-Hua guessed that the loss of his sister still stung his soul.

Haoli took her in his arms. He whispered an ancestral saying, "'Truth is rarely pure and never simple'." He bent and kissed her.

"You are right." She relaxed and snuggled into her husband's arms.

In the middle of a late March most of the snow had melted, and a new storm seemed to be winter's argument against the springtime warmth. During the blizzard, with Bo and Mei's help, Lein-Hua gave birth to her first son. Wang Bo wrapped the newborn in an embroidered red blanket and laid him in his mother's arms. "He will be a pioneer in spirit and devoted to work, and will quest after much knowledge," she quoted the 1885 Cock's zodiac prediction. "But," she hesitated, "he will also be eccentric and somewhat selfish." Then she smiled at Lein-Hua, "He will be perfect, just enough into himself to be of service to others with his wisdom. You are a lucky mother."

"Thank you." Lein-Hua smiled up at Bo, trying to look stronger than she felt. She loved how the older woman knew these things and kept everyone informed of the homeland customs.

"Have you picked a name?"

"Yes, if Haoli agrees, he will be Hong Yun. He will be the namesake for Haoli's cousin, Ming Yun, who died on the railbed crew. He has talked of him much. I think Haoli will be pleased with the name."

After napping, Lein-Hua watched out the window from her bed at what she hoped was the last snowfall. "I remember my first snow here," she mumbled aloud. "When was it? Only a year-and-a-half ago? So much has happened since then. The weddings. The Lunar Year. And Pai, dear, dear Pai. The fires. And now, Mei and I have sons."

"What?" Mei interrupted her musings. "What did you say?"

Mei's voice startled Lein-Hua from her ponderings. Her body jerked, splashing her tea on the bedcovers. "Nothing, nothing at all. I was, ah, just talking, to little Yun." She regained her composure and cradled the feeding baby closer to her bosom. Bo rushed to get a rag to sop up the spill.

Bo and Mei bid the new parents goodbye, telling Lein-Hua to rest when the baby slept. "We'll come and check on you later. Now, sleep." Bo shut the door behind them, but not before a gust of cold blew into the room.

Lein-Hua relaxed, inhaling deeply she tasted his baby-ness as she kissed the top of his soft head. "I've waited a long time for you, my little one," she whispered in his thick, black hair sticking straight up. Sleep overcame her. Haoli entered in to check on his wife, finding her asleep he lifted the child from her and laid him in the cradle he had fashioned.

A year later, after dinner one evening Haoli sighed while reading the newest copy of the Silver Blade, May 8, 1886. "Much has changed."

"What?" Lein-Hua asked as she fed year-old baby-Yun. She slid one hand to her stomach. Her mind was filled with her own worries. "What did you say?"

"Right here. Yost writes that now they are changing the name of Silver Lake to Hauser's Lake."

"Why?"

"To name it after Montana Territory's Governor, Samuel Thomas Hauser. Says he enjoys coming here to fish."

"Oh." Lein-Hua thought for a moment. "So, why change the lake's name? I like Silver Lake."

"Governor Hauser comes here to get away from the Montana's politics, I think." Haoli folded the paper and stood. "He probably does not like his job. He is right, the lake is good for fishing. Pai, Yun, Li, I, and others fished there while we worked with on the railbed," he paused a moment as he recalled some of the men now with the ancestors. "We all fished there several times. It was not far into the mountain from where we leveled the railbed. We supplied the cook with fresh trout and bass for breakfast while we took rest fishing at the lake. The fish was a nice start to our mornings."

"Names here change regular, don't they?" She held Yun up against her shoulder.

"Yes. Westwood's now Rathdrum. And the Mountain, also carries the new name. And, Fish to Twin Lakes. All while I was away. Mud Lake became Silver Lake, and now it's to be 'Hauser's'. What sense comes from all this?" He scratched his head and announced "I do not like this. Why cannot things be as they were? In China, we leave names alone. I am going out to stack wood."

Holding Yun, Lein-Hua went to the window and watched her husband as he split a chunk of wood, driving his frustration out with a chop of the axe. She admired the flex of his muscles. Kissing the baby's head she whispered, "I hope your father will be pleased to learn you will have a brother or sister to play with soon. I will have to tell him—and the girls too. How will Auntie take my news?"

Chapter 22

"Times were hard for my father and mother. Father decided not to open a noodle house like the one he worked in at San Francisco. He feared the whites would not patronize it so he and Ang Li settled on opening a laundry, but of course, they had to get permission. Sometimes, I think father was sorry he had left China. He studied hard, learning to read and write English, and taught the others. But I digress, that is not what my story is about is it?"...

Using his best English, Haoli pleaded his case to the county court judge. "We wish to open a laundry on the south side of the creek. It will not be in the way. Pine and fir trees will veil activity from other enterprises. It will not be noticed." He sat back at the table, folded his hands and waited.

C.L. Heitman rose to make the final plea for the Chinese man. "Your Honor, as you know, in 1882 the Chinese Exclusion Act was repealed, that was four years ago. It was an unjust tax on the Chinese. It is good they no longer are required to pay the quarterly-tax." He rapped his forefinger on the table for attention. Firming his voice he continued, "These men have a right to make a living here in America. We Americans are all immigrants from foreign countries, if not directly, then via our forefathers. Just last week, Your Honor, the new Englishman, William Marsh, celebrated his citizenship to the United States of America. Why is this not allowed for Chinese? The land Hong Haoli and Ang Li reside on with permission belongs to the railroad right-of-way, because the law prohibits them from owning land."

He banged on the table again, emphasizing his point. "The officials of the Northern Pacific authorized me to allow their business as long as there is a need. I suggest you permit them to do so. Have not the Chinese suffered enough? Even the law prohibiting their queues has been overturned now. Where will this ill-treatment end? It is time to recognize them as Americans." He sat, straight in his chair, still looking Judge Melder in the eye.

"So ordered," Judge Henry Melder banged his gavel on the desk. "So long as you, Mr. Heitman, keep close attention to it. Make sure it is managed within the law."

Haoli and Li opened the laundry in July of 1886. They knew their place among the other business proprietors like Orenstein. *Keep out of their way.*

The mayor pressured the others to leave the Chinese alone. "Let the chinamen do it," Mayor McGuire told to the few protestors outside the court. "There are only pennies to be earned scrubbing clothes. Who else is going to do it? Many men here have no wives to clean for them."

Following Fu's suggestions, Haoli and Li built a lean-to shack to house the laundry tubs. Framed with logs of jack pine covered with canvas, they assembled it close to the creek bank next to the lot owned by the Methodist Church. The workers would be shaded from the summer's sun and water was accessible.

By the end of summer, the laundry earned enough to expand and moved indoors. Chyo's teen daughter, Jaoi, who stayed in Rathdrum with Mei, and Jaoi's friends and Yan, Julia, were hired to wash clothes. The pole and tarp hut was replaced with a sturdy log cabin.

Haoli's long queue bobbed up and down his backside as he bowed honorable greetings to patrons who came and left. Between the greetings Haoli, along side Lein-Hua, their partners Ang Li and Sua, washed garments in the huge wooden tubs fashioned from pickle barrels acquired, with permission, from the mercantile discard pile.

Haoli simplified the business with a waterwheel. He fashioned it after the one at the flourmill downstream, southwest of the laundry. His smaller scaled wheel pulled water from the creek and dumped it into a carved out log trough, which filled washtubs rather than powering a grinder like at the mill.

Haoli found he enjoyed analyzing and solving problems especially for industry. His mind whirled, deliberating what to do for a water supply come winter. His inventions became the center of curiosity with folks from uptown.

With resourceful tinkering, he once more improved the washing method. Using an idea he derived for the gold mines' sluice boxes, he mounted several tubs in a row on hewn logs to use as rockers. He added long handles at each end. The workers could easily agitate the laundry by shaking the handgrips with back and forth motions.

This process made the chore more productive with less fatigue. Jaoi, Yan, and Julia liked shaking the tubs rather than having to stir clothing with paddles as before.

The waterwheel was one of Haoli's finest projects. People brought laundry just to see what new thing he had invented. He was not too busy to notice those who moseyed by each day to check out what was up at the creek business.

"Tuu-bits, tuu days." Haoli sing-sang as he accepted a bundle of soiled clothing from a tall man. He bowed several times from the waist. His queue continued to bounce as he bent and repeated his price. "Tuu-bits, tuu days." He used his best broken-English knowing whites preferred to make fun of his pigeon tongue. Twenty-five cents was his usual charge quoted to customers for any sized bundle.

Haoli recognized the next customer as one of the men who had caused trouble for the Chinese when working with Pai, building the courthouse. He did not know the man's name. Taking the safe route, Haoli accepted the man's clothes, bowed his thanks and quoted, "Tuu days, 'tuu-bits. Pleasee."

"Whatcha mean two-bits," the man yelled. "Was only three shirts and a pair of pants. Ain't worth the price of a good whiskey." He slammed his fist on the crate serving as the counter and stomped his foot. "I'll not pay ya at all, ya cheat'n chink!" He hollered loud enough to be heard by passersby.

Sua had come to the doorway when she heard the first outbursts. She vanished to the back room, gathered the girls and hid.

The shouting continued, with obscenities, the man making sure a group of men up the street, within earshot, would hear the commotion.

Orenstein, Wood and Barton jogged with the mayor to the laundry site, giving the man the audience he desired.

"What's going on here?" Mayor McGuire shoved his large frame through the doorway.

"Stinkin' chink is trying to cheat me." The man's voice rose.

"That true?" McGuire questioned Haoli, looking down at him.

Haoli stood still, not uttering a word. His hands spread flat on the counter. He looked past the two men's shoulders and saw that a crowd was gathering outside.

"Of course it's true, I told you already." The customer did not give the china-laundry-man a chance to answer.

Then Orenstein pushed his way in front of McGuire to take charge. "He's a cheat," he pointed a finger at Haoli.

Haoli glued a smile on his face, but did not respond. He understood this kind of anger, and knew that not being white put him in the wrong, and that he irritated them.

With one thrust Orenstein up-ended the crate-table separating him from the Chinaman. He swung at Haoli catching the smile on his fist.

Haoli stumbled backward, fell against a chair, and landed on the plank floor. He stiffened himself, then stood up straight, still smiling.

"I ought to kill ya," Orenstein vowed, then as if an afterthought bellowed, "But who'd clean my clothes?"

"Yeah," the customer agreed and stepped aside letting the bigger man continue the fight for him.

"Now settle down Orenstein." McGuire spoke more to the crowd than to those involved in the fight. "You're always looking for a reason to blame a chinaman."

He saw that the onlookers witnessed him assert his authority.

"Yer always a politician, your first concern is the upcoming election," Orenstein turned his attention on the mayor.

"No need for trouble here," Mayor McGuire continued to try to deflate the tempers, "I'll ignore that political remark for now. What caused all this ruckus?"

"The chink here started it." Orenstein pointed at Haoli. "And I'm gong to finish it," he turned on McGuire. "Are you taking this little cheater's side?" He drew up his knuckles ready to poke anyone who moved, including the mayor. The customer ducked over near the doorway.

McGuire faced Haoli again. "You wash these for free today, huh?"

Hearing the commotion, Ang Li had come to the front of the shop. He now stepped from behind Haoli. "Freee. Yes, freee tuuday." Li grabbed the bundle, bowed and backed out of the room, and in Mandarin mumbled, "I hate having to speak like I am an uneducated foreigner as they think us to be."

Haoli also bowed. His bruised face hurt but he kept the smile in place and repeated Li's words. "Yes, freee tuudae." He stood the crate upright for his counter and looked McGuire and Orenstein in the eyes.

Knowing he'd won his point, Orenstein poked a stubby finger at Haoli's chest. "Free. Today! He'll be back today, ya hear?" He pointed at the customer who was standing near the door, then Orenstein spun on his boot heel and exited past the mayor, out the door and stood in front of the crowd.

A murmuring waved through the gathering outside. Opinions divided between Orenstein and the Chinese. Almost as good at politics as the mayor, Orenstein made his next move count. He hooked his thumbs in his waistband and announced, "See what ya get when ya let them run a business. They cheat ya every chance they get. Next thing ya know they'll be a-

181

wanting to vote and take up with our womenfolk." Orenstein spat the angry words and stomped away. The customer left, grumbling he followed Orenstein with his audience.

Someone shouted from the few who remained. "You tell 'em. We should've never allowed that chink to set up here. What does he think he is? White?" Laughter erupted. Then someone else shouted. "Trouble. That's all these chinks are. Pests. Something has got to be done about them before they get outta hand."

Mayor McGuire stepped up on the stoop, held his arms in the air as a call for silence. "That's enough of that kind of talk. I don't like this any more than the rest of you, but who'd do your wash if the chinamen don't? Even Orenstein there needs their services. Break it up now, and go on about your way."

A few weeks later the August heat exposed the creek bed. The flowing water ceased, leaving only small standing puddles. The hot day took its toll on the crew who now had to haul water from the railroad well.

Li and Haoli placed the washtubs outside on the creek bank under the ponderosa pines. It was somewhat cooler for the girls than in the building.

"Keep working." Auntie Sua encouraged the young staff. "Let the water splash you. It'll help cool the day." She tried to sound cheerful.

At fourteen, Zharg Jaoi and thirteen-year-old Julia, were pleased to work in the laundry. Yan, three years younger than her friend Jaoi, copied the older girls' attitudes.

Jaoi welcomed the water that splashed on her as she moved the handle to rock the tubs. With a playful shake she let the water spray on Julia who was rocking the rinse tubs.

Haoli wiped his forehead with his red kerchief. Even under his large brimmed straw hat with his queue twisted up under it, the afternoon's sun felt blistering. He saw the two girls playing with the water and laughed. The rope he was hooking up to the tub rockers was the last step to connect his newest invention. The girls will enjoy this he thought, they always like new things. He called to them and explained the contraption as he tied the last knot.

"Now. Turn it," Haoli instructed Julia, waving his arm as if he held the crank handle.

Julia rotated the new handle. Jaoi clapped as the connected ropes began to rock the tubs and she figured out the new instrument.

All watched. Then giggles broke out among the girls as they saw the rope spin the wooden pulley-wheel as Julia worked the crank. "This is much better. It's easy and moves the tubs faster," an excited Julia shouted to the others.

Haoli and Uncle Li stood proudly, gazing at the rocking tubs and the girl winding the crank. "Ahh, Haoli's best effort yet." Haoli laughed as he watched the pulley system rotate and sat to observe the masterpiece in full operation.

The sun bore down and Haoli wiped his face again as he spied a man approach across the Methodist lot.

Orenstein, who made it his business to keep track of what the chinamen were doing, had noticed Charles Wesley Wood heading for the creek and followed. "Wait up, he hollered out at Orenstein," and hurried to catch him.

Wood and Orenstein strolled close enough to the laundry to be heard and Wood shouted, "What's that you've done now?" He flipped off his western hat. "If you aren't something, Hong Haoli," he added and slapped his hat against his thigh for emphasis.

"I do not trust the whites—ever," Haoli had told Ang Li and Wang Fu. "They watched when I strung the rope mechanism. I am relieved no trouble was started today. I feel too weary to have another fight with them. We must never take for granted our position in *their* community."

"They are just hoping to find us doing something against the law to report to Heitman and shut us down." Li rose to his feet and stretched and the two friends strolled over to where the girls still giggled, taking turns winding the new crank.

Haoli waved to Julia as she turned the new device. "Yes, Li, you are right. What else can happen? Have we not been careful to comply with all the rules?"

Chapter 23

"We almost had a misfortune on our hands with a young girl falling in love with a white boy. It was Jaoi, Zharg's oldest girl. Remember, she did not go with her parents when they moved to Montana. She was 'of age' and chose to stay in Rathdrum with Mei and my mother—to help with the babies, she did love the little ones so. I only know this because of 'girl talk', the adults never found out about her fondness for the boy."...

Spinning the new crank, Jaoi noticed Jimmy Orenstein's older brother playing in the creek-bed. She didn't know his name, but she remembered him from the springtime's Lunar celebration. Giggling she peeked over her right shoulder at the boy across the shallow creek. Butterflies fluttered in her heart. She hadn't experienced such a feeling before. Then she felt it again when the boy smiled back at her. Shielding her face with the red plaid shirt she had been rinsing and turned away. The butterflies would not stop. Embarrassed, she hurried into the new laundry building.

Julia saw Jaoi's speedy exit from the work area and followed her.

Inside the shack, she found Jaoi in the back corner sorting more clothing to take out to the tubs. "We have no secrets, we are best friends. What's going on? Why did you disappear so abruptly?"

Intent on her chore, Jaoi looked away when Julia approach her. Julia's questioning eyes could not to be dismissed, Jaoi could not put her off. "Shhhhh, follow me."

Not wanting to gain the attentions of the other workers, Jaoi picked up an armload of garments. She stepped closer to the window and nodded, "See him?"

Together they peeked out the open window at the blond boy. Pant legs rolled up to his knees, he bent over and seemed to be catching something with his cupped hands. "Frogs? Waterskippers? Crawdads?" Jaoi couldn't be sure but she liked watching him.

At the window, Julia glanced at Jaoi again. She sighed and both moved to the back corner, away from spying on the boy. Jaoi releasing her armload, "here's a new pile for darks." Then both picked up some clothing from the sorted clothes and headed out to the washtubs.

As Jaoi's eyes adjusted to the brilliant noon sun, she stumbled, dropping the garments she carried. Covering her face with her hands, she ran back into the shack. Now, everyone stared at her. She wished she had not seen the white boy. Pesky moths replaced the butterfly-flutterings. Shame uncoiled into tears.

Auntie Sua hurried to Jaoi. Putting an arm around the girl she asked, "Are you ill?" and felt the girl's forehead with he hand.

Jaoi cuddled into the woman's embrace. "It is this heat." Sua informed the others. "Come with me, child," she led Jaoi to the living quarters, behind the laundry.

Making sure the girl drank some water, Auntie forced her charge to lie down on a straw mat, then placed a cool towel across her forehead. Sua returned to the laundry area, in her high-pitched voice gave orders to the others to stop work and drink some water. "You too, Julia. Jaoi will be fine. She is resting."

At the end of the day, the laundry crew all talked at once, in excitement over the new tub crank. The washing had sped up, allowing them to accomplish more than double the amount of work that afternoon. Only Julia seemed to remember Jaoi was not among them. She hurried to the quarters to find her friend. She found Jaoi sitting at the small table sipping a cup of cold tea.

Auntie Sua saw Julia going to the quarters, and followed to check on Jaoi. "How do you feel, now?" She placed her hand on the girl's forehead again. "No fever." she removed her hand satisfied.

"I am much better. I napped a long time." She swallowed the last of her tea.

"Good. We must take care not to work too long in this heat." Auntie emphasized her words.

"I am ready to leave." Jaoi finally convinced Auntie she felt well enough to go.

Auntie consented as long as Julia promised to go with her. The girls agreed, and turned to leave.

"Oh, just a minute. We could use some more buttons from the mercantile. Do you feel strong enough to fetch some before you go home?" Auntie asked both girls.

"Yes, we can get the buttons." Jaoi was quick to answer.

"Here." Auntie handed Julia a nickel for the purchase. "There have been no troubles of late, but make sure you are careful."

"We will be fine." Jaoi liked going uptown to the mercantile. Fetching items for Auntie was about the only time they were allowed to go there.

As the girls entered Brownson's, the wooden floor creaked under their feet. They stood for a moment, an instinctive reaction to the dim light. Eyes adjusted, together they moved towards the left side of the large room, to the dry-goods.

Jaoi loved the store, so full of wonderful new things. She followed Julia to the shelf filled with thread spools more colorful than a rainbow. A bin holding buttons of different sizes and colors sat next to the threads. Jaoi's excitement heightened when she saw him across the store—the yellow-haired boy from the creek.

His pant legs were full length now and he stood tall. Tall and handsome. Jaoi had never seen such blue eyes. Smiling eyes. The butterflies returned. Her left hand rested on the red threads she had been caressing. She couldn't move it.

187

Julia nudged her friend. Jaoi did not react. "Here are the buttons," Julia announced loud enough that others in the store all heard. She picked up the scoop in the button bin and dipped it deep into the buttons, and brought it up full.

"Pretty." Jaoi moved her hand from the threads down to her side and turned, taking her eyes off the boy—.

Julia leveled off the cup of buttons with her other hand when a large rough hand covered hers. Her body stiffened. She held her breath, unable to move.

The hand, attached to the storekeeper, tipped the cup down, letting half the buttons fall back into the bin. "There," he scowled, "That's a nice cupful for you. That will be five cents." His face smirked.

Both girls pasted large smiles on their faces. Julia accepted his modified cup, bowed her head, and thanked him for his generosity. She handed the storekeeper Auntie's nickel, knowing a white girl could buy any amount she wished.

The storekeeper put the nickel into his register. "Here, put your hands together." He offered no bag, pouring the buttons into her cupped hands.

Several of the buttons dropped to the floor. Instinct warned both girls not to attempt to retrieve them, least they be accused of stealing. Forcing big smiles, both quickly backed out of the store.

Jaoi's shame doubled. The yellow-haired boy had witnessed the affair.

By the time Jaoi saw the tall good-looking boy again, she had managed to learn his name was Buck. "He is the son of the meanest man in town," Julia informed Jaoi what her brother had told her. "We have seen him before. He is the scraggily kid we saw at the Lunar ceremony, remember?"

"He's so cute, now."

"What's the matter with you? He's white! A German no less." The word *white* exploded from Julia's lips. She made a wrinkled face of disparagement.

Jaoi ignored Julia's remark. At the laundry, managing the crank, she saw Buck. Again, wading in the creek. She watched as he bent over and caught something in a glass jar. He wasn't alone. Another boy, Peter was doing the same thing. Her arm automatically turned the crank as she stared.

"Hey! Watch it!" Julia shouted to Jaoi.

She did not stop moving the handle.

"Hey, didn't you hear me?"

"Huh, what? Oh! Oh my." Her arm stopped in mid air with her hand still on the shaft.

"Look." Julia pointed to the overflowing tubs. You let too much water run in the wash and all the soapsuds escaped. What's with you today?"

"Ah. I don't know. I guess I didn't see the water pouring in."

"The way you're acting, I doubt you can see anything." Then Julia saw who was in the creek. "Oh. So that's what's up, huh? He's trouble. Forget him."

As Julia reprimanded her friend, Ang Li came over to the tubs. "What goes on here? Having a difficult time with Uncle Haoli's tubs?" A grin crossed his face and he laughed at the two.

"We kind of got into a mess." Julia was first to answer him. She was quick to keep his attention on the wash so he would not notice the boys below the bank.

Uncle Li helped the girls empty the tubs of the extra water, saving it in a barrel to reuse. "We must be careful with water with so little in the creek." He balanced the tubs back onto the rockers. It didn't take him long to finish, then he left to go back into the laundry shop.

Julia took over turning the crank and completed the wash. Then both girls dashed down along the creek bank to the covering of bushes, giggling until they were out of breath.

"I can't believe you did that. And Uncle Li didn't see what happened. You are about the luckiest person I know. You never get caught and you cause more problems than anyone I know." Julia held her side in a fit of laughter.

"I know," was all Jaoi managed.

It took a few minutes to quiet themselves. Jaoi looked up to see the yellow hair hanging down in front of the bluest eyes—staring at her. "Hi." She managed the greeting.

"Hi yourself. What are you two girls up to? You scared all the frogs out of the puddle."

"Is that so?" Jaoi hid her embarrassment tossing her head. Her hair fanned in the air. Then she looked back into the eyes. "I'm Jaoi. She's Julia."

"I'm Buck. Buck Orenstein."

"I know." Jaoi played coy. Her heart skipped a few beats.

Buck sat next to her. Peter took up residence by Julia. They talked about how hot the days have been for a few moments. Then Buck took Jaoi by surprise. "I saw what Mr. Brownson did—to the buttons."

"Oh." Turning scarlet, she glanced away.

"It wasn't fair. I'm sorry he treated you like that."

"It happens sometimes. Some people don't like the color of my skin or the slant of my eyes."

"I think your eyes are beautiful. And I bet you don't have to worry about being sunburned. Am I right?" his voice was teasing her, but he bent over and brushed her cheek with the back of his fingers."

Jaoi's face flushed. She tried to swallow, but her dry throat would not work. She could not mutter a word. She cast a look Julia's way. She wasn't watching. She was busy flirting with Peter. Finally, finding words, Jaoi whispered, "We have to get back. Uncle will come look for us."

"Meet me. Here again? Tomorrow?" He jumped to his feet. "Come on, Peter. We don't want to get these *ladies* into any trouble." With that, the boys ran off through the pines, undetected by others at the laundry.

Chapter 24

"I don't think I told you yet about Mr. Orenstein's horse, did I?" Jie yawned. "It is not too late for another story is it?" she winked at Molly who nodded ready to listen...

Buck returned to the bushes across the creek from the laundry several different days. Jaoi managed to meet him there alone, without being discovered. "I did not tell even Julia I was coming to meet you," she whispered to him. Buck smiled, took her hand and told her about his job of catching water-skippers and selling them for fishing bait at his dad's saloon. "They pay me a penny a dozen." He pulled a handful of coins from his pocket to show her.

He could tell from her wide eyes that she thought it a lot of money. "It is nothing. I will get more." He pushed them back into his pocket. They talked until Jaoi realized the noon sun was slipping. Fearing her absence noticed, she bid him goodbye and ran back to the laundry shack.

Buck's father caught him coming home. "Where you been off to?" he bellowed when he saw the boy tiptoeing in through the back door.

Buck's feet froze, his head spun to face his father. "Fishing. At the upper creek...up past Chinatown a ways." The fib fell from his lips easily.

"I don't see your fishing pole." Orenstein unhooked his belt from his britches as he spoke.

Buck stiffened, knowing what was coming. "I told you to stay away from *those yeller bellies*." The first lash landed across the boy's backside.

The blow hurt, but he did not let his father see his pain. Expecting another whack he held his breath. It came, along with several more. Buck felt as if life escaped his flesh. When his father stopped hitting, Buck glared up at him. His back burning from the thrashing, his mind spinning, how could he call *her* names? It is *I* who is not good enough for *her*, his shoulders slumped as he cowered from his father. He wasn't strong enough to voice his thoughts.

"I'm going back to the saloon." His father stomped out. "Take care of Lady, I'm taking my stud."

Buck hid in his room until he heard the door slam. Sobbing, he rubbed salve on his wounds. When finished, he ran heedless from the back of the house until he found himself in the barn. Blood throbbed in his ears. His eyes blurred, it was unmanly to cry. His head pounded. He could not think, but it did not matter. He didn't want to think anymore. He kept feeling the hurt of his father's words burn into his mind. "*Chinks!*"

He climbed to the hayloft and flopped onto the hay in his favorite spy corner. He bawled until his spirit died. Sobbing gave no relief and made him feel like a coward.

When he had no more tears, he got to his feet, brushed at the loose hay clinging to his flannel shirt and descended the ladder.

Outside Buck saw Lady still hitched to the buggy in front of the house. "Ah-gheesee, I'm supposed to take care of you when dad leaves you here." He hurried toward the horse and carriage. Lady nickered and Buck reached up to pet her nose. "Wanna go for a good run, Lady girl? I feel like getting out of here." He gave her a last pat on the neck, boarded the buggy, grabbed the reins and snapped the whip in the air signaling Lady to go.

The horse surged forward. Another snap of the switch and Lady stepped into a trot. Once more and she hurled herself into a canter. Buck, Lady and the buggy became as one. Buck could tell Lady felt it too. She ran as never allowed when hitched to the buggy.

Again he cracked the whip over her backside as they raced down the roadway. They turned west onto the main road without losing speed. Feeling the right side of the buggy lift from the ground Buck took a deep breath but he did not pull up on the reins to slow the mare as the wheels bounced down on the road again. Wind blew his yellow hair astray. "If the air could just blow away my troubles," he shouted out to Lady. Then he heard the westbound train coming from behind them.

As the locomotive caught up to him, he got an idea to race it. "Come on Lady, let's beat that old iron horse to the station," he yelled as he split the air once more with the whip. He felt the horse give her all.

They raced for about a quarter of a mile before he pulled away from the engine passing it with ease. Another crack over Lady's back coincided with Buck's voice. "Go Lady girl, you can take 'r."

Like a national champion racer, Lady pulled ahead of the speeding train. "Yeehaw," Buck yelled, "we did it girl. Now, let's show that iron monster who's the boss is around here," and he pulled the reins signaling a left turn. Lady obeyed and whirled her massive bulk onto the road that crossed the tracks.

"Yeehaw," Buck shouted again as the right side of the buggy lifted off the earth.

The buggy, Lady, and all flipped onto the dirt with a loud crack. Dust flew as the rigging came to a halt catapulting Buck from the driver's seat landing him in a clump of grass off the roadway. The left wheel snapped off under the weight of the carriage as it tipped. The right wheel spun on its axle. Kicking her legs and snorting Lady thrashed her head and shoulders against the ground trying to right herself but the harnesses held her down.

The train blasted its whistle as it slowed to stop at the depot, passing the upturned rig. It's whine brought Buck into awareness of what had happened. The stunned boy rolled on the ground, gathering his wits. Holding his head with his left hand, he sat up. "No, no!" He saw Lady on her side shaking her head and trying to rise, to no avail amidst the tangle of harness and the broken shaft sticking upward.

With all his strength, he got to his feet and went to the aid of the flailing horse. "Whoa, girl, whoa there, girl." Buck tried to calm her, not noticing his own injuries. "Whoa, I'll get you out of this mess." Blood dripped from a cut on his arm he couldn't unbuckle the straps that held Lady captive. He slipped his jackknife out of his pocket and cut it. Then he tugged on the halter. "Come on, girl. Up you go. Come on. You can do it."

Lady kicked and threw her head but could not get to her feet. She whinnied and snorted. Her efforts to stand futile. Buck looked closer at her and took hold of Lady's front left leg. Trembling, he ran his hand down the leg. Feeling the break, he pulled his hand away and cried out, "No, noooo!" Tears fell, mixing with Lady's blood, onto the ground. "Lady, I'm so sorry, girl."

He sat on the ground next to the mare's head, petting her nose to soothe her. Breathing hard, she finally stilled, trusting the boy. "This is real trouble, girl. You think father can beat me over a Chinese girl, wait until he gets a hold of me for this."

Denny Barton rode up on his pony. "You all right?" he hollered, jumping down off his saddle. "What happened?"

"Get my Pa."

Denny piled back on his mount and headed uptown to Orenstein's saloon.

"My Pa is gonna beat me good for this one," Buck told Lady. "And I deserve it girl. I never meant to hurt you."

Ahead of Denny, Mr. Orenstein ran to the scene. Orenstein knelt to the horse and rubbed his hands over Lady's back and down her legs in one sweeping motion.

"I'm sorry Pa! I'm so sorry. I didn't mean to hurt her." Buck's fear of his father's wrath overpowered any he had ever experienced.

"It's busted." Orenstein stood and looked down at his son. "You hurt?"

"No sir, not anything to bother about. I'm sorry Pa. I'm sorry." He still sat next to the mare.

"What were you thinking, boy?" he pushed his hat brim back to expose his face and rubbed his chin. "We'll have to put her down. You, I'll deal with later." He left to get his rifle from the saloon.

"Move away Buck," Orenstein aimed at the mare's forehead and shot. It was over. Buck jerked at the sound and shivered. His eyes stared at the blood oozing from the mutilation. More tears threatened to fall. He would not let his father see him cry. He had cried enough already. I'll show him I can handle this like a man, Buck thought. He won't be disappointed in me. I'll show him. Determined, Buck swiped at his eyes and turned to look at his father.

"Come on boy," Orenstein headed to the saloon where his horse stood tied at the railing. Buck and Denny followed, staying a few feet behind the big man. Buck's father turned and spoke to the Barton boy, "Denny, do you think you can find someone, maybe one of those chinks, to come haul the carcass away and bury it?"

"Yes, sir, I think I can find somebody."

"Good boy. Here's four-bits for your trouble. See if you can get it done for five bucks." He handed Denny a five-spot.

"Thank you sir, I will see to it for you. I'm sorry about the mare."

Orenstein mounted his horse, kicked his foot out of the stirrup and held his hand down to Buck. "Come on kid, let's get on home." Buck accepted the hand, put his left foot into the stirrup and flung his body up on the horse behind his father. Together they cantered to the east. Buck glanced back once at the wreckage as they passed it. He swallowed hard, knowing the damage was all his doing.

At home, Buck slid off the horse and his father dismounted. Without saying a word he handed the stud's reins to his son and strolled toward the house.

Buck led the horse to the barn, unsaddled and brushed him. All the while he worked, he could not figure why his father had not wailed on him. Not even yelled, or accused him of the wrongdoing. "I dread when father does punish me," he told his father's mount, stroking its neck. "He must be too mad to do it now, what do you think, ol' boy?" He held back tears that wanted to flow.

Denny Barton rode his pony directly to Chinatown. He stopped near a group of Chinese men. "I need some help," he quickly explained what had happened. "Mr. Orenstein asked if I could get someone to bury the horse. Gave me five bucks to pay ya." He held the money up to them to see.

"I'll do it," Ang Li accepted the duty. "Keep the money, boy. Give it back to Orenstein. It's a shame to lose such a fine looking animal." With the help of his two friends, he hauled the dead horse and buried it at the base of the mountain, away from the creek.

Denny went back to Orenstein and handed him the five dollars, "The Chinese took care of the horse. They said to give this back to you and that they're sorry for your loss." Orenstein pocketed the bill without thanking the boy.

He had only lectured his son about the accident, but it wasn't long before he was uptown downing drinks and bragging, "Stupid chinks hauled my horse away and butchered it after I paid ten dollars to have it buried, the fools ate it."

Buck found out about his father's lie. He waited for a couple weeks before seeing Jaoi. "I want to be your friend. But it's not a good idea for us to...ahh..." His voice trailed off. Jaoi nodded her head, seeming to understand. He did not say anything else.

Jaoi never told anyone about Buck, except Julia. "He's so handsome, but he is *white*." Jaoi left the rest unspoken, knowing her friend understood a mixed relationship would never be tolerated by either race.

Haoli heard the lie Orenstein told his friends. "Whites always find ways to make us a bad people." Li agreed with him. "Will it never stop...this unfair treatment?" He asked the group.

No one had an answer. Shaking heads, they departed to go about their evening chores.

Chapter 25

"One hot day in July, 1889, young Denny Barton stood waiting as the noon locomotive from the east came into sight," Jie began as soon as Molly settled with her notepad. "He and other boys often raced to the depot when they heard the train whistle announcing its arrival. Helping travelers with their baggage and giving directions would reward them with a few coins, like when they delivered messages for the telegrapher. Denny was an enterprising young man. Years later, he told me once how excited he was when he learned he had welcomed the first doctor to Rathdrum. It was the doctor that delivered me into this world."...

The Northern Pacific again jerked to a stop in Rathdrum. The conductor had announced this was a main stopover for loading farm supplies and checking the locomotive. A tall man, dressed in a polished-cotton suit under a black coat, wearing a high top hat, and carrying a medical bag, disembarked. He decided to eat lunch at a café and have a look at the area for the two-hour stopover.

As he stepped onto the platform, the doctor took a deep breath. "Oh my, this is a beautiful place." He voiced his thoughts to no one in peculiar. "This view is breathtaking."

A woman near him heard and agreed, "Yes, it is beautiful."

The tall mountain fronted by a few homes beyond a narrow stream, twisted past pines and firs. He marveled at the height of them. "These trees are not like the ones back in

199

Illinois. No siree, this is like a scenic painting hanging in the university where I completed medical school, back home."

Before the woman could answer, they heard a youngster's voice. "Hello sir, welcome to Rathdrum." Denny made his pitch, hoping for some coins in return for bag handling.

Dr. Wenz heard the voice, looked down and discovered the teen's salutation was meant for him. "Hello, and thank you, young man. Rathdrum you say? That's an interesting name. I'm heading to Spokane Falls. How far away is it?"

"Not far, I think she's just over an hour by rail." Denny informed the stranger. Either of you have any luggage I can get for you from the train?"

"No thanks," the woman turned. "I won't be staying, I must see about my ticket," she disappeared into the depot.

Denny offered his hand to the tall man. "Dennis Barton is my name."

"Dr. Wenz," accepting the boy's handshake. "Do you have a hotel here? I think I may like to stay on for a few days."

"Yes, sir, Dr. Wenz. We have a nice hotel, just up the street. She's brand new, rebuilt after the big '84 fire," Denny pointed toward Main Street at a tall brick building. "I hear they have nice soft beds there." He flashed a toothy grin up at the doctor.

Dr. Wenz made the quick decision to stay over and directed Dennis to his berth on the coach for his bags. "Here's two nickels can you bring my things to the hotel?"

"Yes, sir," Denny accepted the shinny coins and headed to the train.

After looking around Rathdrum for a few days, Dr. Wenz soon forgot about going to Spokane. "This is where I will open my practice." He told a barkeeper while having dinner. "This is beautiful country and the people are friendly here, and in need of a doctor, I'm told."

He set up an office in a redbrick building on Main and McCartney Streets. He soon became well known throughout the entire area. The doctor mixed his own prescriptions resulting in operating a drug store as well as his office. He lived upstairs above his business.

Word of the doctor spread across the prairie. Patients came from Post Falls, and Hauser's Lake, and Moab, Washington. Dr. Wenz cared for anyone who came his way, anyone, including the Chinese. Often he traveled to the far communities to treat patients who could not be moved.

The roads to Moab and Post Falls were too bumpy for his bicycle, and he did not like going by horse or buggy. Perplexed, he asked Wesley Wood one day, "Do you know of a clever man who is good with tools."

"Only one I know of like that is a chink in Chinatown. He has fashioned some crafty contraptions to enable men to work faster on construction sites around town. His name is Hong Haoli. You'll find him down by the creek, just ask any chink there."

Dr. Wenz found Haoli with no trouble and shared his idea for faster transportation.

Haoli accepted the chore and took the doctor's bicycle to Nogle's blacksmith shop at the far end of Main Street. Haoli removed the tires and set to work. He forged wheels fashioned after the original ones, but with extra metal on the circumference of each. Hammering and firing them until finally they molded just the right width with a ridge hanging outward from the edges to grip the rail.

He made many trips to the rail tracks, with the wheels, to make sure of the fit. "I see Mr. Orenstein and McGuire watching, snooping, like always, at what I am doing," Haoli mumbled to Ang Li as they half-jogged back to the Nogle's shop.

A few days later, Haoli and Li carried the finished bicycle to the doctor's office. Together, they went to the tracks with several people following them. Haoli fitted the bike onto one rail.

"This is grand," the delighted doctor mounted the bike and took off.

"He is like a shuriken tossed by a master's hand," Li laughed as the doctor darted out of sight.

More onlookers had gathered at the tracks. "Here he comes." Denny shouted pointing down the rails.

As fast as he had disappeared, he returned, coattails flapping behind and long legs sticking out like that of a grasshopper. Grinning as he peddled, he rang the bell Haoli bolted on to the handlebars. "This is grand," he repeated. "Exactly what I wanted. Now I can travel at a good pace."

"Just make sure no train is scheduled," Wood joked and the bystanders burst into laughter.

Not long after the doctor had his bicycle, Denny ran into his office. "Dr Wenz! Dr. Wenz. I've got a tele-a-mesaage for you from the store at Moab."

"Do say, there son."

"Yes, sir." Denny handed him the note.

The paper read:

Dr. Wenz   Stop   Come quick   Stop   A boy fell   Stop Broken leg   Stop   Will meet you at Moab store   Stop

"Thank you Denny. You are always a great help to me." He handed the boy a nickel for his trouble. The doctor was quick to take his bicycle to the tracks and climbed on it heading to the emergency. Denny stood watching him disappear down the rail, then went about his way.

The doctor traveled easily at full speed to Moab. At the Moab train-stop—no depot, just a passenger stop—he was met by John Warren, with a buckboard to take him to the accident victim. He reset the leg and lessened the boy's pain immediately with his medicines.

Pleased with his success, Dr. Wenz used the bicycle many times. A few years later, he purchased a Hupmobile, the newest of autos made in Detroit, but he kept his bicycle handy.

"This brings me to my family and Dr. Wenz" Jie stretched. "He was a great man. Everyone like him—whites and Chinese. He cared for us without prejudice...I knew him my whole life...well into the 1950s when he sold out to Mr. Dixon and retired." Molly set a plate in front of Jie filled rice topped with quick-fried vegetables that Lilly had fixed for them and poured tea. Between bites, Jie continued...Back when my parent's first child, my eldest brother Hong Yun, was born in 1885, there had been no doctor, not even a Chinese medicine man. But I told you about his birth. Wang Bo, Sua and Mei assisted her. A second son, Hong Li came sixteen months later, in 1887. And in 1889...

"Now, we are lucky. Dr. Wenz is here for my third delivery," Lein-Hua patted her swelled stomach.

Haoli agreed, "Birthing scares me," he admitted to his wife.

Hong Fu was born with the doctor's help in 1889. "I appreciate his medicines," Lein-Hua hugged the newborn.

In 1891 a fourth son, Hong Chang, was born, again under Dr. Wenz's supervision.

The doctor was called upon several times over the years for illnesses, and when second son, little Hong Li, fell from a tree and broke his arm. "I want to be a doctor when I'm big," he announced, rubbing his splinted arm.

"That's fine," the doctor did not try to hide his honor at the boy choosing him as a hero. "You can be my assistant when I come to call on your folks. Now take care not to use that arm until it heals. We don't want anyone saying we can't fix arms," he warned the boy with a smile.

"Then I came along," Jie smiled then sobered, "but it was not all so happy... twelve years since her last baby. Lein-Hua was weakened by her condition."...

Early in the morning of May 9, 1903, Haoli sent young Li to fetch Dr. Wenz to come and assist Lein-Hua with the birth of her fourth child.

Lein-Hua's labor lasted into the night. She still had not delivered as daylight broke through the curtained windows the next day.

Mei brought the doctor a plate of sweet-spiced chicken and steamed cabbage over rice. "Eat," she encouraged him. "I made plenty for everyone." She handed a plate to Haoli, too.

"Thanks," he accepted the meal, but only nibbled at it.

"You're worried?" Mei asked, taking his half-eaten dinner from his hands later.

"I have not seen such a hard time of it for a mother, she is extremely weak," Dr. Wenz shook his head and went back into Lein-Hua's room to check on his patient.

Late afternoon Dr. Wenz called out to the women, "This is it, come quick."

Mei, Sua and Bo rushed into the room, Bo shut the door behind them. The men waited. Haoli paced. "You are going to wear out the floor," Ang Li warned him. Then Sua came out, went to the kitchen, fetched a pot of hot water, and disappeared back into the bedroom with it. The men stared at the closed door. Soon, crying of a babe was heard. It was near dusk on May 10, 1903.

The women came from the bedroom, Sua holding the bawling newborn and announced to the waiting family and friends. "It's a girl."

Haoli peered at the child cuddled in the blanket. Then he turned to his friends, "Hong Jie," he told them. "We decided long ago our first born girl would be the name sake for Lein-Hua's mother, Jie, whom she misses to this day."

"Ohhh," several sighed together.

Bo tried the name. "Hong Jie. I like this name. Jie. She will be a strong girl. Let's see. This is the year of the Rabbit, luckiest of all signs! *She will be affectionate, but shy, and will seek peace her whole life.*" Bo quoted from memory, glad she had learned from Chyo before she moved to Montana. "Jie will live a long, long lifetime." The woman added with authority to her audience.

Dr. Wenz interrupted the happy moment. "I'm afraid Lein-Hua is not strong. She has lost a lot of blood and is failing fast. I have done all I can," he looked at the baby now in Bo's open arms, then to the new father. Haoli rushed past them into the bedroom.

"Little Jie needs to be fed. Her mother is too fragile. You can make a mixture for her." The doctor wrote out a recipe and handed it to Mei. "If you don't have the castor oil drops, send the boy to my store to get some, he nodded at Li Number Two, "he knows where to find it. It is an old cure-all from Egypt and will give her extra strength." He hurried back to Lein-Hua's bedside.

The doctor and new father had been behind the closed door all afternoon, only disturbed by Mei taking tea into them twice. "Will she awake soon?" Haoli asked Dr. Wenz.

"We will have to wait and see," the doctor patted Haoli, trying to comfort him. "She needs rest, Haoli. You can stay with her, but try to let her sleep." Dr. Wenz left the bedroom.

Two more hours passed, Haoli sat holding his wife's hand. He felt her fingers go limp, her eyes blinked twice, and shut again. "Lein-Hua. Leinn-Huaaa." Haoli words strained through tears as he leaned over his beloved wife. "Lein-Hua, can you hear me? Doctor! Doctor, come quick. She does not move. Leinnne-Hhuuaaa, answer me!"

Dr. Wenz rushed to his side and listened for Lien-Hua's heartbeat with his stethoscope.

"Ahweeee! No!" Haoli shouted from the bedroom. "Not so. Lein-Hua. My wife, my love! Can you hear me?"

Haoli felt the doctor's hand rest on his shoulder as he knelt by the bed.

"She is gone, I am so sorry," Dr. Wenz straightened and wound the scope around his arm.

Mei slipped into the room, placed a hand on Haoli's, who still gripped his wife's, and whispered to him, "She is with the ancestors, but the babe is a strong one. A sweet, little girl. I am sorry for your wife, my friend." Tears fell from Mei's almond eyes, down the creases in her face.

The words pulled the last strength from Haoli. He collapsed on Lein-Hua's body. Sobs shook his whole being. "It is my fault," Haoli whimpered. "Too many babies—for one so young. I should not have given you another child. It has been too long—twelve years—too long, now too old for babies."

Mei left the bedroom to allow Haoli privacy. Taking the new baby from Bo's arms she announced the loss of Lein-Hua to the waiting family. Baby Jie made the only sound in the parlor with her soft cooing, her stomach satisfied with the mixture.

An hour later, Sua went into the bedroom to comfort Haoli. "Be happy for your four sons and now, this tiny girl. Your sons are good boys. If you allow, I will care for little Jie."

Haoli nodded, not moving from Lein-Hua.

Sua silently left the room and shut the door behind her.

Chapter 26

"Such a sad time for all," Jie let a tear slide down her face without wiping at it. "I never knew my mother. When I was a small child, I worried that I had killed her."...

Family and friends went into mourning for Lein-Hua. "She will be sent to the next world according to the ancient customs," Wang Fu told the family. Haoli, Ang Li, and I will go pick the place for her final rest.

Together the three men went to the field on the other side of Pinegrove's fence. The graveyard-field now stretched from the roadway's edge, south almost reaching the railroad tracks, and east the length of half a dozen graves. Several hundred Chinese and a few vagrants already were entombed outside Pinegrove with only stones to mark where they lay. "I cannot find the exact place where Ming Yun, Wong Pai, and the others who died in the raid are buried." Haoli cried out in distress. "There are too many...too many of our clans are buried here. I feel the demons. I want my wife to be near my friends so her spirit will be with them. We must please the ancestors to stop the demons."

Wang Fu put his arm on Haoli's shoulder. "Do not worry my friend. This spot is close to them, I am sure. Soon you can place my bones next to her. I will care for her...in the next world...for you."

Haoli nodded, smeared tears across his face with his sleeve drying them, "Yes, but please not too *soon*. I could not bear to lose you now, too."

Ang Li picked up one of the shovels he had brought with him and pushed the blade into the ground. He continued to break the earth, creating the size cavity needed for the burial.

Haoli picked up the other shovel and worked the dirt. Tears rained down his cheeks splattering as they dropped at his feet as if he stood in a rainstorm. Wang Fu sat on a boulder, watching, too frail to dig. Haoli and Ang Li prepared the grave. Tears flowed, stopped, and started again as they worked. They chanted telling the spirits they were about to send them another.

At the age of thirty-four Lein-Hua was laid to rest. The Chinese held a traditional funeral service, all dressed in white they placed her coffin with yellow pieces of paper pasted on it, onto a white donkey cart and paraded to Mr. Potter's field.

Lein-Hua's four sons: Chang now twelve; Fu, fourteen; Li, sixteen; and Yun, a man at eighteen, all in new white garments, walked along the cart, hands on her casket. Haoli hugged the new baby, Jie, wrapped in a white blanket. He saw only darkness in the days ahead as he followed his sons.

"The sun rises and sets each day, but life lightens and darkens as the years go by," Ang Li quoted from the ancestors, trying to comfort his friend, as they stood at Lein-Hua's grave. Haoli moved his head sideways, his thoughts consumed with having to go on without his wife.

Two weeks later they held services for Wang Fu who passed to the spirit world in his sleep. Bo, his daughter, and Haoli held each other, grieving.

PART

THREE

1999

Chapter 27

Jie leaned back in her wheelchair, closed her eyes for a few minutes. "This brings me to telling some of my youth." A smile etched her face. I never knew my mother, but I was told that I followed her footsteps—closely—a good feeling, that comforted me many lonely times in my life. But, I, ah, I am not sure...let me think...my brain does not work like I want it to sometimes. I am confused, too easily these days." She shook her head as if to straighten her thoughts. "It is difficult to be so old," she paused, "What am I now, 96?" Her brows scrunched together as she said the number. Who lives here now...let's see...my grandson, Mack's boy Haoli Number Two, his wife, Lilly, and the three children, Mandy, Bobby and baby Timothy...yes, that's right, she decided.

Then she opened her eyes, looked into Molly's face and continued, "Yes, I do remember. It was the same year I was born, 1903. The railroad gave father title to the land near the creek for the laundry. He built this large frame house next to his business with the help of my brothers, Ang Li and my Pai, Pai Number Two. All moved into the home, along with Mei. I am told Sua took great pleasure in rearing Haoli's baby—me—as she had promised."...

"The child takes the place of the one I never bore. She is small-framed like her mother but driven with her father's determination. She easily steals the hearts of everyone," Sua said as she played with the babe—Jie. Mei nodded agreement.

"They say I became a favorite with the few Chinese still living in Rathdrum. Wong Pai Number Two, took a special interest in me. After all, I was to be his betrothed according to his mother, Mei, and Auntie Sua, too. They had giggled about the old promise several times." Then Jie spoke as though she was telling of someone else, she began again...

"'I am too old for her, mother," Pai Number Two declared. "She is just a child. I am a man, her brother Yun's age. Twenty!'" Jie enjoyed emphasizing how old her husband was when she was born.

"When I turned six years old, Chinese children were still not allowed to attend the public school. Mei and Sua turned the parlor of the big house into a teaching room. Together they instructed me and the other four school-age children of the remaining Chinese living in Rathdrum." Jie stared at Pai's picture on the wall as she searched the back of her memory...

"One morning about age nine, I squatted behind bushes along the railroad tracks and spied on the white children as they walked to school. "What would it be like to go into that tall brick building? Would they let me play games?"

Molly noticed her Nanai faded out again as she let her head drop. It happened so often these days. "Would you like some more tea, Nanai? Do you want to rest? Take a nap?" She refilled the teacups waiting for an answer from her elder.

"Oh well," Jie looked at Molly and continued her tale. "I consoled myself on the path back to the house, "the studies would be hard, probably all in English." I could speak the foreign words, but my tongue could not seem to forget its original twang. I remember I hurried so as not to let Auntie think I was too long at the morning chores." Jie sighed again.

"I liked feeding the chickens." Then Jie looked straight at Molly, "I was told mother had liked chickens too." Staring down at the teacup, she began again. "I usually took my time at the barn. Now, I headed straight there and bent to pickup the basket of eggs I had gathered earlier, only to find Wong Pai looking down at me.".....

"What have you been up to little one? I've cleaned all the stalls and did not find you here."

"Without lifting the basket Jie stood to look into his shining eyes. He was tall. It was not in her to lie, so she confessed, "I strolled up near the whites' school."

"Ahh, and what did you see?"

"Children. Lots of them. Boys and girls. Why can't I go to school there?"

"It is not fair, little one, and I don't blame you for wondering about them. But, it is the law. Maybe one day it will be different. I do not know. Best you get the eggs up to Auntie, she will want them."

"Quickly I grabbed up the basket and headed for the house. Never did I mention the school to anyone. But, several times before the snow came I would steal away and watch from afar before going into the parlor for my own studies.

"I always concentrated on twisting my tongue around English words to pronounce them without my native accent. All my youth Pai would come after work and taunt, 'You place too much importance on speaking the language'." Jie's face shone and she smiled at the memory.

"When we were together, he always chuckled at my attempts to cover embarrassment. He knew I liked him." Jie smiled at

Molly "He was special to me, my whole life." Then she added, "I must rest now, take me to my bedroom."

Molly obliged, and with her cousin Haoli Number Two's wife, Lilly, helped to make her comfortable for a nap.

Chapter 28

Jie napped and dreamed—or was she awake and simply remembering? Her thoughts took her back to 1913, she was ten-years-old—again...

A noisy chorus of erratic crowing had awakened her that memorable day. In one hardy motion she stretched her arms and legs and sat up on her mat. "I hear you," she scolded in a whisper, aware she would not wake anyone whom the cock-a-doo-ing-ruckus hadn't already disturbed.

Two Irishmen who had started alley cockfights approached Chinese men about supplying cocks for the rink. Haoli and Ang Li, industrious providers, found gamecocks profitable. They separated young roosters from their feeder chicks and groomed them for fighting. The gambling sport caught on rapidly and Jie earned the right to tend them, displaying a talent in caring for the animals.

Hurrying, Jie slipped a fresh tunic on, splashed cold water on her face at the basin and inched out the door. Shuddering from the chilly wind, she pulled her shawl tight over her shoulders and headed down the hill behind the house to the barn and cock pens.

At the barn, she filled a broken-handled bucket from a barrel of corn and wheat kernels. Usually the trek to the cock pens was enjoyable, but today she could do without the wind and with a fixed handle. "It wouldn't be busted if Ol' Red hadn't attacked me yesterday. Brainless rooster!" He had vaulted in a fit when she tossed his food causing her to fall on the pail, snapping off the handle, and land in chicken dung.

When she saw the broken handle she ignored her bleeding knee where Ol'Red's spur stabbed it.

The crowing volume increased as Jie approached the pens, limping, favoring her wounded leg. A pathway flanked by two rows of pens was just wide enough to walk between the tethered cocks. Each bird had his own space with a small two-foot-high fence to perch and a box-house served as a shelter. A water pan nested against each railing. Leather straps attached to one leg and rail contained the birds to their own territory. To keep them from agitation a small leather cap hindered vision.

Roosters perched on railings crowed at Jie. She enjoyed this part of the daily ritual of feeding the proud lot. Their pretty array of orange-brown to golden feathers tapered down their necks into a mixture of blues, greens and brown-reds that draped across the saddlebacks to their tail feathers. Bright golden-orange leggings showed off spurs sharpened to a luster that made one fear the exquisite animals.

Haoli had bred the gamecocks to achieve physical power, speed, and courage with a killer instinct. On some, spurs were trimmed so artificial ones of steel or brass could be attached. The game birds used the deadly weapons to rip and tear at their opponents but also managed to split open a girl's leg. Jie glared at Ol' Red and tossed him a handful of grain. He pranced, challenging her.

"Easy Ol'Red. You'll not get a piece of me today, you devil." She tossed him more kernels. "Think you are a descendent of dragons don't you?" she scowled, careful to keep clear of his reach. "Fancy, ohhh Fanncy booy," she cooed, changing her tone calling to her favorite rooster at the end of the row, pitching grain to the others along the way to Fancy's perch. Jie had named him when just a chick because he strutted with an air of importance. She taught him tricks and told him her woes and secrets. Now that he was fully-grown, her father insisted he be penned like the other cocks. Jie stooped to Fancy with a handful of grain. "Here you go my pretty boy." Fancy lifted his freed leg as if to shake hands, then jumped from his perch to peck at the offering, never harming the gentle fingers holding the kernels. "I love you Fancy." She petted his little bright head, the only cock without a hood, raised to meet the hand.

Finally, she spread the last of his meal in front of him. After she finished feeding the two-dozen cocks she returned to the barn, filled the bucket again and headed to feed the hens and gather eggs, singing as she went.

A fresh bowl of hot rice waited for Jie when she returned from her chores. The open-pit fireplace warmed her as she ate alone by the fire. Her thoughts were on the big fight tomorrow. Father had agreed she could go and help with the birds, but she had to stay out of the way. "Just because I'm a girl, father looks upon me as if I am nonexistent. Boys!" She scooped up another bite of rice, swallowed, then took a drink of the rice-water from the bowl. What was wrong with her? She loved her brothers. They always got along. Although Chang was now a man of twenty-three, he always protected her and taught her their mother's aphorism she'd come to live by: *'There are three choices in life; be good, become good, or give up.'* Giving up was not in her. Never. She took another bite of rice. Jie repeated Auntie's favorite words, "Cold rice is no good." That always made her eat up and stop complaining. With new energy, she finished and cleaned the dishes.

Chilled, Jie shivered and pulled the blanket up around her fragile shoulders, still thinking back—eighty-six years ago—to that fateful day of the cock fight, the first she was allowed to attend. Recalling it, clearly, she had taken extra care feeding the birds that morning...She stared out the window letting her mind drift back to the dream...

The next day as Fancy had crowed his special hello to her, she held out a handful of corn to him, she petted his beautiful feathers. "You are so perfect, Mr. Fancy." As if the rooster understood the compliment, he arched his back to press against her hand as she stroked across his saddle to his tail plume. "Don't worry. Father will never put you into the ring. You are my friend. He promised." She knew she was taking too much time and her breakfast would be cold, but could not help spending extra time with Fancy. She bid him goodbye, hurried to finish the hens, and dashed towards the house.

On the path she met her father with Mr. Barton. She recognized the man as Denny Barton, Jr. from his red hair. Once, he had spoken to her when she was at the mercantile and held the door open for her. It surprised her because no one ever talked to Chinese girls. She guessed him to be over thirty, older than all her brothers yet not as old as her father. And now, here he was with her father.

"Good morning," greeted Father. "Daughter, this is Mr. Barton. He has come to look over our birds. Will you help?"

She dismissed the thought of cold rice and followed the men back to the cocks. The crowing increased as the three approached. Father extended his arm, giving permission to the white man to proceed. Barton entered the walkway between the noisy roosters. He carefully inspected the cocks and picked one up. The bird squawked, flapped its wings and aimed spurs at the arms that captured him. "I like this one." Denny released the cock. The bird jumped up on his perch and crowed. "He looks like a good fighter."

"He is. That's Ol' Red. One of my best." Haoli bragged.

Jie knew her father was thinking this would be a grand day. Ol' Red will win and everyone would know he was from Hong Haoli's champion cock farm. "He is a good one." She heard her father say. She followed him as Mr. Barton picked four more cocks. Then as he started to leave, he turned about and faced Fancy. "And I like this one, too."

Wide-eyed, Jie stared. The promise! He was not to fight. Ever. "No—oo!" she screamed, her voice trailed off in the middle of the two-letter word.

Both men stared at her as though they had not noticed her before.

Haoli spoke. "He is a good bird. Belongs to the girl, here. She has taken good care of him." He bowed in respect to Barton, glanced at Jie then bowed again.

Fancy stretched his head high, plume spanned as he perched in a one-legged stand, his performance hindered by the leather strap attached to his leg.

"A good fighter too, I bet" Barton studied Fancy a bit longer. "Add him to the lot, will you, Hong."

"Yes, sir." Her father nodded approval.

Jie gawked at Fancy as the men left. "No. No, nooo." She plopped down next to the fence and hid her face in her hands, moaning. "Father, you promised. You promised!" Fancy tipped his head sideways and looked at the girl. She cradled him in her arms and rocked. "You'll be all right Fancy. You are smart. And, quick. You will be fine? Won't you?" She cuddled the bird for a long time.

Hearing stomps of feet on the path, Jie stood as her father approached. "He picked my Fancy. He cannot fight. Remember?" She pleaded.

"I am sorry, daughter. But I cannot deny a white man. You know this. He appreciates a good bird, has good taste, do you not think?" Haoli pasted on a smile but his eyes did not shine.

"Oh Father." Jie wanted to hug him and beg him not to let the man have Fancy but knew it unbecoming and not allowed.

"Come, help me crate the ones he wants. You can carry Fancy. I am sorry little one, but it must be. You know it must. We want our birds to make money. Now come. Get your bird and bring him into the barn."

They put the cocks in wooden crates, used for transporting them. Jie did not leave the barn. Most of the day, she cleaned stalls and spread fresh hay between spurts of sitting next to Fancy.

That evening Jie rode on the driving seat beside her father, with six crates stacked in the back of the donkey cart. They arrived at the Barton farm on the northeast side of town. A large crowd of men had already gathered around a roped area. Friendly men greeted Haoli—all white, Jie noticed. A few Chinese men were there too, most had arrived with crated roosters. She only saw three women in the crowd. Wives of

Barton's friends, she presumed. They kept to themselves, and later disappeared into the house.

While the men carried the crates over to the assemblage, Jie stayed by the donkey cart. Men shouted, placed bets, and argued with profanity at which cock was best. Jie paid no attention to them, but kept an eye on the crate that held Fancy.

The hollering increased as two men, each holding a cock, stepped into the rope ring. The handlers squatted facing each other. On the Odds Layer's count of three, the men removed the cap from the head of the cocks. They held the agitated birds, jabbing them towards the opposite fighter several times, until each cock struggled against his handler's grip to get to its opponent. On a second count of three, both tossed his bird toward the other and jumped over the rope, out of the way.

Jie saw feathers flying. The cocks jumped into the air, landing atop the other, stabbing spurs as if daggers. In only a few minutes one cock lay still on the bloodied dirt. The other hobbled away, blood spraying from its side. Jie ducked her head, hiding under her forearms. For the first time she was thankful for the large sloppy sleeves of her tunic.

"That was awful." She spoke the words aloud and hid again by the wagon near the barn. She studied Fancy as he pecked at the wood holding him captive. Several more fights took place. Jie dared not go to Fancy. It would shame her father. She listened to the cheering and hollering as bets were won, lost, and paid to the Odds Layer.

The man who handled the crates came again and picked up Fancy's. She eased closer and spied from behind a wagon, the closest she could get without being observed. "Good luck, my Fancy." Jie spoke so low she did not hear her own words above the yelling.

She heard the Odds Layer's count begin. "Three. Two. One. Go." Like an expert Fancy used his shiny brass spurs and attacked his rival, who quickly retaliated. Feathers flew. Blood spattered. Men cheered. Wide-eyed she could not turn her head away. The cheering stopped. Bets collected. Fancy lay in the dirt, dead. Jie ran to the cart, climbed in and hid her streaming eyes under her arm.

Jie blinked. Had she been dreaming? It seemed so real and the hurt as deep as it had been so long ago. She wiped her moist eyes with her nightgown sleeve, and called out for Molly.

Molly rushed to her grandmothers' bedroom. "What is it, Nanai? Did you not rest well?

"I have more to tell you, come sit with me." Jie told Molly of the dream she had just relived about Fancy.

When Jie ended the story, Molly hugged her. "What an awesome story, Nanai. Your life was so hard. Thank you for telling me these things about you. It is near dinnertime. Lilly has made your favorite rice noodles. I'll help you get ready."

At the dinner table, Jie told more about her and Pai...

"I had turned seventeen when Wong Pai Number Two celebrated his thirty-fourth birthday. It was the 1920 Lunar Year. After opening presents, he turned to me with a mischievous grin. "I was hoping you would give me the best gift of my life."

"Don't you like the scarf I made? It took me two months. I was confused by his question," she grinned slyly.

"What did he mean?" Mandy asked, her junior high mind was a romantic one, she stopped chewing, waiting for the answer.

"Ah, my Pai was a clever man." He said, "'Yes, I take pleasure in it very much. It is perfect. But what I want cannot be wrapped in pretty rice paper'."

"Oh, what is it then?" my eyes questioned his. He explained it alright, little Mandy, do you know what he said?" Mandy shook her head sideways. Jie smiled, knowingly at the girl.

"I want your hand in marriage. Will you be my wife? We are predestined to be together." He took my hand in his. "We both know it. I realized I wanted to marry you when

221

mother gave us her blessings, just before she died. Remember? She was right. I have loved you since—well, since forever."

"Ohhhh!" Mandy let out her amazement. Everyone at the table looked her way.

"I studied Pai's face for a moment. That's what I did." A grin lit Jie's face, eyes sparkling, she nodded. "Then I answered him, 'Yes, you are so handsome, I have hoped this day would come. Our mothers would be pleased, would they not?'"

"'There are not many Celestials living here now,' Pai told me, factually. 'We will have no traditional fanfare of firecrackers, dragons and lions, parade, or feasts,' he had said. So our wedding took place in a private celebration after I turned eighteen in 1921, the year of the Cock."

"That is so cool," Mandy ohh'd. "What happened next?"

"Well, the next year, I gave birth to my first son, Mack." She looked into Mack's smiling face. "He was three when Kai was born, and two years later, Hua, named for my mother, came. Our last son, Ming, arrived as Mack turned eight years old." Jie took a sip of tea. "But let me back up to when I had only Mack. You were three, Mack, when the 1924 fire burnt the town—again." Jie glanced into the expectant faces as she spoke.

"Pai said it was worse than the fires of 1884," she paused, rubbed her chin, and explained. "There were two fires in '84, the first burnt our Chinatown—started by the vigilantes—when they hung my father-in-law...and the second destroyed the downtown area...before I was a babe, father told me about it many times. Then Jie stopped talking, closed her eyes and sat still for a minute.

She looked up and spoke again. "'The world is changing. It is a good thing.' Pai took my hand in his, squeezing it gently. 'This is only the beginning, I think. We will see many good things happen for our sons. We must make sure we keep these days alive in their memories. We will talk of it often, and tell them of our kin.' He had spoken the words softly. Together we made an oath that our descendents would know the truth of our family's past."

"What about the fire?" Mandy impatiently asked of Nanai.

"Oh, yes, the fire. Terrible." Jie gave a shudder. "Remember I told you about the boys playing with the firecrackers they found after the '84 Lunar celebration?...well...

"Now it was 1924. Pai and I had been married four years with two babies, Mack and Kai. I was about your age, Molly" Jie glanced at the college girl, then her eyes twinkled and a mischievous sparkle lit her face. "It was an *arranged marriage* to—Mei's son, Wong Pai—but I loved him, you know that, right?"

Her face still glowing, she forgot about the fire again recalling her marriage to Pai. "Mei, Auntie Sua, and my mother had made a pledge long before any of them had children—their first born male and female would marry. It was a Chinese custom from our homeland. The three friends did not experience it because their families did not accompany them to America. I did not mind, you know. I loved my Pai. Since my childhood, I loved him," she repeated without realizing it. "We were close, even though he was already a man at seventeen when I was born. Both of us grew up knowing of our parents' *wish*." She stressed her meaning. "I think my Pai kept an eye out for me because of it," Jie winked at Molly, grinning widely, and then blew a kiss into the air.

Mandy could wait no more. "What about the fire, Nanai?" Everyone gave her a quick look.

Molly, Lilly and Mack shared glances.

"Oh dear, did it I forget again? The fire, yes, the fire." Jie regained control of her thoughts. "I digress. I started telling you about the big fire that destroyed downtown Rathdrum, worse than the 1884 fire of Westwood, they all said so. It was 1924." She thought for a moment. "Yes, same town, different name and time."

Nanai pointed her index finger at her other hand, counting to herself, making sure of the time. "Yes, it was this second fire, when again, so much damage was done to the city.

So many buildings burned. Gone. No longer could I enjoy my beloved *Spot Beverage*, the Wings N' Cola Bottling Company was ashes. Grape was my favorite flavor. I remember drinking the last bottle we had in the icebox after the fire. I didn't open it for a long time." Jie licked her lips as if tasting it. Then she added, "The Creamery burnt. And, the Beer Brewery. All destroyed." She paused, like she did so often when recalling the past. Then added, "Oh, and the Northern Pacific Depot, too. Gone.

Then Jie stopped talking again, as if recalling it all she added, "Wesley Wood died in the fires. And father. My father, Haoli, ran into a burning building to warn Mr. Wood. Neither came back out." Jie cried out in a sudden gasp. "Father! Oh Father!" She stopped talking, and sat quietly for a several minutes.

No one, not even Mandy, spoke a word.

Jie finally opened her eyes and gripped Molly's hand tight. Her lips moved but no sound came. She found her voice. "Girl," Jie looked into Molly's eyes, "do you know what they did?"

Molly shook her head sideways and waited. Lilly look horrified, but kept quiet.

Jie uttered, "They held an immense funeral for Mr. Wood. I saw them. *We* all did. All the people in town. Stood there at his grave. All dressed in black, what a shame they dress in black. White is our tradition. The few of us Chinese left in town stood at the same time...outside the *real* cemetery at father's grave—in the *field*." Another tear fell from the old woman's eye as she pressed the words from her mouth.

Lilly handed her a new tissue.

"They, the *whites*," she spat the word, "did not acknowledge my father's life. We all watched as they left, turning, away from us. Leaving, as if we did not exist. They placed a carved stone on Wood's grave. The newspaper wrote, 'there is no room for the scum of alien lands'." Jie became quiet and sat with her hands folded in her lap, staring at them.

Without looking up, she continued. "Nothing marked my father's grave except a few rocks my Pai piled on it. I could not find the place where my parents rest a few years ago when your uncle took me there. But I know. I *know* they are there!" She leaned back in the chair again, as if all her energy had drained from her being.

Molly wiped Nanai's face again and put a new tissue in her hand. Lilly dabbed at her own eyes.

Jie stared into Molly's face. "Do not forget the truths I tell you. Promise me?" The elder one clenched Molly's hand then pushed back in the chair and closed her eyes. "I want to be buried by them," Jie whispered.

"This has been a long day, Nanai, let me help you to your room for the night." Molly got up from her chair.

"Yes, I need to lie down. But one more thing I must tell you first." Jie added. Then she spoke of when her husband died. "In 1962, I believe, he had reached age seventy-six, Pai suffered a heart condition and we laid him to rest—the first Chinese to be buried *inside* Pinegrove Cemetery. Mack and Kai were unable to get the city to let Pai be buried with our family ancestors. Said they had no proof of graves existing outside Pinegrove. Remember Mack? You could not prove to the city fathers where the graves were. We had to lay Pai with *them*. Another sad day for us."

"What will happen to me, now that I've lost you, Pai?" I asked, but no one was there to answer me. The words slipped from my lips as I placed a miniature temple for him on the mantle and lit the candle in it. Then I stood a framed picture of him next to the temple. I pushed it over a few inches, to leave a space so my sons might put something in my memory someday."

Jie glanced up at Lilly and Molly, 'I suppose will I be denied burial with our parents, too. How long will it be before I, too, lay at rest?" She kissed her forefinger then reached out and pointed it at Pai's photo still on the mantle. "Now, I am ready to go to bed, if you please."

"I'll help you," Lilly got up from the table and took the handles of the wheelchair. Together they left the parlor.

Molly had lot to think about on her drive home to Spokane that evening.

Chapter 29

A week later on Saturday, Molly rested her chin on her left hand holding dark hair out of her face as she read the newspaper. Her feet, now bare of her flip-flops, took turns fanning the air as she read articles.

"Listen to this, Nanai." Jie tipped her head a bit forward to hear. Molly read:

> "The Rathdrum Lions Club voted to preserve burial grounds from over a hundred years ago. While making plans to pave the area for extra parking, the club discovered the cemetery's existence. Chinese, evidently not allowed to be buried in Pinegrove, were placed in the field next to it."

"Isn't that something Nanai? The city must have found where your parents are buried." A single tear fell from the natural slant of the aged woman's eye, unnoticed by the college girl. She continued to read from the Sunday morning Press:

> "It is unknown how many Chinese were buried in the plot, discovered outside Pinegrove. The graveyard is estimated to be from the late 1800's to early 1900's. It is thought to have been called Potter's Second Field, named after the man who owned the land, later purchased by Fredrick Post."

Molly's voice trailed off as she finished reading the story. She looked up at Jie, "Why would they do that, Nanai? Why wouldn't they let our ancestors be buried in the town's cemetery? You told me about this, but I don't understand. Just because they were Chinese? I'm only twenty-three, but I have a hard time imagining what you and our ancestors endured."

"It was the way then, child. We Chinese were looked down on, treated as diseased creatures." A second tear ran down Jie's face, this time capturing Molly's attention.

The girl sat up and studied her elder's worn face. Molly let the newspaper fall to the floor, landing on the old rag-crocheted rug grandmother insisted on keeping next to her bed, atop the light blue carpet. She plucked a tissue from its box on the nightstand, and sat on the bed's edge next to the woman she loved so much and wiped the silky, withered cheek it felt cool to her touch.

"I want to be buried by them. You are young and know the ways of the whites. Will you promise to see I am put to rest with my family and friends?"

"It is a promise, Nanai. I will do all I can." Molly fluffed Jie's pillow and cuddled next to her. She wrapped her left arm around the frail shoulders, took both creased hands in her right palm and gave a gentle squeeze. They sat in silence for several minutes. "Are you still with me Nanai?" Molly recognized the distant look in Nanai's eyes, the withered memories consumed the elder one.

"Yes," whispered Jie, "I *will* be buried with my parents and the others. Pai would want me to do this. People today do not understand. Dennis Barton Junior would have. Denny had told about the drifters and unknown men from the poor house west of town also buried in *the field*. Of course, there will be no funeral procession like the ones in my youth, with decorated white chariots, firecrackers popping and flutes playing softly. Those things do not matter, not now. Not the burning of money, or loud mourners. Surely, Molly, with your education, you can find a way for me to be at rest with the clans. It would make history, a stand for the rights of the Chinese." Jie felt the coverlet slip from her shoulders again and shuddered. "Is my mind playing tricks on me? I am not sure I remember it right."

Molly watched as Nanai drifted into her youth again. Jie's face turned pasty, eyes distant—it always happened when her thoughts wandered back to her childhood.

"You know before I was born, Idaho had become a State in the Union on July 3, 1890. Judge Melder helped write the Idaho State Constitution. He was a friend of my father, 'a fair man.' father always said of the Judge. Father and his friends wrapped many firecrackers for the town's Statehood celebration."

Wrinkling up her face, Jie stated, "You see, when *they* wanted something from *us*, they were kind—yet they brutally killed my husband's father, Wong Pai, for making the same kind of noise at our Lunar Year? But, that was then, times have changed, somewhat, they have." Jie relaxed with a pleased look on her face. "We never celebrated the Lunar in the full traditional ways after Wong Pai was hung. Father told me the clans were afraid. No one was ever prosecuted for Pai's death. Father and others knew—they all *knew* who the vigilantes were."

When she ventured back from her woolgathering, Jie added, "I was just a little tot of five years when Rathdrum lost the county seat, but my husband was older. My Pai told me much about that time. The privileged seat moved to Coeur d'Alene. That was, let's see, 1908. Yes, '08. Rathdrum folks were upset about the county changing and stood guard with shotguns over the county records, to keep Coeur d'Alene people from stealing them. They were not successful. Coeur d'Alene took all the files by court order. Rathdrum's population had dwindled to less than 500, with only a few families of our kin remained. After the railroads connected Coeur d'Alene, it became the newest booming town." Looking downward, hands folded in her lap, she whispered, "most clans moved away, many to Butte, Montana. A lot went to mines in Montana as well as Silver Valley."

They moved into the parlor, a favorite place Jie liked to sit and visit. "Nanai's memory is getting confused more often these days," Lilly whispered to Molly in the hallway.

"I noticed." Each time I visit she seems more 'spacey', if there is such a word," Molly returned.

"The doctor says her memory loss is dementia, common for the elderly." Lilly hushed as they joined Jie again.

Molly curled up in a chair next to Jie and took her hand. Lilly and Uncle Mack joined them. Do you feel up to one more story, Nanai?" Molly urged her to speak.

"Ah, there was the day of triumph for we Chinese Americans. It came in 1929. With the new baby, Ming your father, in my arms and toddler, Hua, holding my hand, I walked Mack and Kai to the three-story, redbrick, schoolhouse on Main Street for their first day of school. 'If only my father and your mother could witness this day,' I told Pai over a special dinner that night to celebrate the occasion. I wish my father could have seen it. I grieve every time I think of him running back into that burning building to save Mr. Wood." The elder blew a kiss into the air.

As Pai predicted, 'many good things shall come to pass for us Chinese.' We were the last family in Rathdrum, left from the Chinatown community of the 1880s. We kept to ourselves, residing here, in Hong Haoli and Ang Li's big house. Our family grew, our boys moved on to careers. Ming was the first to attend college, where he studied law, like you Molly. You are following your father's footsteps. I am so proud of you, Molly girl." Jie gave her a half wink.

"Thank you, Nanai, I do love you so." Molly patted Nanai's hand and pulled the shawl back up on her shoulders. Sitting in her wheelchair, Jie took a sip of tea, and set the cup on the end table.

The musical ringing of her cell phone drew Molly's attention to the present.

"Hello Kim.

"It is.

"Oh goodness, I'll be right there.

"Bye." She pushed the off button.

"That was Kimmie. She is already at the study group. I promised I'd be there tonight. I must go Nanai." Molly began gathering her things and stuffed them into a purple backpack.

"Girl," Jie whispered, "I do not know how one college girl can have so many books. And, I sure don't know how you can talk to friends on that tiny phone with no wires attached."

Molly smiled, "Modern technology is a good thing." She bent over the delicate woman, kissed her on the cheek. "Bye for now, dear Nanai." Molly gave a quick wave goodbye to Lilly and dashed out the door.

Jie didn't seem to notice Mack's daughter-in-law prepare her for bed that night. Automatically, she lifted her arms as Lilly slipped a fresh gown over her head and arranged it around her. Her attention strayed, again, back to 1903, and the stories she'd heard of her birth, of her mother, Lein-Hua. "Was mama thirty-three-years old at the time of her death, my birthday?" She had heard the story until she could recite it backwards. To be sure, Jie counted on her fingers. "Yun, my eldest brother was seventeen when I was born, he was the same age as *my* Pai. Yes, that's the right age. Then my brothers Li, Fu and Chang, all gone now...am I repeating myself? I think my brain is not working..."

"What did you say?" Lilly asked as she tucked the blanket around Jie's shoulder. "Your brain is working just fine, dear. It is alright to recall often, it will keep you and your mind young. Good night." Lilly left the door ajar as she left the room.

Jie continued to track her own children, they were easier. "Mack is seventy-three, Kai named for my father's uncle; and Hua, named for my mother, lived up to his name's meaning 'brilliant'; and my youngest, Ming, Molly's father," she pointed her fourth finger. She sighed letting out a deep breath. "Ming would have been sixty this year." Molly, poor dear, her parents died only a few years ago in a car/train accident on the Rathdrum Prairie. Ming did not marry until in his late thirties and Molly, his only child, was born nearly a dozen years later. "I miss you Ming," she mouthed blowing a kiss then leaned against her pillow. She smelled the tall pines from the open window. She could envision the mountain behind, and the blue, blue sky. And, hear the flowing creek. She saw them all from long ago. Clearly. "Soon, I will join my parents, brothers, Ming and the others."

Chapter 30

A week later, Molly walked into the city hall auditorium. A large gathering already filled the room. Many sat on the metal folding chairs visiting amongst themselves, some in whispers, some boastful, greeting one another. "Please sign our register, Miss." Molly picked up the pen and scribbled her name.

Molly stood just inside the door, sucked in a deep breath, spotted an empty chair in the corner and headed for it. The seating faced a raised bench at the end of the room wood paneled walls matched it. The room smelled as if an antiseptic cleaning spray was used just today. She inhaled again almost tasting the air. She noticed nameplates marking places for the mayor and council members, a powerful atmosphere. Reading the names, she decided she did not know any of the people on the council, but did recognize the mayor's from newspaper articles. Small microphones poked up from the bench in front of each high-back leather executive chair.

Two council members sat at their place, chatting quietly. The mics must not be turned on yet she thought watching the two men. The audience quieted as the other council members seated themselves. The mayor then took her place at the center, tapped her gavel and called the meeting to order in a low foghorn voice. "All rise."

Chairs scraped against the tile floor and feet shuffled as people rose to their feet making a clatter. Then the room fell silent. The mayor started reciting the Pledge of Allegiance and in unison all joined in, giving emphasis to the words "under God."

The mayor acknowledged visitors, thanking them for attending. The agenda for the night approved with a unanimous vote. After a dispute over a contractor's fee for installation of the city's new sign for a park the council finally voted approval of payment for the month's bills. Then the mayor opened the meeting to visitor comments.

As Molly listened to grievances and requests, she realized she must make her presentation in front of all these strangers. Unconsciously her fingers twisted around each other in her lap. She wasn't afraid to speak publicly. She often addressed large classes at college without hesitation. The subject matter worried her. Surely these decision-makers would see fit to grant her request. They would understand, wouldn't they?

Her attention came back to the matter at hand, a request to pave the road up Reservoir Hill. The man droned on, Molly thought, listening to his voice but not his words. Concentrate, she scolded herself, annoyed that she was nervous. He finally took his seat, and another approached the podium. The mayor requested the man speak into the microphone so the recorder could pick him up.

Recorder? Oh dear, what next? Must I do that too? She couldn't see any equipment in the room. She had assumed the microphones were for amplifying, not recording. The man moved closer to the protruding mic on the podium and his voice echoed though the room. He was making the same request as the woman before had. "Why is the city letting the railroad close off McCartney Street? The town would be divided in half." That wasn't good, Molly agreed silently, but couldn't be sure why it mattered to her, since she lived in Spokane.

"Fine," the mayor thanked the spokesman as he made his way to his seat in the back row. "Anyone else? If anybody has something to bring before the council tonight, this is your last chance before we go into executive session. I see none." She raised her gavel ready to end the visitor session but stopped as a hand in the audience had caught her eye. "Welcome, young lady," she invited Molly with a smile and a wave of her hand, indicating the visitor podium. "Come right up."

Molly took in a shallow breath and bit her lip as she stood. She heard whispers and felt eyes following her as she approached the podium. Her legs moved her to the front of the room almost against her will. She tugged at the edge of her blouse. At the stand, her voice barely audible she began, "I am here on behalf..."

"Please. Speak into the mic," the mayor prompted her.

Smiling meekly, Molly stretched her head upward and spoke again. "I've come on behalf of my grandmother," she began, but the mic didn't pick up her soft voice. A man in the front row came to her aid, grabbed the mic and pushed it downward to meet Molly's shorter height. He gave her a quick grin, nodded politely and took his seat.

Molly murmured her thanks, which boomed across the room. She jerked at hearing her voice, regained her composure, and began again. "You see, Your Honor, my grandmother is breathing her last. She wants to begin life beyond with her ancestors. She has but one request of you so that she can go in peace." Molly's voice rose with new confidence. "My Honorable Grandmother, Wong Jie, wants to be buried with her forefathers. She understands your city has found our ancestral burial grounds, outside the cemetery. She wishes to be laid to rest there. We are told we must ask the city's permission. Please, Your Honor, let my grandmother be with her family. It is a small thing to allow an old woman who has lived here nearly a hundred years to die with respect." Molly's voice rose, "I beg you, do not deny my grandmother's deathbed wish. Let her be buried where her heart desires. I thank you for your time to hear me."

Just as quietly as she had approached, Molly returned to her chair in the crowded room. She heard a hushed buzzing of the audience. Several in front turned to stare. Her heart raced. She sat motionless, but her eyes darted about the room trying to study people's reactions. The woman sitting next to her gave a sympathetic smile of approval and patted Molly's knee.

She gave the woman a quick grin and locked her fingers together in her lap trying to steady her shaking hands. It was over. She had carried Nanai's request to the City Fathers.

Finally, the mayor's voice rose above those still talking and banged the gavel twice. "Quiet. Quiet please."

The assemblage settled down with abrupt silence.

"Thank you for sharing your request with us tonight. The council will take it under advisement and will discuss the situation further. This unusual request is a complete surprise and will require investigation of the laws concerning it."

Icy stares from several in the room felt like shurikens thrown at her. At the first opportunity Molly left the meeting and hurried down the stairs to the door. Outside, she took a deep breath of fresh air without noticing the evening chill. What should she do now? "Calm down," she warned herself as she headed across the street towards her '87 blue Toyota. She pulled her keys from a pocket as she reached the car. She unlocked the door, got in letting her body collapse in the seat, and pushed the lock, "Whew," the sigh of relief escaped her.

After school the next day, Molly found Jie sitting in her rocker. "Nanai, listen to this!" As she spoke, Molly lowered her backpack to the floor next to the rocker then straightened Nanai's hand-quilted lap cover and planted a gentle kiss on the aged woman's cheek. "We made the news." Molly sat on the footstool near the rocker, unfolded the newspaper and began to read:

> "A young Asian woman approached Tuesday night's Rathdrum City Council with an appeal to bury her grandmother in the original Westwood Chinese Cemetery, known as Potter's Second Field. The woman, identified as Molly Wong, according to the meeting registry, stated that her elderly grandmother wants to be laid to rest with her ancestors. Wong left the meeting without leaving a number where she could be contacted. An unidentified man in the audience spoke out against the request, stating that it is unlawful to bury a body outside an established cemetery and to consider it could only waste the council's time. The council members

took no action, stating that at this time there is no body to bury, therefore, the issue would not be considered for immediate action. The mayor concluded that they would need more information for any further deliberation or discussion on the matter."

"Oh! Why do they call us names? 'Young Asian woman,' indeed. I am an American!" Molly let the paper fall to her lap. "What does it matter I am Asian? Why do they point that out as if I suffer from some dreaded disease?" Molly's temper flared only to be smoothed quickly in her grandmother's presence. She would not dishonor her beloved one by her mood.

"It is nothing," Jie's voice mumbled. "They do not know better." She cleared her throat. Molly stilled as Jie's gentle, bony hand patted hers.

"You don't think that they will say no, do you Nanai? Surely they will see what this means to us! What shall we do now?"

"Hold family meeting. Soon." Jie's soft voice gave the answer.

"Yes, of course. We will call the family together. We will make the city see the importance of your heart's desire."

"Good. Now, read more news."

Molly lifted the paper. She read aloud an article about the shortage of teachers and nurses that was posing a problem for the local economy. Her voice floated in the air, but her thoughts remained centered on city hall. What would happen now? Surely they would see the significance of Nanai's last wish.

Chapter 31

Molly busied herself in her aunt's kitchen, folding the last of the eggroll appetizers and arranging them on a silver tray. Usually she enjoyed working with the women for holidays and special occasions, but this was different. This was serious family business.

She glanced at Nanai sitting near the dinning table. The familiar lap quilt covered Nanai's frail legs in the wheelchair. Jie pointed to the floral arrangement, directing Lilly where to place it.

"I'm amazed at Nanai's eloquent style," Molly told the others, "even to this day she remains the perfect lady." Molly turned her attention back to her chore of decorating the tray just the way the elder woman had taught her long ago.

Aromas from the kitchen drifted through the dining room into the front room and den where the men visited. A mix of English and Mandarin filled the air almost as tantalizing as the smells from the kitchen. "I'm so happy the family agreed to gather and support Nanai's quest," Molly finished with her tray and took it to the dining room.

"My, how you've blossomed. A beautiful young woman," Uncle Hua acted surprised, "and in law school too, Mack tells me."

Just how long had it been since she last saw him? One? No, two years. "I feel the same about my young cousins, and I see them more often." Baby Timothy was already in preschool, Bobby in third grade, and Mandy entered junior high this year. She studied the young faces now sitting at the dinner table.

"Let us enjoy this fine meal our ladies have set before us." Kai pushed his mother's chair to the end of the table, the customary place of honor.

The family quickly took their places at the large table. Each man reached for a serving bowl set by his plate. Uncle Hua dished a spoonful of noodles with sesame sauce onto his plate, and passed the bowl to his left. Dishes and utensils clattered as each filled their plates, but no one ate. Uncle Mack set his fork down after taking the first bite, smiled and announced, "Is good." On cue, everyone began eating and chatting in Mandarin. Lilly's new sweet and sour chicken recipe received agreeable comments.

Wong Kai brought back the subject on all their minds. "I do not know why the city is causing such a problem," he stated. "Mother Jie is still very much alive and in sound mind." Jie smiled up at him from her wheelchair, chewing a piece of chicken. She did not try to speak.

"I believe it is a problem," Uncle Mack pointed to his mother. "You know, it is not just for mother, but for all of us." The finger circled, pointing at each one. "I would also like to rest with our ancestors when my time comes. We've known this field of graves exists. Now its true location has been identified. This is very important. Mother, you knew it as a girl. You insisted clan members were buried outside Pinegrove's fence, but we never found the graves. It has all changed. The cemetery is much larger and there is the highway, wider than the first road along there, and buildings too. There are no grave markings anywhere."

Jie spoke up in her slow silvery voice. "Some thirty years ago, Ming took me to the field. I could not recall the exact location. They have changed the area so much. Distressed, we sobbed with our prayers."

Uncle Kai nodded his head. "I remember that day. Mother was sad indeed. Ming and I could not get her to eat for two days. I do not think that she let the memory leave her. Ever. It is essential this final desire of her heart be fulfilled."

Molly was remembering her own trip to the field near the cemetery with Nanai, when her thoughts interrupted by Wong Mack's baritone voice. "Our meal has been one of the finest our good ladies can prepare." He turned towards her, and nodded, "Our niece will share her news. Molly." He pointed a finger at her and flexed it as if to pull her to her feet with the motion.

She stood, cleared her throat, reached for the water glass, took a sip and set it back by her empty plate. Glancing around the table at all the expectant faces she paused then began with new courage. "I do have news." She repeated her story about attending the city meeting, including how nervous she had been. "I feel as shaky now as I did that night," she admitted. Involuntarily she fingered the locket hanging from its chain at her chest. She released it and reclaimed her confidence, thinking *my uncles should not make me anxious.*

"Question?" Uncle Kai lifted his hand a few inches from his plate where it rested.

"Yes?" Molly nodded to him.

"How long before the city will let you know its answer?"

"Ah, that *is* the problem." Her confidence returned, she continued, "They have not given a date. But if we are serious at helping Nanai Jie achieve her goal for final rest with our ancestors, we should attend the next council meeting in full force. *All* of *us*," she stressed her words. "At law school I learned there is power in large numbers. It will be difficult to ignore a group of us."

"Yes, Molly is right," Uncle Mack agreed. "We can be strong with many. I will bring my entire family." He gestured towards his wife, children and grandchildren at the table with a sweep of his arm.

"I, also." Uncle Hua stood, making the same motion towards his family. "And I mean my whole family." Big smiles were returned to him from his son-in-law who was white, and their two children, who resembled both parents' features.

"And mine too," Uncle Kai rose and included his family in the same manner. "We will all go. It is important." Even Timmy, the youngest family member, sat up taller in his highchair as his grandfather smiled at him.

"I love seeing my family together. It is grand how you hold fast to customs, an honor to the generations." Molly looked at Uncle Kai, the most like her father, then glanced at

Uncle Hua thinking he displayed mannerisms that continually reminded her of her beloved dad. She missed her parents so. "Yes," Molly answered, bringing her thoughts back to the present. "The city council will have to take notice of us. I am so proud to have you all as my family."

"We shall wear traditional Chinese robes," Uncle Mack added. "It will make a statement for us, that is, for our cause. We will show we belong to our ancestors and that mother's mission is also ours."

"Wearing that old blue dress with the dragons embarrasses me." Mandy muttered. As if realizing she'd spoken, she explained louder, "The boys at school always make fun of me, like I'm some backward, antique weirdo."

At realization of her words the entire family went silent.

Finally, Molly spoke. "Mandy, I am sorry you have suffered for our customs. Junior High boys can be so cruel. It is ignorance that makes people act so. It is this same attitude that brings us here today. You see, my little cousin, Nanai has lived a lifetime under such *lack* of *knowledge*. It is for her that we must prove to others our heritage is important and to be Chinese is not *shameful*." Molly turned to Nanai and smiled.

Nanai lifted her right arm, pointing her index finger as straight as it would, then spoke slowly. "Accept it as character building. It is only beginning in your young life."

"I *am* proud to be Chinese," Mandy apologized, "It will be my pleasure to wear my *qipao* for you, Nanai." She covered her face with her hands.

"Good girl. We will always be Chinese. It is up to each of us to be proud of our birthright." Mandy's mother put her arm about the girl and hugged her.

Their business concluded, Mack stood and declared, "We will all go to the next city meeting and convince them the Chinese cemetery must be reopened." Then he went over to Jie and kissed her forehead.

Uncles Kai and Hua rose from their places simultaneously. Each also honored their mother with a kiss. As the men left the table and went to the parlor to visit, the children were excused to the den to continue their video game, leaving the women to clean up.

"I think you have had enough excitement for one night, Nanai. Say your good nights and I will help you get ready for bed." Lilly gripped the wheelchair's handles.

"Good night, my loves," Jie threw a kiss towards her family.

"Good night," the group replied almost in unison.

Lilly wheeled Jie to her bedroom and made her comfortable, tucking her in for the night.

The media announced the burial request eagerly when Molly called them. Channel 6 news aired an interview with her. They jumped at the chance to be the first to identify the young Asian woman challenging city hall. Channels 2 and 4 fell into line, all broadcasting in depth the news about the abandoned Chinese cemetery in Rathdrum, Idaho. Letters to the editor followed, arguing pros and cons of the issue in both local newspapers. For over a week, Chinese and Rathdrum were the hottest topics in the news.

A week later at a special city council meeting, the room filled to over capacity, leaving standing room only. Folks stood at the back of the room and along the walls. The door to the foyer was left open, allowing the overflow of people to observe the proceeding on a monitor hanging high on the wall. The Chinese, who had arrived early, were seated at the far-left side of the room. Over thirty of them, all dressed in traditional clothing sat straight, heads high. An old woman in a wheelchair was among them.

The meeting began, taking care of various business items. Finally, the mayor tapped her gavel on the table, officially beginning the public hearing for the request to open a closed cemetery outside Pinegrove for another burial. "We will now hear comments and will start with a spokesperson pro this request."

Mack approached the podium. He straightened his ceremonial robe and manipulated the mic for his height.

"Madame Mayor, council membership, ladies and gentleman," he began. "I am Wong Mack and am here with my family to make formal my mother's request. It is a heavy burden on our hearts and has caused much turmoil for our family. We come here tonight so you may see how important this issue is. My mother, Wong Jie is failing in health in her ninety-sixth year of age. It is for her that we approach you tonight. We are pleased the Lions Club did not choose to pave the entire area as part of their new parking lot. They made a kind gesture by erecting a fence and designating the area as an ancient cemetery. We are here to verify that their information is correct to a point. But, the area of the gravesites is much larger. We would like to reopen the Cemetery on the other side of the fence. Please consider resurrecting our ancestors' resting place. I thank you for your time tonight." Mack spoke in his usual articulate manner then returned to his seat.

Grumbling filled the room. The mayor slapped her gavel twice but received no response from the audience. Now, she slammed it. The room fell silent. "That's better," she stated in a firm voice. "There are many who would like to be heard tonight. Now, if you have a comment, please wait your turn, approach the podium, state your full name and keep your comments brief." With that, she rapped her gavel again.

Several men raced toward the podium. The mayor slammed her gavel against the bench. "Let's be civil here," she ordered. "Those who wish to speak form a line."

Half the people started moving from their chairs and stopped short when the gavel banged the desk again. "This is definitely a problem. Raise your hand if you intend to speak." Almost every hand not belonging to a Chinese waved in the air.

"Very well, we must have order," the Mayor kept her tone strong. "I will take comments from the left to the right side of the room. Please wait your turn and move about only when a speaker is finished. Please keep comments to two minutes. I am sure many of you have the same thing to say, so please state your comment quickly without repeating your neighbor. We will be here as long as it takes to hear everyone." The mayor nodded towards the man at the podium.

"My name is Jerry Samuels. I am a fourth-generation member of my family to live here. I do not know of any cemetery other than Pinegrove, which is where I have family buried. I feel to create or re-create a new cemetery at this time would be a disaster for our town. Who will be buried in the new one? Will you only allow one ethnic group or will it be open to everyone? And how many Chinese will want this same privilege? They seem to have a large family here. The grounds are not large enough, and isn't it on private land? Would it be illegal? I think so. Thank you." As Mr. Samuels left the podium to return to the back of the room where he had been standing, a cheering in the crowd had to be quieted by the mayor.

The second speaker stated, I am in favor that the Chinese cemetery be reopened and allow Wong Jie to be with her ancestors." As he finished, another eruption of the crowd had to be quieted by the mayor.

An hour and forty minutes later, having heard over fifty, two-minute speakers the mayor called for a fifteen-minute recess.

Uncle Mack had been the only member of the Chinese to speak in the public hearing. "Our point of view is best served with only one spokesperson. Our strength is in our multitude of attendance." Molly nodding her head agreeing with him.

The room was still full as comments resumed. As the hour grew late, part of the crowd had slipped out of the room. Those who had been standing left or took the vacant seats.

At ten-thirty, the mayor interrupted the hearing again, before another speaker approached. "We have been at this since seven o'clock and I think it's time to stop for tonight. We will continue in two days on Thursday evening. We will start at six o'clock, earlier than our usual time. We still have to complete city business that was set aside for this hearing," she reminded the council as well as the audience. She again tapped the gavel for dismissal and stood to leave the bench.

The audience dispersed mumbling amongst themselves. "It will be interesting to see how the city rules." Molly overheard one man say as they exited. She felt dizzy as she left the room. She had never imagined Nanai's request would stir up so much emotion or that so many people would involve themselves.

She was in awe that her great-grandparents had lived in this town so long ago, yet faced the secluded lifestyle the Americans pressed upon them. She felt it now, too.

That night sleep escaped Molly as she replayed stories of the old days in her mind. She would never forget the softness in Nanai Jie's voice as she told the tales of her own grandparents, Lein-Hua and Haoli. How would she survive without Nanai's wise guidance?

Epilogue

Two months later, a half-mile-long procession of cars followed a white painted donkey cart. Police barricaded the route from other traffic. It started near the Methodist Church, moved slowly up the hill, crossed highway 53, the railroad tracks, passed the redbrick Catholic church, traveled down the slope to highway 41, and turned left, towards the cemetery. Elderly Chinese men, beating drums and playing flutes and cymbals, marched behind the cart. Along the way teenage boys set off firecrackers. Onlookers lined the highway to watch, as if a parade were performing. Some cheered, while others yelled crass remarks.

Ahead, lay Pinegrove Cemetery. Approaching it, the procession stopped on the highway before reaching the gate. Past the eastside fence, the Lions Club parking lot was outlined by yellow police tape. Reporters and TV cameramen crowded at the entrance. Onlookers close held their breaths. Which way would they go? Beyond the cemetery's fence, under tall pines and firs, tombstones of various sizes and shapes leaned as they pleased. Stones framed other aged plots. Plants and cut flowers, some old, some fresh, among other items, decorated different gravesites.

The cart driver turned into Pinegrove under the arched sign. He led the motorcade through the oldest part of the cemetery into the newest section, an open area without trees, to the far fence line, where it came to a halt. White-robed men unloaded a white casket splotched with torn pieces of yellow paper glued to it.

Wong Mack took his place at the head of the open grave. The cart, emptied of it's cargo, moved away. Cars parked along the pathways as over four-hundred people gathered. The clans walked silently to surround the grave. Prayers were chanted as red paper money and pieces of cloth were burned in traditional ceremonial fashion.

Members of the clans lowered Jie's coffin into the pit, but not far from her husband's grave, also inside Pinegrove.

Bowing his head, Mack prayed in Mandarin. Then he looked up and spoke, using both languages he repeated himself.

"We are here to honor a resident of Rathdrum, who has lived almost a hundred years." Mack paused and pointed towards the Lions Club area. "Her greatest desire was to be at rest with her ancestors, there, on the other side of the fence. That cannot be, because of rules. But a fence cannot separate our loved ones. We trust she is happy to join the ancestors from here and her spirit will be at peace. As we remember her today, please do as she did. Make her promise yours, 'I will not forget.' Take this one step farther. Let us treat each other as one family." He bowed his head and recited a final prayer. Then he looked up and spoke again:

"We are here this day to honor our loved one. Wong Hong Jie was born ninety-six years ago in Rathdrum, Idaho, May 10, 1903, to Hong Lein-Hua and Hong Haoli. She was preceded to the ancestors by her parents, and four brothers, Hong Yun, Hong Li , Hong Fu, and Hong Chang. Her husband, Wong Pai Number Two, and a son, Wong Ming. Jie's mother-in-law, Wong Mei, and her husband Wong Pai, hung by vigilantes long ago before she was born. We count her friends, who have gone to the ancestors before her also as family, Ang Li and wife, Ang Sua, so diligent in helping Jie through her motherless, childhood years. All are buried...there...beyond this fence, in the *field*—as if punished for being Chinese." His voice wavered, as he lifted his eyes toward the ancient cemetery. "Jie, my mother, knew. She knew where their graves were over there. She knew. She did not forget."

Composing himself, he continued. "In 1920 at seventeen, Jie married Wong Pai, age thirty-four, who went over to the ancestors at seventy-six in 1962, after providing a good life for his bride of forty-two years. Jie is survived by her sons, Wong Mack, Rathdrum, Wong Kai, Missoula, Montana, Wong Hua, Spokane, Washington, ten grand-children and six great-grandchildren.

"She suffered the past eight years with deteriorating health but was determined to tell her stories to make known the injustice forced upon her family. She was a tenacious woman. Her life started with the loss of her mother, Lein-Hua, also a strong lady.

"Under the guidance of four older brothers, her father and women she came to know as her aunts, Mei and Sua, Jie learned to love and honor other people, regardless of ethnic influence. She repeated family historical accounts, always saying, 'do not forget' to us.

When odds were against her, she learned to look for the best way to handle things. She attributed her life's longevity to giving her utmost to accomplish whatever she set out to do. As we remember her today, please, do as she did. Make her promise yours, and take this one step further. Make a difference. Let us not discriminate against others."

As Mack bowed his head lower, and prayed in Mandarin, Molly blinked blurred eyes, and whispered, "I will not forget."

The End

Acknowledgements

It takes a lot of help to complete a project like this. My special thanks to my critique group without whom this novel would still be a jumbled pile of words on paper without form, meaning, or message. My special appreciation extended to Pat(ricia) Pfeiffer who used several red pens bleeding on my manuscript teaching me the art of fiction. It is my prayer her time was spent for the best of my ability.

The cover Artwork is a painting by my artistic friend and author of eight books, Pat Pfeiffer. After a multitude of ideas for title and cover, Pat, 84 years young, painted what this story said to her. Cover design by Jim Kelly.

Honorary Mention to Patty Elliott, Deasa Stein and Sheri Patik; my cheerleaders in supporting this work.

After eight years of working, researching, writing, and storing this on the back shelf, this manuscript is now a published work of much labor. If you have ever been discriminated against for any reason, take to heart; it is the result of ignorance, therefore my motive to not let this story go untold. Please consider others in the manner in which you want to be regarded.

Contact Info

Visit our webpage at <u>writeoffsite.net</u> where you can find history facts, pictures pertaining to the story taken during research trips, and more. Please feel free to take the survey and let us know your comments about this project.

Email us at <u>writeoffsite@verizon.net</u>; or write to P.O. Box 999, Spirit Lake, Idaho 83869.

To purchase copies of this publication visit your local bookstore; amazon.com; writeoffsite.net; or email directly to writeoffsite@verizon.net.

About the Author

Joyce Nowacki, is a freelance writer and owns Write Offsite Publishing, a marketing and business-management company on consultant basis, since 1995. She has authored news columns for both the Post Falls Tribune and Spokesman Review for a total of eight years. Periodically she teaches writing classes for North Idaho College Workforce Training.

Joyce resides in Spirit Lake, Idaho, with her husband, Wayne, of 43 years, whom she swears keeps her around to see what she will do next. They have two daughters and five grandchildren. A native of North Idaho, she served three terms as Trustee on the Lakeland School Board of Education, Rathdrum, Idaho.

5692313R0

Made in the USA
Charleston, SC
21 July 2010